LONGING TO GO HOME

Author, Richard Jan

ISBN
Hardback: 978-1-964289-76-2
Paperback: 978-1-964289-75-5

LONGING TO GO HOME, is the sixth book in a twelve-book series, **DYING TO SUCCEED,** exploring our fragile human existence.

Other books in this series include:

Book 1, Winds of Success
Book 2, Living with Death
Book 3, Pretending to be Alive
Book 4, Presumption of Sanity
Book 5, Running from Regret
Book 7, Afraid to Hope
Book 8, Waiting in Infinity
Book 9, Chasing after Time
Book 10, Casualties of Words
Book 11, Traveling into Chaos
Book 12, Snows of Fear

God willing and the spirit strong, I hope to write more books in the future.

As I write, I often play music in the background. May I suggest you do the same when you read this book, choosing music you enjoy.

This book like all the other books in this series, is a continuation of the adventures of one character, John Van Laan. The people and places in the book can be better understood after reading the preceding books.

In order to make the book more readable, each episode is identified at the beginning by place and time, along with the name of the primary person who is speaking.

Should you have questions or comments, please feel free to email me at rhoekstra@sbcglobal.net. I will do my best to reply.

Richard Jan

Light is sweet.
It pleases the eye to see the sun.
It is good to enjoy the day.
But remember the night, the darkness.

Contents

AUTHOR'S NOTE

Although I am familiar with the colored gemstone industry from having worked in it for ten years, I don't pretend to be an expert on any level. My knowledge can best be described as that of a man traveling through a city without ever stopping for an extended period of time to experience the living conditions up close. And yet, as I contemplated my journey after it came to an end, I thought it was interesting and perhaps worthy of being a wonderful subject for a book.

But what I discovered as I wrote was that the real story was not the gemstone industry but how the cast of characters reacted to the challenges they faced, challenges similar to what we daily endure. And it is my hope that knowledge gained from existing for a time in their shoes as you read this book; may encourage you to live a fuller, more purposeful life.

ACKNOWLEDGEMENTS

It is only fair that I acknowledge the help and encouragement that I received from New York Book Publishers. I went to them initially looking for guidance in editing, cover design, marketing, and distribution. They promised me that they could fulfill my needs. I accepted their proposal and began working with them virtually while living in the Midwest with their company's resources located in New York City. Our journey together has been an adventure; one not taken lightly, but traveled with some trepidation and concerns. Special thanks go to Victor Hughes, who guaranteed me they would not let me down. And thanks to my daily contact, Serena Hoffman for understanding my concerns and assuring me that everything was progressing as it should. And to Jim Bannister who took the time to talk to me when I needed a conversation. And to the many editors and artists who have contributed greatly to the final product. Thanks to them all for helping me achieve what I had hoped for when I first contacted this New York Book Publishers.

Page Left Blank Intentionally

AMBERGRIS ISLAND, BELIZE, WEDNESDAY, NOVEMBER 18, 7:15 AM,1998, JOHN VAN LAAN

It was early morning when I went for a swim.

An ugly nightmare had woke me. I couldn't remember the dream, only knew it was unpleasant and I was happy to be awake.

Ilana and Sandy, my two lovely girlfriends, were sleeping peacefully beside me at the time. Not wanting to disturb them, I crawled gingerly out of bed and went upstairs to dress in shorts and a T-shirt. Still mentally and physically exhausted from the torturous ordeal I had recently suffered at the hands of kidnappers, I shuffled outside at a slow, meandering pace, lacking any real motivation, headed for no apparent reason toward the dock in front of the house.

I felt strangely different that day; stronger than the day before, closer to accepting the fact that I wasn't going to die any time soon. A good night of sleep helped. I was still very weak, but nothing like before, nothing like those days and nights of torturous existence, tied to a bed with nothing to eat and very little to drink, waiting for my fate, waiting for my life to be over.

The rising sun lay low in the sky over the Caribbean Sea, warming the air. Black-headed seagulls floated lazily in a fresh breeze. Shallow waves could be heard lapping on the shore, playing a melodious tune in my head, somehow reassuring, as if I was meant to be here after all, to be alive in this place.

It was too early for beachcombers. The white sands of the seashore near the dock were wind-swept smooth, uncluttered by human traffic as God intended. Palm trees could be seen growing in the virgin sand at odd angles to the beach, sculpted by the wind, their leaves waving in the gentle breeze. It was, I had to admit, a glorious morning. Warm and bright with not a hint of storm clouds near the horizon. The early morning sunlight flashing off the rolling waves of the sea made it difficult to look out over the vast expanse of ocean. Turning my back to the sun at the end of the dock, I sat down to rest.

Even though I didn't want to think about him, about what he had done to me, about all the pain he had caused me, it was almost impossible. Sophon, my kidnapper, my torturer; he was on my mind. In a way, it seemed impossible to believe he was gone and I was still alive. After all his promises to execute me, I couldn't help but wonder why he didn't do it. Was it something I said? Had I actually convinced him not to kill me? Or was it just not in him? He couldn't do it. He wasn't a man who could kill another man. He didn't have the mental makeup to do what he had traveled from Thailand to accomplish. He couldn't kill the man who had murdered his father. He couldn't kill me.

I didn't know the answer to my riddle. I only knew I was alive. He had tried to shoot me several times, but each time, his hand fell to his side, still clutching his gun. Perhaps he didn't know the answer to my riddle any more than I did.

I wondered where he was now and what he was thinking. Even though he had caused me great pain, there was something about him, something I didn't understand...

I stopped... suddenly tired of thinking about Sophon or his father or what I had done. Or why I was alive when I should have been dead. I needed to stop thinking about any of it because every time I did, I became afraid. Afraid that someone was coming to kill me. But more than being afraid of dying, I was afraid of what I had become, a murderer I didn't want to be. I was almost more afraid than him, of me, of being me, afraid that I had died to the man I was, and now I was forced to live with the man I had become. I was almost more afraid of him than I was afraid of dying. And these fears had been living with me for so long that I was having difficulty placing them on a dark shelf in the back of my brain where I didn't have to think about them anymore, where I didn't have to be afraid all the time.

The warm Caribbean Sea looked quietly inviting, an escape from my morbid mental meandering. After taking off my shirt and shorts, I dived naked into the clear blue, rolling sea, a rush of warm water washing over my body as I lazily floated to the surface, thinking perhaps a short swim might help clear my head and strengthen my depleted body.

I told myself to take it easy. Don't overdo it. I was still very weak. I just wanted to stretch my aching back and shoulder muscles. Swim slowly and stop thinking about Sophon. Stop thinking about what I had done, stop thinking about who I had become, stop thinking about dying. Concentrate instead on simply pulling and breathing and kicking in slow, even rotations; stroke, one arm over the other in the warm sea. Turn your head to breathe, kick, pull, and feel the water wash over your aching body, cleansing your troubled soul.

No more sorrow, no more pain; only the sea and me in unison... like a dance... like a dance.

My arms began to ache, but I did not stop.

It felt too good to stop.

Something is relaxing. Something is restful about the repetitious motion of swimming. Steady strokes, arms rising one after the other, slow and steady, the feel of the sea, the comfort of the sea was wonderful. I wasn't thinking about the ache in my arms. I wasn't thinking about anything. Just being one with the sea, letting the warm water glide over my back, over my mind, take over my thoughts, let the gentle flow of the sea wash away my fears. No need to argue. No need to try to justify my life or my actions to anyone... just the gentle roll of my shoulders, each stroke bringing me closer to being one with my mother, the sea.

Several times I rolled over on my back when I became too winded to continue, resting, catching my breath. My eyes closed, just for a few seconds while kicking lazily to remain afloat, I rested in the gently rolling sea. After finding some reserve, some new source of strength, I rolled over and once again continued to slowly swim, one arm over the other, kicking less frequently now, slower strokes, but still steady progress out to sea.

Finally, my arms grew tired, and I could go no farther. I rolled on my back and rested as I breathed in the warm morning air, closing my eyes as the sun warmed my tired body. Thinking how glorious it was to be alive, kicking slowly to maintain my balance in the sea. After a few minutes, I tried to swim freehand again, but it was no good. My arms felt like dead weights. I could not lift them out of the water. I turned over to rest on my back again, kicking slowly until my legs began to tire.

That was when I realized how far out in the sea I had gone. The beach house looked miniature on the shore. I had made a mistake. I swam away from instead of parallel to shore, as was my normal habit. I wondered briefly why, but the reason seemed unimportant. Truth was, I was happy to be in the sea, to be one with the sea... never having to return to dry land again, to the house on the beach that held so much pain.

I didn't dwell on my mistake.

I simply accepted its consequence, judging my odds of making it back to shore and calculated they were long. I probably was not going to make it. Still, I had to try. It seemed somehow wrong to simply give up and die without trying. Not after everything which had happened.

Reluctantly, I turned over and began to swim, alternately lying on my back when I became tired, then turning to slowly breast-stroke towards shore.

Tired is a state of mind.

I have been tired many times in my life, but it never meant I couldn't do more if I pushed my body. But what I felt that morning was more than tired. It was a deep fatigue which began in my brain and spread through my body like a disease. My muscles began to feel like they were fusing to my bones, my joints growing together, becoming one unmovable stone. No way to continue. I began to realize it might not be possible to save my body from drifting to its final destination: a deep hole in the sea.

7:25 AM, ILANA

Ilana got up before Sandy.

Lazily rolling over, she sat up and put her feet on the floor to walk sleepy-eyed to the bathroom to freshen up. After wandering around the house for a few minutes, she began to wonder where John was. A little anxious at first, perhaps even a little frightened, she searched for him as a random question passed through her mind, followed by a wave of panic igniting nerve ends, causing an involuntary shiver of fear to run rampant down her spine.

Had they returned, she wondered, those bad men? Did they come back to kill John after all?

Instantly, insanely, fearing the worse, something was wrong, very wrong; a thorough search of the house did nothing to calm her fears. John was nowhere to be found.

She woke Sandy with her panicked question on her lips. Frantically, they searched together, Sandy retracing the steps Ilana had taken through the house while Ilana wandered outside, calling his name, searching his sailboat, finding nothing except some clothing lying discarded on the far end of the dock. A shirt and shorts that looked like they could belong to John but offered no clue as to where he was.

The sun lay low over the sea to the east, making it difficult to see a lone head bobbing among the reflections of the waves.

Ilana retraced her steps in her mind, remembering she had seen no new indentations in the morning sand, no fresh footprints; no evidence he had gone for a walk. But the shorts and a shirt on the dock, they were clothing that could belong to him. She deducted he was in the water. Squinting into the bright sunlight, the vast empty rolling sea revealed nothing... until... unless... something caught her eye, some small speck of movement on the water far out in the sea.

Her heart raced as she strained to see if it was him.

'I think I see him, Sandy,' she yelled while running down the dock toward the house, knowing she needed help.

Sandy came outside.

'Get the dingy and follow me,' Ilana screamed.

Never hesitating, stripping off her clothes as she ran to the end of the dock, Ilana dove into the water, swimming as fast as she could toward the dark speck she had seen far out in the sea.

Untying the dingy from the dock, Sandy began to row behind Ilana, following her lead. But unfortunately, she was not practiced in the art of rowing and it took her a few minutes of frustrating, splashing activity before she finally acquired the knack of rhythmically rowing in the direction she intended to go. Making steady progress through the shallow waves, every once in a while, she stopped to see where Ilana was, making sure she was rowing in the right direction.

More than once, she had to adjust her efforts, trying to catch up to Ilana's steady swimming out in the sea.

4:45 PM. JOHN

I learned long ago that you can rest on water by floating on your back, especially in salt water, which is buoyant. Kick slowly to stay afloat and let the sun warm your body while you breathe deeply, keeping your head above water. I was doing this, but it wasn't working very well. I was finding it difficult to continue. Every time I stopped kicking, even for a few seconds, my body would begin to slip into a restful sleep as the sea gently rocked me and took me into its arms. When my legs stopped moving, they became dead weights, pulling my body down until my head slowly submerged below the water and it was only the unpleasant sensation of salt water seeping into my nostrils that revived me. Not having the ability to breathe ignited some primeval urge to live, aided by a shot of adrenalin which gave me strength to swim again; slow breaststrokes, halfhearted kicks, until I became winded again and turned over on my back to rest, to dream.

It was one of those times when I was laying my back when she arrived and wrapped her arms around me. I didn't know it was Ilana. I only knew I didn't need to work anymore. I could rest in her arms. I could rest in the arms of the lady of the sea.

Sandy eventually caught up to Ilana, and together, they somehow dragged my limp body into the boat and rowed slowly back towards shore in silence.

I slept off and on for most of the day after being rescued, dreaming of slipping calmly into the deep waters of the ocean to rest forever. It was a good sleep because every time I opened my eyes, I saw light. It was comforting to see daylight; not frightening like waking at night when it is dark and nothing but imagined tragedies roams through your mind.

Finally, when I could sleep no more, I simply lay in bed with my eyes closed and forced my mind to think about everything that had happened.

I sensed I was not okay. I was existing in some sort of state of assumed normalcy... while not really being okay at all.

Fear was my predominate problem. No place to hide, no place to run; fear found me wherever I went. Facing my fears head on seemed my only option, hoping this might prevent fear from wandering around like a shadowy monster through the dank dark caves of my mind, attacking me at will without notice or pity.

I decided Sophon was where I needed to begin, forcing myself to think about the son of the man I killed. Details of my exhausting meeting with him returned to me in bits and pieces when I could think clearly. He had kidnapped me to avenge the death of his father, but first, he had questions he wanted to ask me. He wanted answers, demanded answers. Mostly demanded, I admit to murdering his father.

The problem was that I had no good answers for him, not the answers he wanted to hear. I was willing to admit nothing that implied guilt. Not because I didn't kill his father. The truth was I shot his father, and the man died from his wounds. But I argued my actions were a reaction to his father's countless acts of violence against me. His father had attempted to kill me on more than one occasion. Therefore, it was self-defense in my eyes. His father's death was not my fault. It was his. At least, this was how I saw it.

Sophon had disagreed.

He said his father was only trying to scare me, not kill me. His father wanted to scare me into voluntarily giving up control of my company, which had taken resources from his family. My company had diminished the value of Thai businesses, which had economically empowered his family and made them wealthy for hundreds of years. Sophon said his father simply wanted what they considered was rightfully theirs for generations, wanted it returned. And to accomplish this, he needed my stock so they could control my company.

Sophon reasoned his father never intended to kill me because if his father had actually wanted me dead, I would be dead.

That's what Sophon said. Said my act of killing his father was not self-defense. It was murder, and it demanded justice.

We argued long and hard into the night. I knew I was losing and going to die. And that's what happened. Eventually, he tired of the game we were playing, and sometime before dawn, he decided it was time to kill me. But for some reason, he couldn't do it. Perhaps because I finally convinced him I was not responsible for his father's death... or maybe not. I didn't really know. I was too tired and stressed at the time to make rational observations. All I knew was Sophon wanted to kill me, but for a reason; he did not do it. Instead, he had his men unceremoniously throw what remained of my tortured body on the bed occupied by the ladies.

After hours of arguing with Sophon, I was so stressed and exhausted that I passed out. I remembered nothing of being dragged to their room. I lay in a deep coma-like sleep. That's what they told me. Ilana and Sandy said they could not wake me. They thought I was dying, and they were helpless to do anything to help me.

When I finally woke up, they were happy I was alive but still afraid, scared the men were still in the house. Although nothing had been heard for hours, they were not convinced silence was evidence of an empty house. They were afraid their tormentors were lurking outside their bedroom walls.

I got up slowly to go to the bathroom.

A person who was alive and looked like me returned my stare in the mirror after I splashed cool water on my face. Summoning what courage still resided in my wasted body, I feebly crossed the bedroom to the hall door as Ilana and Sandy silently watched from their bed.

If the Chinaman, the man who had been my guard when I was Sophon's captive, if he was outside the door, I reasoned he could do what he wanted with my wasted body. I had no control over him. I was too exhausted from my ordeal, from being tied to a bed for days without food. I had no strength, no defense. I almost didn't care. I reasoned it would be game over if he was waiting for me.

I hesitated... standing by the door and listening... hearing nothing.

Ilana's house by the sea was quiet, but this did not mean Sophon and his men were gone. Our kidnappers could be waiting for me to revive so they could kill me when I was conscious. Kill me when I knew I was going to die. Revenge would be sweeter then.

I remembered. While arguing with Sophon through the night, I had only one desire. I wished to see the sun for one more day. I had prayed, more than anything, to see the sunrise one more time. For some inexplicable reason, I was not afraid to die, but I didn't want to die at night when it was dark. I wanted to die during the day when it was light.

As I stood by the bedroom door, I wondered if perhaps my prayer had been answered and I had lived to see one more day, nothing more. See the sun on this day, which would be my last day, my day to die. If Sophon was in the house waiting to finish what he had traveled thousands of miles to accomplish, then this would be my day to die.

It was time to find out.

Either he was in the house, and I was dead... or he was gone, and I would live.

I opened the bedroom door. It was empty and quiet in the hall. My footsteps on the wood floor echoing down the hall were the only sounds I heard. This and sounds of waves breaking on the seashore and a seagull screeching in the wind.

The living room was as I remembered from the previous night. Nothing had changed; nothing except now it was day. The deep shadows that had lay across the room from the light of one lamp were gone. Sunlight filtered through the windows overlooking the Caribbean Sea, casting a warm glow over the soft tan cushions on wood-framed furniture. An empty glass sitting on a table caught my attention. I remembered seeing Sophon drinking from this glass while he questioned me. I had wondered if he had alcohol in his glass, but he had not acted drunk. It could have been filled with water. I didn't know. I only remembered wanting some water, but I was afraid to ask.

The kitchen was empty: dirty dishes in the sink, crumbs on the tables, a mess everywhere, but no kidnappers. I searched every room before I was finally convinced. Kidnappers were gone. The house was unoccupied, no one here except the ladies and me.

I should have been elated, but I was almost too tired to care.

'Should we call the police?' Ilana asked after I returned to the bedroom to tell them the good news.

I didn't reply.

Sandy, my tall, beautiful, blond-haired Sandy, my Dutch girlfriend from my hometown, my former teenage flame, the woman from San Francisco whom I now loved; she helped me take a shower. After turning on the hot water, she helped me undress. Then she came into the shower and held me. She was probably afraid I would fall and hurt myself. And she had every right to be concerned. I could have fallen; I was very weak. I didn't refuse her help. She washed me as I held her, reveling in every smooth, wet curve of her naked body. I should have become aroused, but relief was all I could muster. I was too weak. I held her thinking she was a dream. Last night, I thought I was dead. Now, the soft lines of her body helped me accept the reality of being alive.

When I stepped out of the shower, Ilana, my petite black-haired island girlfriend, the woman who had brought me back to life from an emotionally crippling experience, my lover from Belize, brought me clean clothes. She let me hold on to her while I put on a pair of shorts. She buttoned my shirt, brushed the wet hair off my forehead, and smiled at me. She looked so alive, so wonderful, her rich tan skin literally glistening with life.

I was in love with them, loved them both, loved them deeply and without reserve. And they in turn loved me, held me, cared for me. Food was prepared; chicken soup, a peanut butter and jelly sandwich. They asked me if I wanted anything else.

Mostly water, I replied. I told them I wanted water. I think I drank every fifteen minutes for the next hour. I was so thirsty. Then I went to the bedroom to sleep and didn't wake until the next morning, the day I almost drowned.

I didn't drown because they saved me.

I was alive for another day, a day I never thought I would see.

After my rescue in the morning and after a day of resting and reflecting, a welcome calm came over my mind. I got out of bed feeling renewed for reasons I did not try to understand. That evening was filled with wonder. We went for a walk on the beach, and everywhere I looked, I marveled at how glorious it all appeared. The moving blue-green Caribbean Sea, the sun, the sky, the birds; it was like I had never seen any of it before. Everything appeared to be new. The ladies, especially the ladies, were so new and beautiful, the way they moved, the way they smiled. I was acting like an idiot, smiling back at them, grinning self-consciously. I knew I was acting like an idiot, but I didn't care. All I wanted was to be with them and smile, my idiotic smile.

Thankfully, they were nice to me.

The ladies didn't scold me for acting so dumb, for swimming out to sea and almost drowning. They smiled back at me, their hair blowing in the wind. They were so beautiful, especially how they walked, Ilana bouncing along, Sandy more graceful, slower, and methodical, both of them wondrous: straight black hair, curly blond hair... I stared at them, thinking I should be dead, dead for a second time, this time from drowning. I should be seeing none of this. Every minute was a joy, a pleasure.

The sea beckoned me. The sea looked alive. A wave of soft water washed up on the shore, covering my feet. I couldn't resist wandering alone out into the water, drawn to the sea on an impulse. The warm water washed over my tired body, cleansing my mind from the memories of those dirty, smelly, torturous nights I had endured in a stained bed upstairs. My strained muscles rested in the moving warm water of the sea. Ilana followed me in to assist me. Even though she was dressed in a skirt and blouse, she walked out into the water with me. She said she was afraid I might fall over and drown. I put my arm around her shoulders and leaned on her for support.

'Stay with me,' I pleaded when she tried to lead me back to the shore.

She smiled and kissed me as waves washed over her shoulders, soaking her blouse to her skin until the full, rich round of her breasts could be seen in all their wonder. I ran my hand through her hair. Silent tears fell from somewhere deep inside me, tears which melted into the sea. She held me while I silently cried away all the agony of the last few days.

I'm not sure she knew I was crying. I didn't want her to see my tears. I hoped the sea would disguise my tears, drown my sorrows. Maybe she knew, but she didn't say anything, just held me until I slowly turned to walk back to shore. I had cried enough. It was time to move on.

We didn't talk on the beach as we walked back to the house. I didn't want to talk. I wasn't ready.

'No,' I finally said when we were sipping wine on the front deck before dinner. I had not answered Ilana when she asked about calling the police. I was too tired to think about it at the time. Her question required a response.

'What are you talking about?' Sandy asked.

'I don't think we should call the police,' I replied.

'But what if those men come back?'

'If they had wanted to kill us, we would be dead. I don't think they are coming back.'

They didn't argue with me; simply sat with me in silence. My ill-considered and unintended attempt at suicide came to mind as I rested with them sipping wine. It was wrong. I owed them an explanation. If no one else, I owed them. They had rescued me. They did not let me die. I reasoned that my life no longer belonged to me alone. It belonged to them now. I needed to take them into consideration in everything I did.

'I want to thank you both for saving my sorry ass today,' I apologized. 'What I did was wrong and it will not happen again.'

'It's okay John,' Sandy said.

Ilana nodded.

'It just happened. I didn't think about doing it,' I tried to explain.

'We know,' Sandy replied.

'I wouldn't have done it if I had thought about it.'

'We understand, John,' she reiterated. 'You don't have to apologize.'

'You have been through a lot, John. No one is blaming you,' Ilana added.

That night with the two of them once again curled beside me in bed, I thanked God for these ladies and promised I would always try to take care of them. I didn't know how, but I knew I owed them.

As for Sophon, I also thought about him. I wondered if maybe I owed him too.

He also had kept me alive.

GRAND HAVEN, MICHIGAN, FRIDAY, NOVEMBER 20, 11:35 AM. PHILLIP PALMER

His phone rang as Phillip was preparing to leave his small office in Grand Haven for lunch.

Intuitively sensing Sophon might be on the line, finally returning his call, Phillip stopped to answer the phone before walking out the door.

All week long, Phillip had been trying to reach the young man. He knew where Sophon was, in Belize. And it didn't take a genius to assume the reason for his trip would not be good news for his nemesis, John Van Laan.

Phillip had never suggested Sophon kill John. This was not Phillip's method. Instead, he simply made the case for John's execution. Like a lawyer to the jury, Phillip had primed Sophon until Phillip had no doubt about what the young man would do once, he located John.

The fact that Phillip had been an eye witness to Sophon's father's death had been very helpful. Phillip had been at the scene when John shot Sophon's father at close range. Point blank pulled the trigger and shot him dead. Phillip saw it all. He verified to Sophon that it was John who killed his father, no one else. John was a murderer. The verdict: guilty as charged. If the CIA had not intervened, covering up the crime; John would now be on death row.

It was easy for Phillip to make the CIA the bad guys. The US Agency possessed a poor reputation in Thailand. In this respect, his case was not difficult to make. In fact, it had all been easy. So easy, Phillip never questioned his assumptions. He assumed Sophon would execute John.

Phillip's only unanswered question was who would take control of John's company after John was dead. And even though Phillip was not absolutely assured of getting the job, again he had few doubts about his conclusions.

Before confronting John in Belize, Sophon had traveled to Grand Haven, Michigan to meet with Phillip. Aside from convincing Sophon that John was his father's murderer, Phillip used the opportunity to act as the young man's mentor. Like an actor on a stage, he regaled Sophon with story after story, illustrating his experience in the gemstone business and patiently demonstrating his technical knowledge of gemology. He told Sophon stories of the history of gemstones in Thailand, stories even Sophon did not know. Phillip had expertly played his part until he was convinced Sophon would naturally turn to him to run the company as soon as John was dead.

Now it was only a matter of time until it all happened. Phillip only had to wait. But Phillip hated waiting. Not that he couldn't wait. Phillip had taught himself to be a patient man. Patience was a matter of discipline. Phillip could be disciplined when he chose to be, and he had been very patient. For a week he waited for the phone call he knew would come from Sophon. But when it took longer than he assumed it should, Phillip became impatient. He badly wanted to know what was happening. Temporarily putting aside his disciplined behavior, he called Sophon's cell phone. Then he called it again, a second time when the first call was not answered. And again... same result, the phone rang, no one answered.

Frustrated, Phillip called Sophon's uncle in Thailand. The old man refused to talk to him. Phillip then tried calling John's office in Charlottesville, thinking someone there might tell him what he wanted to know, tell him John was dead. He learned nothing. Phillip was simply told John was currently not be answering calls, out of the country on business.

His frustration now in high gear, Phillip began calling anyone and everyone he could think of to receive the news he desired: the news of John's death. He discovered nothing, nothing new. Every call was unproductive. No one knew anything.

So, when his phone rang before lunch on Friday, Phillip badly wanted it to be Sophon calling and as it turned out he was not disappointed. However, the subdued tone of Sophon's voice on the other end of the line immediately caused him to be suspicious that something was wrong.

'I don't understand,' Phillip pleaded with Sophon after receiving a brief account of what happened in Belize.

'What do you not understand?' Sophon responded. 'I met with John Van Laan. We talked. Then I left. What are you asking?'

Phillip knew he should not ask Sophon why he had not killed John. This was never Phillip's plan. The decision to kill John had to come from Sophon and Sophon alone. It was not something Phillip could ask. Still, he needed to understand.

'I...I just thought that... Well, I guess I thought...' Then he stopped because he did not know where to go with his question.

'You thought I would kill him,' Sophon interjected.

'Well... yes, I guess I did.'

'I did not.'

'Why?' Phillip blurted in frustration even though he knew he should be keeping his mouth shut. But their conversation was wrong on so many levels. First because Phillip didn't think he would ever have to ask. He simply assumed it would be done by now. John Van Laan would finally get the reward he so earnestly deserved. Second, because he knew his emotional outburst would reveal to Sophon a side of his personality, a side Phillip did not want Sophon to see. This was not how Phillip wished to play the game. This was not his plan. It was all wrong.

But he had asked, and he couldn't take his question back.

Sophon replied, 'Because I decided not to kill him.'

BANGKOK, THAILAND, SUNDAY, NOVEMBER 22, 5:30 PM. LUANG

Sophon's great-uncle never got a call.

He didn't need one. He received news of what was happening in Belize in daily reports from one of the men assigned to be with Sophon. Every afternoon, his assistant promptly delivered a folded sheet of paper to Luang, simply placing it on his desk. The assistant never spoke to the old man. It was not his place to question Luang. His task completed, he retreated from his master's office quietly, closing the door quietly behind him.

Luang was upset, but not surprised after he read the report. After days of disappointment, he had come to think this might happen. His nephew's son had always been unpredictable.

In contrast, the boy's father, his nephew, simply called Nue. Nue was never hard to read. Luang always knew what his nephew would do. Luang's challenge when dealing with his nephew was to counsel him, to moderate his behavior, and to calm him down from time to time. Nue was impulsive, always rushing off on some sort of mission, never content, always looking to make things right quickly, never really considering the consequences of his actions, intent only on achieving his goals no matter what the cost.

In contrast, his nephew's son, Sophon, had his father's determination, but also dominant in his character were some of his mother's qualities. She was more introspective, more aware of her world and all that existed in it. She saw the complexity of life. She was more content to enjoy its beauty, less desiring to damage it. Luang liked his nephew's wife. He was sad when she died at a young age. Sophon had never known his real mother, never had the opportunity to be educated by her, taught to see the world in a different light, through her eyes instead of his father's. Luang was sure the boy would have loved his mother. They were very much alike. And now that Sophon was becoming an adult, the qualities which his mother possessed were beginning to be evident in her son.

But this made it hard for the boy. It was difficult because what his heart often told him to do was often the polar opposite of what he had been taught by his father. As a result, his behavior was often erratic, like a bouncing ball, bouncing this way and that. The old patriarch could never predict what Sophon would do.

When Luang read about what happened on an island in Central America, he was not surprised. But as he sat in his garden with evening tea, after having time to consider the implications, he was also disappointed. Although he personally abhorred the use of violence, some circumstances demanded excessive force. Every rule had exceptions.

This was one of those times. This was the one time when he wished his brother's son was still alive. His nephew would have done what needed to be accomplished. This was one time when his nephew's straightforward way of viewing the world was missed. One time when justice should have been quickly served, the family's honor avenged.

The foreigner should be dead.

BELIZE, MONDAY, NOVEMBER 23, 3:40 PM, JOHN

They never let me out of their sight.

Even after I told Sandy and Ilana, I was fine, they simply nodded as if they believed me and then continued to keep an eye on me constantly. Whenever I thought I was alone for one brief moment in time, one precious moment of freedom; I would look over my shoulder and discover one of them nearby, pretending to be doing something, looking innocent, but always watching over me.

I knew what they were doing, taking turns. I assumed they were afraid I would do something dumb again, something suicidal like swimming too far out to sea. That's why they were keeping an eye on me, but their efforts were ridiculously obvious. I finally confronted them when I couldn't tolerate their intrusive attention any longer. I told them I loved how they cared for me, but I would never do it again, never try to kill myself. I pleaded with them to please let me be.

They played dumb, simply asked what I was talking about. They said I was delusional. Said I was getting paranoid. Assured me I was wrong. But I knew what they were doing, always watching me. They had a schedule. I knew it. They were alternately assigned to watch me for certain hours every day.

It wasn't bad really. I loved them both. I liked having them around. They were beautiful in their skimpy bikinis, strutting their lovely bodies in the sun. It was great to be near them. Still, it felt confining and dismissive, like they were babysitting me. Like they didn't trust me. I guess this is what bothered me, the fact they didn't trust me. After a few days, it started to get on my nerves.

So, I began to make a game of it. I tried to ditch them. That afternoon, I slipped off the end of the dock and dove under water, swimming madly under the dock, rising slowly and quietly, hiding on the other side, waiting to see what would happen next.

Of course, I knew what would happen. I knew she would come looking for me.

Ilana was my assigned babysitter at that time, innocently taking a walk nearby. I could feel the dock instantly began to vibrate from her footsteps as she ran out to find me. Saw her shadow pass over the wood slats as I treaded water under the dock. Standing at the end of the dock, she searched for me. Seeing nothing in the water put her in a state of panic. She quickly dove into the water. Hiding behind a post, I peeked around it to see her swim under the water looking for me. When she rose to the surface for air, I dove under the water and rushed from behind, grabbing her around her waist. She struggled at first, causing a bikini strap to become loose, dangling at her side while she attempted to escape the clutches of the sea monster who had grabbed her.

Releasing her, I rose to the surface, grinning at her broadly.

The disgusted look on her face told me she was not too happy with my game. She quickly began to swim toward the ladder at the end of the dock, but I caught her before she got there, took her in my arms, kissing her hard on the mouth. She struggled to be free before relaxing in my arms as we treaded water.

Stepping on the bottom slat of the wood ladder, I held on to the side to let her go up first. She smiled, but when she took hold of the ladder with one hand holding her bikini top with her other hand, I took the opportunity to slip the bottom of her bathing suit down around her ankles with a grin. She turned to hit me. I let go of the ladder to avoid her flailing arms, falling into the water while grabbing her ankles and pulling until she released her hold of the ladder, splashing into the sea. Wiggling out of her bikini bottom she playfully wrapped her tan legs hard around my waist.

The Caribbean Sea on the shores of Belize is warm, almost like a preheated bathtub. The gently rolling water caresses your body and soothes it, rocking away stress. The sea is like a living breathing organism caring for you, taking you in her arms and holding you. I love the sea and I loved being in the sea with Ilana. I couldn't help it. It seemed only natural, an action so right that nothing at that moment could be wrong. It was wonderful to hold her, pressing her naked body against the ladder, entering her while the warm waters of the sea gently washed over our heated bodies.

She held me, eyes closed, moving to the rhythm of the waves, like this was the way making love should always be. This was her place, my island girl. She understood the sea and all its currents, all its movements. She was one with the wind and the waves. She was one with me. I breathed deeply and cried inside as we moved in unison until my pain and sorrow were released, washed away in exaltation, and my mind cleansed for one fleeting moment in time.

When we were done, she clung to me, her head on my shoulder for a long time as I held her body while standing on the ladder. Finally, she climbed up on the dock and sat there naked, waiting for me. I dived to the sea floor, searching for our swimming suits lying on the sand. Climbing the stairs with the suits in my hand, I saw Sandy quietly talking to Ilana.

When Sandy saw me on the ladder, she walked away.

BANGKOK, THAILAND, TUESDAY
NOVEMBER 25, 9:25 AM. SOPHON

Sophon casually viewed the streets of Bangkok as he rode in a taxi from the airport.

It felt like the first time he had ever been in the city; like everything looked new and different somehow. The trees, the flowers, the buildings, the streets... the constant flow of the people of his city; he took it all in. He breathed it all in. It felt good to be home again. He had been gone too long.

Arriving at his ancestral home, the large stone mansion his family had occupied for hundreds of years, the seat of power his family maintained, the symbol that designated his family as a power in the hierarchy of the political landscape that was the culture of Thailand, he didn't bother to greet his great uncle. He ignored the servant who held the door for him. Without saying a word to anyone, he went directly to his room to rest.

Perhaps it was jet lag... or something else... like possibly understanding that nothing could be gained from speaking to Luang at this time. Sophon had accomplished what he had traveled to do. He didn't feel the need to justify his actions to Luang or to anyone else. Soon the reins of the family's businesses would be in his hands. Before the trip he had not been anxious to take control. Now, after returning home, he was impatient with Luang's patronizing ways. He felt it was his time. He had dealt with the ghost of his father, something he needed to do first. Now was the time to get on with his life's work.

The only man standing in his way was the old patriarch, his great-uncle. But not yet. He was not ready. He was tired. He needed to rest. He needed time to think. Then, when he was ready, he would confront Luang and demand his birthright.

It was only natural and he was confident it would happen.

BELIZE, THURSDAY, NOVEMBER 26, 7:15 PM. JOHN

It was inevitable.

I always knew paradise did not exist, not on this earth anyway. Living with two exquisite women on a lush island in the Caribbean and in love with both of them... and more importantly, they in love with me... Couldn't last forever... It was too good, too perfect.

Perhaps the truth was that it never really existed in the first place. It was a myth found only in my mind. I believed it because I wanted it to be real. I wanted to live with and love them both.

Eventually, that became impossible.

If it ever was real, and I'm not sure it ever was; it disappeared the day I impulsively made love to Ilana off the end of the dock. Sandy never admitted it mattered to her, but something changed after that. Sandy was not the same. It was as if she stepped back from us, stepped aside; just a little. Not much, not enough to notice if you weren't paying attention, but enough to be noticeable to me.

It was as if she were trying to stay out of our way, like an intruder in our lives.

It was probably a result of everything; being kidnapped, scared we were going die, those days in hell when we were held captive. We tried to shrug off the memory of that agony. Tried to pretend it never happened, but that wasn't possible. The suffering was on our minds ever when we tried not to think about it. It was like driving through mountain valleys filled with pockets of fog. Even when you couldn't see the fog, you knew it was out there, ready to obscure your view of the road, threatening to be around the next corner, blinding your vision in an infinite gray haze, unable to see the rocky walls that life obscured behind the next curve in the road ahead... until it is too late... too late to avoid a crash.

It had to be the same for Sandy and Ilana, it was bound to cause us problems. We just didn't know when until it was too late. So, we laughed, we swam, we ate. We tried to act like it didn't matter. But it did... even though we didn't admit it. It did.

That evening, I sat on the front deck as the lime blue sea darkened and clouds near the horizon caught the sun's brilliant receding light in the west behind me. Normally I wasn't alone. They would be sitting with me, the three of us together having a drink before dark. But for some reason, I was alone that night, and Sophon was on my mind. Wondering why I was still alive. What had stopped him from killing me? Questions I could not answer.

Problem was, I'd had too much to drink, one too many glasses of beer; not an activity conducive to clear thinking.

Sandy appeared to be the convenient distraction I needed, sitting in the living room behind me reading a book.

'Hey Sandy,' I lazily yelled through the open door without bothering to get up.

She didn't respond.

'Come out here and sit with me,' I listlessly begged.

She shook her head, no.

'Ah, come on.'

She continued reading, ignoring me.

I went inside, her big blue eyes beckoning, and her blond hair falling easily around her shoulders. Wearing a light blue T-shirt and white shorts, her skin seemed to literally glow with a golden tan after days in the sun, looking absolutely irresistible.

'Want to go for a walk on the beach?' I asked.

Although it was obvious from the look on her face that she didn't want to be disturbed, I reached for her hand anyway, gently pulling until she reluctantly rose from the couch and followed me outside to the shore.

It was twilight and the wind normally becomes calm on the island. The sands on the beach cool, and the frantic activity of the day slows, the water and the land gracefully resting together in harmony. Seagulls along the shore could be seen standing on one leg with their beaks under their wings. Pelicans assume statuesque poses on dock posts. The sky fills with a soft evening light that never lingers long. Belize is too near the equator. The sun dips into the earth at a sharp angle. Day turns quickly into night.

I found myself wondering why some days are so different from others. It is as if we live in a house filled with many rooms.

We may occupy one room of our house one day but live in a completely different room the next day.

As Sandy and I continued our walk along the shore, night took up residence in one of the rooms of the house we occupied together. Stars quickly assumed their rightful place on the ceiling. A dark night sky painted the eastern wall of our room while the western wall was colored with the golden light of the setting sun beyond graying edifies to civilization built along the shore. Sea water cooled our feet, seeping harmlessly into grains of pale beach sand covering the floor of our peaceful room of solitude.

Yet, we were only too aware of the angry ghosts who lived in other rooms of our house. Rooms which also existed in the house we now occupied. These were rooms we did not wish to visit. These rooms could be filled with pain. Phantoms of fear had invaded our privileged abode, taken up residence in the rooms of our house; making our lives miserable, threatening us with death. Angry ghosts had come uninvited through open doors into the house we built for shelter. Ghosts of death desecrated rooms we built for contentment, coloring the walls of our peaceful rooms with streaks of blood and damp tears.

I wondered who was to blame for opening doors to these merciless intruders. Was it us? Were we responsible for welcoming these fearful apparitions into our house? Did we purposefully destroy our cherished abode, ushering peace and grace from some of our rooms like unwanted guests? Was it our greed and hate that welcomed these evil merchants of chaos into our house? Did we invite them?

Or are we not responsible?

Do we have no control over who enters our rooms?

A palm tree embedded in the sand near the shore was a natural bench. Its long, sloping trunk, sculpted by intense storms, had grown low, parallel to the beach sand, before rising into the sky, with leaves waving in a gentle breeze. I took her hand as we sat on the tree to rest, but she pulled away.

'What's wrong?' I asked.

Sandy never answers a question hastily. She hesitated, considering her answer for what seemed a long time before finally saying, 'I want to go home.'

'Then let's go home.'

'It's not that easy.'

'Why not?'

'John, sometimes you can be so dull.'

'Am I supposed to know what that means?' I asked as I turned to her. It was dark, too dark to see her face clearly, but I knew the look on her face all too well—a quizzical look that always begged the question: How can you be so stupid?

'Okay,' I said. 'You're right, we can't stay here forever. If now is the time to go home... Let's go home.'

'What? And just leave Ilana behind?'

'She lives here.'

'John, she loves you. Do you think you can just walk in and out of her life like she is a hotel?'

I didn't respond, hoping she was done, but Sandy was not done with me yet.

'She cares for you,' Sandy implored. 'She has helped you through some difficult times. You owe her if nothing else.'

'How about you?' I asked. 'Weren't you also kidnapped? And weren't we having a good time together before it happened.'

'Yes, we did, John. Do you regret it?'

'No, of course not. It was fun.'

'Yes, it was fun for a while. But now... well... things are different now.' She sighed.

'So, it isn't fun anymore?' I asked.

'No.'

'That's it? It's over for you and me?'

'That's it,' she stated.

'But that's not it for Ilana? It's not the same for her? Is that what you are saying?' I asked stupidly.

'Yes,' Sandy confirmed.

I tried to see her face in the shadows. I sensed something more, something Sandy was not telling me, but I couldn't see into her eyes. It was too dark. We were sitting in an isolated section of the beach, with very little light from nearby houses to illuminate the shore. Something invisible lay resting quietly on the water, whispering in the wind and brushing over us—something I had to know.

'Why... Why isn't it the same for...' the words stuck in my throat.

'It just isn't,' she responded simply as if she had been anticipating my question all along. 'I like you John, but that's it... I hope I have not misled you. I don't think I have... Have I? Have I misled you, John?'

Her voice in the darkness sounded like a rehearsed speech, like she was an actress, a good actress, playing a part. Telling me everything was different now, different than I understood. She wanted me to understand my relationship with her was different than what I had with Ilana. But I didn't want it to be different. I didn't want anything to change, not with her, not with Ilana. But this was not how she saw it. For her everything had changed and I was being foolish.

'No, Sandy,' I finally replied. 'You have never misled me.'

'Good, I'm glad.'

'Except maybe now.'

'What do you mean?'

'I don't believe you,' I said, not totally sure why I was questioning her, just instinctively knowing I was right.

After a short pause, she said, 'John, I want to go home. If you don't arrange it, I will buy my own ticket. I'm going home because this is not my home. This is where you and Ilana live and I don't belong here anymore.'

'Okay, I'll arrange a flight for you.'

'Thank you.'

The room we now occupied had walls stained with sadness.

GRAND HAVEN MICHIGAN, 11:50 PM.
PHILLIP

Thanksgiving, like all holidays, was nothing more than a minor inconvenience for Phillip.

He was only happy when he was in his office with his phone in his ear, verbally castrating enemies, scheming and calculating, lining up allies; always something new, something grand in the great drama that was his life where he was the hero. Holidays were nothing more than undesired delays in his well-orchestrated plans, blips on the radar screen of his life. He tolerated holidays. He did his duty to his family. He spent time with his mother and his sister. He never complained, but secretly he loathed the obligation. Especially the time he had to spend with his sister's family. Her two young boys were undisciplined terrors. Her husband was a worthless car salesman. And his mother, well, she was another story in his sorry life, a long story.

He had more important matters on his mind, matters which required his attention. His grand plans had not progressed as he envisioned. It was time for action. He had spent his Thanksgiving thinking about what to do next, when the holiday was over, thankfully over.

After careful consideration, Phillip had decided what he would do and now was the time to put his plan in play.

Thousands of miles away a phone rang in another part of the world as Phillip listened. It was already a new day where he was calling, not a holiday weekend across the ocean. People would be working where he was calling. It was a typical Friday morning there. He waited patiently, staring into the night through a dark window in his office. Finally, a female voice answered the phone speaking Thai.

Phillip spoke English in reply, speaking slowly and clearly so she would understand. He asked if he could speak to Sophon. He told the young woman who he was and where he was calling from. He spoke with a voice of authority, so she would be impressed and assume he was an important person.

She asked Phillip if he could wait.

'Of course,' he replied.

After a brief pause, 'I'm sorry, Sophon is unavailable.' she said with quiet sincerity,

Phillip was prepared for this possibility. If Sophon was not available, he asked to speak to Luang.

The girl hesitated. 'I'm sorry sir. Luang is not accepting phone calls at this time. Would you like me to tell him you called?'

Phillip knew this was how it worked. He did not expect to speak directly to Luang when he called. He knew the procedure: Leave his name with the house secretary. If Luang wanted to talk to Phillip, he would return his call, and the same would be true for Sophon.

Phillip hung up his phone reluctantly after responding 'Yes' to the secretary's question.

It promised to be a long night for Phillip. If either of them returned his call, it would be sometime tonight.

And if Phillip was not awake at the time of their call, he would be out of luck.

BELIZE, SUNDAY, NOVEMBER 29, 4:10 AM. JOHN

Ilana lay quietly sleeping beside me.

Her bed was big, king-size, big enough for three bodies to sleep comfortably. But tonight, like the last few nights, it was occupied by only two warm bodies: Ilana and me.

This was not what I desired. It was not something I had requested. It was something Sandy did. She wanted our sleeping arrangements to return to what they were when she and I arrived on the island, three separate bedrooms. This was not going to happen. No way was I sleeping in that upper bedroom ever again, the place where I had been tied to a bed for days and nights of agony. Plus, I couldn't sleep there even if I wanted to. The bed was gone. Ilana had it dumped it when I wasn't around. I wouldn't have noticed except when I went there to get some fresh clothes, the room was empty. I understood. The bed contained a world of horrible memories. I was glad it was gone.

Sandy was sleeping in the other upstairs bedroom. She had gone there to sleep the night she told me she wanted to return home.

So, everything was different now.

Ilana took the change in stride, never said a word, nothing to me, nothing to Sandy. They were still good friends, or at least they acted like they were friends. Nothing appeared to be different during the day. They still did all the same things together, made meals together; chatting up a storm most of the time. Nothing had changed on the outside, but inside we all knew it was different.

I tried to buy Sandy an airline ticket to San Francisco, but it was Thanksgiving weekend and flights were booked solid. To make matters worse, a big storm was moving through the Great Lakes and up the East Coast. Chicago's airports were closed and New York airports were running hours behind schedule. Air traffic delays were epidemic across the country. It was a mess. I finally gave up and called a jet charter service. They said they could send a plane down late Monday. I thanked them and hung up.

Sandy didn't know what I had arranged. I hadn't told her. And I hadn't told Ilana, not yet. I was putting it off.

It was time to get out of bed. I was tired of being awake with a hundred thoughts running through my troubled brain. As quiet as possible, so not to wake Ilana, I got up. It was warm outside, but without the heat of the sun, the early morning air felt cool. I put on a shirt, sweater and pair of shorts before wandering into the kitchen. An open bottle of wine sat on the counter. Thinking a half glass of wine might soothe my troubled spirit, I settled on a couch on the front deck and took a sip, letting a gentle breeze cool my overheated brain, hoping the wind might blow away the nightmares which had been running rampant inside my head. Ever since Sandy told me she wanted to go home; I could not stop thinking about what she said.

'John.'

Startled, I looked up, expecting to see Sandy, but it was Ilana who was standing over me dressed in her short night shirt.

'John, what are you doing out here?' she asked as a half-moon cast a line of shimmering light across the troubled sea, lighting her shadowed face.

'Couldn't sleep,' I replied. 'Go back to bed. I'm fine.'

'Do you really think I can let you be out here all by yourself?' she asked like it was the most logical question in the world.

I looked at her pale face. I was trying to chill. Night dreams and night thoughts had driven me out of bed. I was not looking for a confrontation. But ...

'Sit down, Ilana. I think it's time we talked,' I sighed, motioning her towards the couch where I was resting.

She looked very pretty in her nightshirt as the breeze played with her long black hair. When she raised her hand to brush her hair off her face, the love I felt for her was still there. Despite everything that happened, she was still the same wonderful woman who cared for me when I needed someone. I didn't want to have this conversation, but I knew it was something that needed to be done.

'I'm returning to Virginia,' I began, 'I'm leaving late Monday.'

She stared straight ahead without speaking.

'Say something, please,' I half begged.

'What do you want me to say?'

'I don't know, just say something.'

Silence.

'You know I have to go back some time,' I continued.

'Do you?'

'Ilana, my work, my home is in Virginia. You know I have to go.'

'I was hoping you would stay this time,' she said without emotion.

'You know I can't.'

'Why, have you not endured enough? Have you not learned anything, John Van Laan?'

'I can't give up my work. My company depends on me. You know this as well as anyone.'

'And if you are dead, will your company still need you then?'

'Ilana.'

'I know you are going, John Van Laan. I know I cannot stop you.'

'Do you want to come with me?' I asked.

She took her time answering, perhaps trying to decide if I was sincere. I was. At that moment, I was. If she wanted to come, she could come with me.

Finally, she answered. 'No. This is my home, John Van Laan. You will always be welcome here. This is your home too, if you want it to be...

After pausing, she continued, 'I will not leave my island. This is where I belong. Now you go where you need to go, and if you decide you wish to see me again someday, you know where to find me.'

She stood up and walked away, leaving me to sip my wine in discontent while staring absentmindedly out over the water. Slowly, my head fell on the back of the couch, and my eyes closed in sleep.

They came to me in a dream, rising out of a moon stream of dancing light, vacillating over the restless sea. She came first like she always did at times like this, the ghost of my beautiful dead Monica.

She knew I needed her. Riding on a wisp of misty vapor rising out of the sea, soft and kind, like a big gray heron in the night, rising on the wings of my imagination, she came to me slowly assuming the shape of a woman, a beautiful woman, her red hair streaming behind her streaked with blood falling like tears into the sea. She lingered near the shore for a moment while looking at me, looking at me with pity in her eyes, talking to me without saying a word.

He was standing beside her with his arm over her shoulder. His dark black complexion lay like a shadow over his handsome face. An expression of amusement was in his smile, like he too knew what I needed to do. And like always, he was mocking me for being a fool. Arny, my friend, my companion, the man who took care of me for so long. He stood next to her. They were friends in life, Arny and Monica, friends in a way I could not be their friend. I was his boss, and she was my lover. But they were friends, and there were times when I was jealous of their relationship.

They were talking about me and I understand what they are saying, but I did not want to listen to what they were suggesting.

I did not want to do what they were telling me to do.

BANGKOK, THAILAND, 6:35 PM. LUANG

Painted red wooden posts supported carved sculptures at the four corners of a ceramic tiled roof, which provided shade in the heat of the day and shelter from rain over a large deck. A nearby garden of flowering bushes and palm trees had been cultivated on the shore of an untroubled, small pond beside the deck. A bamboo fence surrounding the deck, pond, and garden served as a real and visual barrier to intrusions from the outside world.

In the middle of the deck, a tea setting for two had been placed on a simple wood table. Matching wood chairs surrounded the table, only two. Luang never allowed more than one guest to sit with him in his garden retreat. He had been waiting patiently for his nephew's son to join him, rehearsing what he planned to say to the young man. This evening was unusual. First, because Sophon seldom visited the old man. And second, because Luang rarely asked anyone to join him on his deck in the evening. This was his place. This was his time to rest after work.

He preferred to be alone.

More than anything else, this deck and garden surrounding a pond on the mansion's grounds belonged to him. He had changed nothing else on the estate. History and tradition rested in the magnificent abode of his ancestors. He didn't want anything else to be different. He wanted it to remain as it had been since he was a boy, no different than the first day he had come here with his father. All the great pictures on the walls of the house had not been moved, their ornately carved frames overlaid in gold leaf depicting scenes from the history of the family. The highly polished wood floors were as they had been for years. Statues carved from stone throughout the mansion are untouched. Nothing had been altered. All the shrines were as he remembered when he walked through this house for the first time, seeing everything through the eyes of a small boy, eyes filled with wonder looking at all, the rooms, the halls leading to more rooms, more halls, more rooms, high ornate ceilings. This grand house symbolized the prestige his family enjoyed: its history, its strength, its place of honor in this thriving city, as nothing else could.

His garden was his only contribution to the estate. It had taken him years to cultivate the soil surrounding the pond. With his hands and help from servants, he had removed overgrown native plants and replaced them with flowering bushes. Great palms had been planted to shade the edges of the pond. He had worked in his garden until he became too old and no longer had the stamina or the will to trouble the soil with his old, arthritic hands.

To better enjoy his garden, he had a wood deck built out over the edge of the pond many years ago. When it became obvious the deck needed shelter from rain and sun, the roof had been constructed over the deck. That's when this place had become his own. It was where he went to rest. Whenever he had a difficult problem to solve or when he simply wanted to be alone, away from the pressures of running the family businesses, he would sit on this deck and let his mind wander.

Eventually, he habitually came to his deck every evening. Sometimes,, he sipped tea; sometimes, he drank wine. It was his place at the end of the day, his place to find peace.

So, it was with some reluctance that he invited Sophon to visit that evening. He doubted their discussion would be restful. And yet, this seemed an appropriate place to have the conversation.

Luang closed his eyes for a moment and rested. It had been a long and difficult day. He was weary. It was not like when he was young when he could work for long hours and never get tired.

When he opened his eyes, Sophon was standing over him, tall and strong.

Luang suddenly felt very small and old.

SAN FRANCISCO, CALIFORNIA, TUESDAY, DECEMBER 1, 3:05 AM. JOHN

We slept only briefly on the flight home that night.

She more than I. Perhaps because I was desperately trying to think of something to say to make it right with her. Finally, after an extended period of painful silence, our chartered plane began to descend despite the fact I had yet to accomplish my mission.

The skyline of San Francisco appeared below, obscured in a gray fog concealing all but the tallest buildings. Thousands of lights shining through the dense mist made the fog appear to be a living, breathing life form as it rolled in off the bay, devouring the city. The view from my window seat turned quickly gray as the plane descended towards the runway. I turned to Sandy, who was silently sitting across from me in a tan leather armchair. Only one strained, tense conversation had passed between us during the flight. It was obvious she was not a happy camper.

Turbulence rocked the plane as the pilot jockeyed for the runway on instruments, causing her to raise her head briefly from a book she had been reading.

'We're landing,' I interjected lamely, hoping for some meaningful dialogue.

All previous attempts had gone nowhere. Only this one last opportunity existed before landing, then she would be gone. I wasn't being naïve at the time. I was fully aware the odds of success were slim. To begin with, she was very unhappy with me. This had been unambiguously communicated to me even before we left the island. She informed me that I was my mental health was in no condition to return to work. She was worried I might do something stupid again, and this time, neither she nor Ilana would be around to rescue me. I assured her I wasn't planning anything remotely suicidal. Told her she didn't need to worry. But from the look she gave me, well... it didn't appear I was very convincing.

My initial attempt to talk with her on the plane had ended in utter failure, with her berating me in no uncertain terms for leaving Ilana behind. She made it eminently clear she thought I belonged in Belize, nowhere else...end of conversation... Well almost. She did add that chartering a plane to fly her home was a big waste of money. She said she would have been perfectly content to fly on a commercial flight. Said she didn't need, nor want, this kind of expensive attention anymore.

I explained that all commercial flights were booked. A big winter storm in the East had disrupted flights across the country. People were stranded in airports trying to get home after Thanksgiving. A private plane was the only method available to transport her safely.

She said she could have waited.

I countered; said I was returning to Charlottesville anyway. San Francisco was merely a detour in the flight plan.

Now, that comment didn't go over well. She looked at me as if I was as stupid as my remark warranted.

'Okay,' I admitted. 'San Francisco and Charlottesville, Virginia, are not exactly in the same direction from Belize, more like at the opposite ends of the continent. So, what?'

I then confessed to booking a chartered flight because I wanted to talk to her in private?'

No comment.

BANGKOK, 5:10 PM. LUANG

The long, glossy conference table in the great hall of the family's mansion was uncharacteristically covered with papers scattered with unaccustomed consideration.

Constantly blinking laptop computers added to the undisguised confusion. The meeting had been long and difficult. It was well past time when it should have adjourned. Family members were restless. Usual ceremonious order had dissolved into disarray hours before. Decorum had been tossed aside as the participants talked over each other while failing to resolve absolutely anything.

This unexpected lack of progress and order did nothing to deter the old patriarch's foreboding worries of disaster. Without order, Luang feared greatly for the future of the family. Generations of wealth and power could be lost forever. Only Sophon seemed to be content, sitting stoically at one end of the long table. While everyone else was looking decidedly anxious, Sophon looked unconcerned.

This emergency session of the family council had been called by the old patriarch. He urgently wished to discuss an important matter. His call for a meeting had gone out on a Sunday evening. That in itself was very unusual. No meeting had ever been called on a Sunday night. Most meetings were called with a minimum of two weeks' notice. Naturally, family members were both surprised and concerned when they received a late call telling them a meeting would be held in two days. Due to the short notice, an unusually large number of chairs at the long table were empty. Not everyone found it possible to make it to the meeting. Those who were physically unable to be in attendance were listening on several conference telephones placed in the middle of the table.

As the meeting drifted on monotonously without resolution, Luang occasionally could be seen looking down with his hands holding his head. The truth was he was tired. He was starting to think he lacked the will to proceed. Yet he knew he owed his brother's son this one last effort to make things right. It was his duty as the head of the family.

He had reluctantly called this meeting only after a frank conversation with Sophon failed to achieve his desired result. While sitting on his garden deck Sunday evening, they had discussed the matter openly. Luang had hoped that talking to the boy face-to-face would resolve his concerns. He told Sophon exactly what he expected of him. He explained to Sophon in detail what he needed to do and why. He used all the tools at his disposal to make his case. Quotes from the young man's dead relatives were invoked. Stories of valor and honor from the family's history were told.

Nothing produced the desired result.

It wasn't because Sophon had not listened carefully to his great uncle. He did, but when Luang was finished; Sophon had simply said it was over. He had met with John Van Laan. They had talked and Sophon had decided killing this man would accomplish nothing. It was time to move on. More important work needed to be considered.

Luang had pleaded with the boy and told Sophon plainly it was his duty to avenge his father's death. But even then, the young man had refused to be moved; unwilling to discuss the matter further. In the face of such bold insolence, Luang had stormed out, leaving his nephew's son to enjoy the flowers in his garden alone. Luang was angry. Immediately, he issued a call for a meeting of the family council.

Sophon understood why Luang desired the meeting. He knew Luang had no choice but to seek support from the family if he wanted to accomplish his goal. But Sophon had his own reasons for wanting a meeting.

'Well, great uncle. What is your decision?' Sophon finally asked from across the long expanse of the table. Discussion had continued long enough. It was time for a decision.

Luang looked at the young man. Unpredictable as always, he mused. Far from getting what he wanted from Sophon, Sophon had raised a new question.

Luang had called the meeting for the sole purpose of dealing with the problem of John Van Laan. He had hoped that the family might convince Sophon to avenge his father's death. Luang wanted this man killed for murdering his nephew. And even if Sophon continued to refuse, even then the meeting might not be a total loss. Because if this happened, Luang planned to ask the family to appoint someone else to do the job. He wanted the job accomplished as soon as possible. Everything depended on it. It had to be done. Only after the American was dead, only then could the business of the family move forward.

But Sophon had taken Luang by surprise.

After Luang explained what he wanted, Sophon raised a separate issue. He suggested it was time for Luang to step down. Sophon said that he should be allowed to sit in the chair at the head of the table. Sophon asked the family to give him what was rightfully his by birth. His father was dead, and he was the true heir to the seat of power at the head of the table, the seat his great-uncle had assumed after his father's death. Sophon said he was ready. He had thanked his uncle for his service in a time of need, but now it was time for his uncle to step aside.

His great uncle had objected, suggesting revenge needed to be accomplished first; the American intruder needed to die. Transferring power to the Sophon could wait until later.

Sophon disagreed. Argued it wasn't necessary to wait.

And so, a discussion began among the members of the family. It had been long and hard, voices coming from the teleconference phone sounding exhausted after almost two hours. A decision was needed.

Sophon looked at his great uncle. The old man's strength was ebbing. His resolve was weakening. It was time. Only one solution could solve their dilemma. He would offer it now.

'Uncle,' Sophon spoke very slowly with caution and dignity. Sophon knew he needed to choose his words carefully if he wished to succeed, speak with authority, and act like a leader. This was his opportunity to demonstrate maturity.

'I know how much it means to you to deal with the American,' Sophon began. 'But as I have said, I think action is ill-advised, and I will not participate... However, I will allow this matter to move forward with my approval after the seat of power has been transferred to me. I promise you; I will not stand in your way.'

Luang looked at Sophon. Once again, the boy had surprised him. He wondered if he could trust the young man. He took a moment to stare into Sophon's eyes. Even though the distance between them was long, Luang could clearly see the sincere eyes of the boy's mother looking at him. Instantly, Luang felt he could trust this young man.

'I nominate Sophon to sit at the head of this table,' the old patriarch stated simply without further explanation.

If anyone was listening closely, they may have heard a sigh escaping from Luang's lips at the end of his sentence. Luang was ready to step down, more than ready. His duty was done. He was tired. His garden was beckoning him.

'Great uncle,' Sophon said. 'I humbly accept your nomination, and I thank you for it. But before this matter is concluded, I want you to know that I will place one condition on your desire to have the American killed.'

'And what is that?' Luang asked in exasperation. Just when it seemed the meeting could be concluded in a positive manner, Sophon wanted something else.

'You must be physically present when my father is avenged,' Sophon said without emotion. 'Your eyes must verify the American's death.'

SAN FRANCISCO, CALIFORNIA, 3:25 AM, JOHN

The plush leather seats in the interior of the chartered plane vibrated in harmony with the plane's revving engines, alternately accelerating and decelerating as the silver bird rolled and bumped uncomfortably down long cement airport taxiways, headed for the San Francisco airport terminal building, which serviced private planes.

Sandy sat belted into an opposite seat from me, still steadfastly refusing to look in my direction. After hours of traveling through the air at close to the speed of sound, I sensed I had been going backward in everything I had hoped to accomplish on this trip, going nowhere fast in terms of coming to an understanding with her.

The plane came to an abrupt halt outside the terminal, its engines winding down. Through my cabin window, I could see a black limo drive up to the plane. It was the car I had ordered for her. It was the middle of the night. The thought of Sandy wandering around town alone made me uncomfortable.

'I ordered a car for you,' I explained.

'I don't want your car.'

'Please take it. I will feel better knowing you will get home safely.'

'I can make it on my own,' she stated emphatically.

'Sandy, please,' Taking hold of her arm, but she pulled away. 'Sandy, wait, just one minute, please.'

She turned.

'You know I have loved you since high school,' I blurted because I didn't know what else to say. 'And I still do.'

She looked at me long and hard. Turning away without a word, she headed down the aisle. As soon as the copilot opened the door and lowered the stairs, the lady was gone. Overhead lights illuminating the tarmac witnessed her walking away. I wondered if this was the last time I would ever see her.

An airport employee took her bags from the luggage compartment in the rear of the plane and placed them on the ground. Throwing her black and brown overnight bag over her shoulder, she grabbed the handle of her wheeled suitcase and trudged towards the doors to the terminal building in obvious discomfort under a load of baggage, walking steadfastly past a surprised limo driver who had opened the trunk of his car for her.

Her blond curls flowed in the wind as she hurried away.

GRAND HAVEN, MICHIGAN, 6:50 AM.
PHILLIP

He was in his office early waiting patiently for over an hour, waiting for a call.

Phillip knew all about the meeting in Bangkok. He had a spy inside the mansion's grand hall. Not a spy really, more like a friend who was a member of the family, a man he had befriended when he traveled in Thailand.

Most of his calls to this man had no purpose and asked for nothing. He didn't want to jeopardize his source. However, this morning was different. He was feeling uncharacteristically anxious because this morning, Phillip wanted something from his friend, something he had been unable to get from either Sophon or Luang. Information which was desperately important to him.

What he wanted to know was had the Thai family decided to seek revenge. Make John suffer the consequences of killing Nue. If the answer was yes, then Phillip would be happy. In fact, it couldn't happen soon enough for him.

Although Phillip would never acknowledge it, he would miss John after John was dead. Because more than anything, Phillip loved having an enemy. He loved them in ways few men understood. His enemies gave him life. They gave him energy. They were the reason he got up in the morning. They gave him something to think about: plans to be made, allies to be gathered, telephone calls to be dialed. His enemies were his life. So, after John was dead, Phillip would feel sad, but the feeling wouldn't last long, only as long as it took for Phillip to identify his next enemy.

For now, Phillip was excited. He was convinced the Thai would decide to kill his arch-enemy. And this meant Phillip needed to be prepared; ready and able to offer them assistance because Phillip assumed it would be good to be helpful. Not so helpful as to get in trouble with the law, but helpful enough that when it was over; he could ask for something in return for services rendered.

All part of the plan, his brilliant plan.

CHARLOTTESVILLE, VIRGINIA, TUESDAY, DECEMBER 22, 4:25 PM. JOHN

I owed my friend Charlie a call that I had no desire to make.

Charlie and I have an unusual relationship bred out of a complex history that was not always cordial but which had forged a formidable friendship that demanded attention from time to time if it is going to last.

However, work was piled high on my desk when I returned to my office in Charlottesville. My secretary, Helen, had a 'to-do' list a mile long, which made it easy to avoid thinking about Charlie or anything else like what happened in Belize. All the pain, all the trauma, the problems I had with Ilana and Sandy... Sophon, the whole mess. Work allowed me to put the whole stinking affair out of my mind and concentrate on something else instead. It was a relief, like a tonic for my over-wired brain. Work became my life again. The everyday duties of my job allowed me to shove the whole Belizean lurid affair into the back of my brain where I didn't have to think about it.

And I needed this. I needed it badly. I needed to think about something else for my mental health if nothing else.

So, I worked. I worked long, and I worked hard. I immersed my tangled, messy mind in my job as never before, working twelve, sometimes fourteen hours a day. Taking only time to eat and sleep. Then it was back to my office in the morning, back to the place where I didn't have to think about what happened in Belize.

However, as Christmas approached, the demands of my job slowed. And like a bubbling seeping volcano which had been slowly working its way to the surface by great pressure from beneath; it all returned to me; all the memories from Belize began to haunt my sleep again and occupy my thoughts during the day. Every time the work slowed, every moment I had nothing else to think about, the past came back to visit me.

And so, I reasoned that as long as I was thinking about what happened in Belize again, I should probably call Charlie and tell him the story. He deserved to know if for no other reason than I owed him. He had saved my life on more than one occasion. And he might have to do it again. It was time to call him, past time. Even so, I resisted and procrastinated. However, my desk was uncharacteristically clean that afternoon. Nothing required my immediate attention. And my phone seemed to be staring at me, begging me to call Charlie.

Almost everyone was gone at the time or preparing to escape for Christmas break. Even Helen, my secretary, was planning to be away for a week. It was time for her semiannual visit with her daughter in another city. Which city, I didn't know. She seldom visited her daughter. Apparently, she didn't get along with her son-in-law. Or maybe it was the other way around, she didn't say. I just knew she had grandchildren and a daughter, but she seldom traveled to see them. She blamed him, her son-in-law. That's what she told me. It seemed a shame, but then, everyone has their problems.

It occurred to me that Charlie might also have gone home. I could only hope. Then I wouldn't have to talk to him. It was almost Christmas, after all. Maybe I could simply call and leave a message on his answering machine, not have to actually talk to him, putting it off until another day. I decided it was worth the gamble.

Dialing the direct number to his desk, I was relieved to hear his phone ring several times at CIA Headquarters in Langley, Virginia, ringing and ringing plaintively with no one to pick it up. I envisioned an empty office, happy Charlie was not present to answer his phone. But as I was thankfully anticipating an obnoxious greeting from his voicemail, a real person answered instead.

'Hello.' Charlie said. 'Hello... Come on, John, say something; I know it's you. I have caller ID. This is the CIA, after all. You can't expect to call anonymously and then hang up... Say something.'

'Charlie?' I replied somewhat hesitantly.

'Who else did you think was going to answer? Did you dial the wrong number, John?'

'No, I mean, well... I just assumed you might be gone. So...'

'Would you rather talk to my voicemail?' he asked. 'I can arrange that. Hang up and call back.'

'No, that will not be necessary. I'm happy to talk to you.'

'Well, good. Now that we have that settled, why did you call?'

'Okay, Charlie, it's just... how do I say this?'

'I don't like how this conversation is beginning, John,' he interrupted. 'You didn't call to wish me Merry Christmas, did you? And you probably don't have good news, do you?'

'Not exactly... well, some good news. The good news is I'm talking to you.'

'So, am I to assume that means you are not dead,' Charlie asked. 'Even though you should be dead?'

'Yea, right, I should be dead.'

'And that is your good news?' he comically countered.

'Right, Charlie. Good news for me.'

'Okay, enough theatrics. Tell me what happened?'

I told him the whole story even though I didn't want to. I didn't leave anything out. Well, nothing important was left out. For instance, I didn't tell him about my relationship with the ladies. I kept this information to myself. It was personal.

He listened without saying a word. One of the attributes of a good CIA agent is the ability to listen. I couldn't see him, so I didn't know if he was taking notes, but I wouldn't put that past him. He was very good with details.

When I finished, my phone was silent.

'Okay,' he finally asked. 'So why did you call? Do you want something from me?'

'No, I just thought you should know.'

'Okay, thanks for the information. I do have one question, though. I'm a little confused about why you waited so long to call. When exactly did this happen?'

'About a month ago.'

'And you waited until now to tell me because?'

'Look, Charlie. It's over. I just thought you should know. That's all.'

'That's it. A guy commandeers your boat and takes you captive for several days. Subjects you to torture, threatens to kill you, and you wait a month to call. And when you finally call, you say you don't want anything from me. Is that right?'

'It's over, nothing to ask.'

'And you think it is over because?'

'Because he walked away. He could have killed me, but he chose not to.'

'So, you have concluded he won't come back?'

'He won't.'

'John, you killed his father. And apparently, from what you just told me, he knows this. In fact, if I heard you correctly, you admitted it. So now he has proof positive his father didn't die in a helicopter accident, right?'

'I guess.'

'Look, John, just because he didn't have the balls to kill you the last time doesn't mean he won't come back to finish the job. Or send someone else to do it.'

'It's over, Charlie.'

'I don't think so.'

'See, this is why I was reluctant to call you,' I responded.

'So, my trying to keep you alive, so that's a bad thing?' Charlie said with a hint of exasperation in his voice.

'It's over, Charlie. And I don't want to think about it anymore. I called you because I thought you should know. That's all. I didn't call because I wanted something. Do you understand?'

'I only understand you are not thinking clearly.'

'Charlie.'

'John, do you remember what happened the last time you refused to take my advice.'

'That was different.'

'I don't think so.'

We talked some more but got nowhere. He said he was on duty for the next few weeks. Someone had to be. The CIA doesn't close for Christmas. He said he might swing down from Washington, DC, to see me.

I told him not to bother.

I was going home to Grand Haven for a few days.

GRAND HAVEN, MICHIGAN, MONDAY, DECEMBER 28, 5:50 PM. JOHN

Apple pie, ham with a dark brown sugar crust, laughing children, presents, family; my brother's obnoxious kids and wife flew in from Seattle for the Christmas festivities.

Dad and mom were happy to have the family together. I guess it was alright and I did my part, the proper family Christmas obligation to make everyone happy; I showed up. Truth, was I didn't want to, but I did anyway. Mostly because there wasn't much to do at work. I took the opportunity to fly to Grand Haven.

Now it was over, thankfully over, one more Christmas complete with presents and kisses and, well... you know, family hassles. Mother had a little talk with me. Seems she was not happy with my lifestyle; no wife, no pending grandkids in her future... not a proper way to live in her mind. Dad remained silent. I listened without comment, wishing my dad would tell her to leave me alone while sensing my brother was grinning behind my back.

The outside temperatures during the festivities hovered between single digits at night and the teens during the day. No ice on the lake shore yet, but it wouldn't be long. The ice would come soon.

Alone inside my cottage, listening to a cold, hard-metal wind whistle through barren trees outside, whitecaps dotted an angry, dark green Lake Michigan outside my windows. A few seagulls could be seen playing in the wind, rising and falling through a gray sky. It would be dark soon. Night comes early this time of year in the north country. The sun had already disappeared and dropped below the water, vanishing anonymously into a cloud-dominated sky.

I was finally alone, no relatives to tolerate. It was time for solitude, time to think and plan. This was my usual habit, use the holiday lull to plan for the coming new year. Trouble was I didn't want to plan. Planning took thought and thought meant thinking about what happened in Belize. And I didn't want to think about Sophon or any part of that ugly mess.

Ilana called during the holidays. She sounded cheerful. It was impossible to get that woman down. She was a survivor. She had her island, her house, and more money than she could spend in a lifetime. But she wanted more. We all do. She was no different. However, disappointment never affected her for long. She was too busy living in the moment. I wished her well. I told her I would visit her soon. She wanted to know when. I told her I didn't know.

Truth was, I wasn't telling the truth, and I think she knew it. Our conversation ended with a whimper, a genuine lack of enthusiasm, a quick goodbye. She didn't sound too terribly disappointed in the end. Maybe she had experienced enough bad times with me. Maybe she was beginning to think life without me was better than life with me. I didn't know, and she didn't say.

I sipped some wine and watched the clouds fade to a black night sky. Sandy was on my mind. Our last conversation on the plane was playing in my subconscious as white caps appeared like gray ghosts rising out of the invisible mist over the waters of the big lake, marching to shore on cold night winds like an invading army of anxious thoughts. I would have preferred to be outside on the front deck facing the elements head-on, living with the wind and the sound of crashing waves, but wisdom dictated otherwise. The icy wind was simply too cold.

It was time to turn on some lights. The cottage was almost completely dark inside. But turning on lights would cause the picture outside my windows to disappear. I hesitated because black windows always make me feel alone.

Sitting in the semi-darkness with a half-filled glass of wine, my thoughts naturally turned to Sandy again, wondering how she was doing. I had considered calling her a few times, but it never seemed like the right thing to do. The last time I saw her, she was visibly upset with me. I couldn't blame her. She had endured something terrible with me. I was sure it left scars on her mind, scars which would not easily fade away. Her wounds might heal with time, but it could take a long time, and there was nothing I could do or say to help.

I didn't call.

TUESDAY, DECEMBER 29, 6:50 PM. JOHN

David called while I was at the cottage.

He is my best friend and legal advisor. He lives in Grand Haven where we grew up together. His life is the life I probably should be living; the life my mother would prefer; you know, a wife, kids, and a good job; a normal life.

We have remained friends and David has helped me through some rough times. His advice has always been welcome, but that day it was not. Seems Charlie called him and apparently, they had decided to tag-team me like two wrestlers. They both wanted me to do something about what happened in Belize. They thought I should take it to the authorities.

David gave me his usual carefully prepared legal spiel, like a lawyer to a jury. I listened patiently, but I wasn't buying. I cut him off after a few minutes. Told him it was over. I didn't want to do anything. He said that was crazy. I said the only thing that was crazy was me, so drop it.

My last comment didn't go over very well, but after a brief pause, he asked if we could get together for lunch. I said I wasn't leaving until Monday and I would meet with him only if he promised no more talk about Belize. He agreed.

As soon as he hung up, I got another call.

I was inclined to let the phone ring at the time. It was evening and David's call had interrupted my reading a book by Nelson De Mille. The book had been helping me take my mind off all the stuff I didn't want to think about. I was trying to relax. David's call, on the other hand, was not relaxing and I was not motivated to talk to someone else who might make my life even more miserable.

I answered the phone anyway, assuming for some unknown reason, that the second call was probably from my mother. She had promised to call me after our last unfulfilling conversation, said we needed to talk some more. I wasn't so sure I wanted to talk to her, but I decided to get it over. I knew she wouldn't let up until she had given me another blast of motherly wisdom.

The caller was not my mother.

His accent was Thai, but I could easily understand his English because he spoke slowly and carefully. Said his name was Luang, and he wanted to know if he could meet with me. I asked him what did he wanted to talk to me about? He said he was Sophon's great uncle and he wanted to talk to me about Sophon.

I was shocked.

Nothing coherent escaped my mouth for a second or two. I didn't know what to say. Finally, I managed to mumble something about when he would like to meet. He said he was in the US for the holidays. He wondered if he could visit me this week. I asked him if he knew where Grand Haven, Michigan, was. He said he did. He suggested we meet in a public place of my choosing if I wished. Or he was willing to come to my home if that was more convenient. It was my choice. We settled on Saturday afternoon at my cottage. I gave him the address.

His call was completely unexpected, like an accident which happens so fast and is so out of the ordinary, it throws you into circumstances for which you are totally unprepared, no time to analyze what is happening, no time to make logical decisions. Just react instinctively and then it is over before you have the opportunity to consider the consequences.

The Nelson De Mille book lay open on a table near my favorite armchair after the phone call. I thought about returning to it to settle my mind, but when I did, the sentences were incoherent. I couldn't concentrate. I kept thinking about the phone call. Luang, Sophon's great uncle. So why did he want to talk to me? What could I possibly do to help him with Sophon? I couldn't think of anything. And now that I had time to think about it, how did he know where I lived? And how did he get my cell phone number?

Too many questions, too many unanswered questions.

I badly wanted to call him back and start over, but that seemed inappropriate.

FRIDAY, JANUARY 1, 1999, 1:45 PM. JOHN

Ilana called in the afternoon to wish me a Happy New Year.

We talked, nothing special; small talk to pass the time; like casually mentioning I had talked to Sophon's great uncle, and he was coming to see me.

'Who is coming?' she asked.

It was a clear blue day, not a typical day for cloudy West Michigan in the winter. A cold, crystal clean wind blew off the big lake from the northwest. The sun was bright and shining through the sliding glass windows, warming the interior of the cottage. Waves crashed ominously outside, cascading high into the air, spraying newly formed chunks of ice and water rushing up on shore. A few boot tracks marred an otherwise smooth, snow covered beach.

'A man named Luang,' I replied. 'He said he is Sophon's great uncle. He wants to talk to me about his nephew.'

'Sophon's uncle?' she asked skeptically. 'Do you remember who Sophon is? He's the guy who kidnapped us and almost killed you in Belize.'

'He sounded nice on the phone, very polite.'

'John, I am afraid for you.'

'Why?'

'Where do you plan to meet this man?' Ilana asked, pressing the issue.

'Here, at my cottage.'

'You are at your cottage now?'

'Yes.'

'Are you alone?'

'Are you asking me if I have any other girlfriends here?'

'No, I am asking if you have anyone to protect you in case this man has come to kill you.'

'He's an old man.'

'How do you know that?'

I didn't answer.

'When are you going to meet with him?' she asked.

'Two, tomorrow afternoon.'

'Have you told anyone about this meeting?'

'No.'

'John, this man could be dangerous.'

'I don't think so.'

'Why not?'

'Because if Sophon wanted to kill me, I would already be dead.'

2:35 PM. JOHN

'John, are you suicidal? Have you lost your mind?'

No hello. No, how are you? No pleasantries before diving in. Sandy wasted no time before letting me have it with both barrels. It was as if no time had passed between when she walked off the plane in a huff and now. She was in the same bitter frame of mind, which meant nothing but trouble for me.

I, of course, knew who she was even though she did not bother to introduce herself when she called. The gentle inflection in her voice, the soft underlining tone behind her harsh words, the self-confidence; I knew it was her.

'How are you, Sandy?' I inquired. 'It certainly is good to hear from you again. How is everything in San Francisco?'

'I didn't call to talk about me,' she instructed. 'I called to talk about you.'

'Okay, I guess if that's what it takes for you to call, let's talk about me and whatever else is on your mind.'

'You know what is on my mind.'

'Indulge me, please. In case you haven't noticed, it has been several weeks since we last spoke. How could I possibly know what is on your mind?'

'John, don't play dumb with me. I just got a call from Ilana. She told me you are planning to meet with Sophon's uncle. And she mentioned you planned to do this alone at your cottage. I said, not possible. The John Van Laan I know is not that stupid.'

She paused, I assumed, for effect.

I said nothing. Because I could think of nothing to say in my defense, nothing she would accept.

'Well,' she asked. 'Is it true? Are you that stupid?'

'I don't think the meeting is going to be a problem,' I replied, even though I knew I couldn't win an argument with her. Oddly, at that moment, I remembered my recent conversation with Charlie, something about Sophon sending someone else to do the job. But, could it be an old man, would Sophon send an old man? Seemed highly unlikely.

'It's his great uncle. The guy has to be ancient.' I argued.

'John, are you trying to get yourself killed?'

'Sandy...'

'No... you listen to me, John Van Laan. You need to get out of there now. Do you understand? Get out of that cottage. And John.'

'What?' I asked, now resigned, no way could I argue with this woman, never could, especially not when she was in one of her moods.

'Call me when you are safe. Or...' she hesitated.

'Don't bother to ever call me again.'

4:55 PM. JOHN

Snow blew sideways across the road, accumulating slowly.

Not enough snow to stop me, but enough to make me slow down. My car's heater was on high. It was comfortable inside, but outside, the weather was deteriorating. It was starting to snow, and the wide tires on my Porsche were making my trip into town difficult. The tires were great for dry summer roads, but low-profile sport tires are nothing but trouble on snow-covered highways. I had to slow down. Going any faster could result in losing traction and a spinning exit off the highway.

I was heading south along the lake towards the highway after changing my mind and deciding to leave town. Or rather, it would be more correct to say Lana and Sandy had changed it for me. They said I needed to avoid meeting anyone from Thailand, especially someone related to Sophon. I didn't necessarily agree. However, somewhere in my feeble brain, I had to admit they might be right and it was probably the better part of wisdom to leave town.

It only took a few minutes to pack my bags and load the car. Snow started falling soon after I was on the road. And unfortunately, the cold white stuff was accumulating quickly, swirling in my rear-view mirror, making for slow but steady progress. Fortunately, a stiff crosswind was blowing some of the slippery stuff off the road, but only as fast as it was accumulating. And the wind was no help when it came to visibility. Seeing more than a short distance down the road through the falling snow was becoming difficult. As much as I wanted to increase speed, the weather demanded I take it easy, drive with a soft touch on the accelerator, make slow turns, and always be alert.

In good weather, a road trip to Grand Rapids from the lakeshore might take forty-five to sixty minutes. Today, it was going to take considerably longer. I planned to stay in a hotel near the airport for the night and catch an early flight out of town the next day.

Get on the road quickly, get away from the cottage as soon as possible; that was my plan. As I drove, I frequently checked my rear view mirror for any signs of a tail. So far, I didn't think I was being followed. I saw nothing. In fact, very few cars were on the road due to the snow storm.

Visibility suddenly disappeared into a white, snowy haze as I strained to see the road ahead. This can happen sometimes when traveling near the lakeshore. A brief downpour of snow from warm, evaporated lake water can dump over the stark, cold land, making it almost impossible to see. All but the edges of the road disappeared. Couldn't see anything except an occasional guard rail along the road and a few tall trees, gray shadows in a white blizzard marking the boundaries of the road. I slowed, feeling my way along the highway, searching visibly for the gravel shoulder to make sure I was on the road. Lights appeared suddenly in my rearview mirror, swerving to avoid hitting the back of my car. A big black monster SUV rushed past, blowing swirls of new snow across a moving white canvas. Thankfully, the wind quickly blew the snow away. Objects along the side of the road once more appeared against a white background after the cloud burst lifted.

I reached for my cell phone on the passenger seat while keeping my eyes on the road. I had one loose end I needed to clear.

'David.'

'Yes.'

'Sorry, I'm not going to be able to make lunch tomorrow.'

'Why not?'

'Have to return to the office. Work calls.'

He was silent for a moment. I wasn't sure he was buying my excuse.'

'Okay,' he finally replied.

'Look, I'll call you as soon as I get back to Charlottesville.'

'Okay... John?'

'Yes.'

'Is everything all right?'

'Yes.'

'You would tell me if it isn't?'

'I would tell you.'

'Okay, talk to you later.'

The phone went dead. I held it in my hand, thinking I probably should have told him the truth, but I didn't want to worry him.

The phone rang in my hand.

'Hello.'

'Mr. Van Laan,' a clipped Thai voice said.

'Yes.'

'My name is Luang.'

'Sophon's great uncle?'

'Yes, I am calling to confirm our meeting tomorrow.'

'I'm not sure I can make it,' I replied honestly.

'I have traveled a long way,' he interjected. 'I would like to talk to you.'

'Sorry, but I'm not sure I want to talk to you.'

After a pause, he said slowly, 'That is not possible.'

'I don't care. Every conversation I have had with someone from your family recently has turned out badly. I'm done talking to all of you.'

'Mr. Van Laan. It is better to prevent trouble before it comes to us. That is all I am asking. We need to talk.'

His words sounded like he was quoting something Zen. Perhaps I was wrong about this man.

'I'll think about it,' I responded. 'But if I meet with you, it will be on my terms. The last time I met with someone from your family, it was on his terms. And, as I'm sure you know, it caused me a great deal of grief.'

'I accept your terms. All I ask is to meet with you. The meeting shouldn't take long,' he added.

'Okay, let me think about it. How do I contact you?'

'I will call you.'

'Give me a week.'

'One week, yes, I will call you in a week. Where will you be?'

'I will be in my office in Charlottesville.'

'Thank you,' he replied. The line clicked off.

The snow slowed. A few miles down the road I passed a black SUV sitting upside down off the side of the road. Blinking lights from a cop car were already on the scene. A wailing siren from an ambulance cried in the distance. Thankfully, I did not have to stop to help. I wondered briefly if this was the guy who had passed me in a big hurry.

A few rays of sunshine miraculously peeked through puffy white clouds, and the road began to clear. My speed increased. The pavement, covered with a thin coat of melting wet snow, eventually dried.

Soon, I was traveling at close to the speed limit.

CHARLOTTESVILLE, VIRGINIA, SATURDAY, JANUARY 9, 4:35 PM. JOHN

The sound of rain dripping off the eaves of the roof, fell with monotonous drum-like regularity on the deck.

The TV was on in my apartment. It was playoff time for the behemoths of professional football fame. Announcers searched their limited vocabulary for voluminous sentences capable of filling silent airtime with anything remotely approximating an intelligent analysis of the game. Most of the time, they could be heard quoting irrelevant statistics or verbally replaying what could plainly be seen on the field, adding nothing material to the broadcast.

I had been watching because I had nothing better to do on a dull Saturday afternoon. Finally bored with football, I hit the off button on the TV. Searching my library for a book was tedious. I badly needed something to help get me through the afternoon. There was work I could do, but nothing important, nothing which required my immediate attention. I had been back in my office for a week, and I was caught up. My to-do list could wait until Monday. Besides, I wasn't motivated. I found a book that looked interesting but quickly placed it back on a library shelf for another day. I just couldn't get interested. The constant dull drip of rain disturbed my anxious thoughts, drip, drip, dripping into the caverns of my mind.

Luang.

I didn't want to admit it, but he was on my mind. Tomorrow he was scheduled to call. Problem was, I had not given him much thought since arriving at the office. I spent most of my time working instead. Truth was, I didn't want to think about him and all the attendant problems which came with him. Besides, I knew I could always say no, say I didn't want to meet with him and that would be the end of that.

But somehow... saying no didn't seem right.

Rain continued to fall tediously. It was too wet and cold to go for a walk. And it was too early to have a drink... or maybe not. What difference would it make? I was alone in my kitchen; no one to tell me what to do, tell me I couldn't start drinking early, no one of the feminine gender, that is, Ilana and Sandy, to be specific. I opened a bottle of wine, something red from Canada. Featherstone was the name on the label.

Security had been increased as soon as I returned. Just knowing Luang was in the country was enough to make me nervous. Dealing with his nephew had been a nightmare. And despite the fact I did not want to admit it, I had to admit that Sandy and Ilana were probably right. His arrival signaled a renewed interest in killing me.

Plus, I was still healing from the psychological wounds inflicted by Sophon. I didn't want to go through anything even remotely close to being kidnapped again. Office security staff had been doubled. I explained the danger and outlined the cause. Told my staff to be alert. Doors were locked down at all times. No one entered the building without an appointment.

A phone ringing in my apartment caught my attention.

I briefly hoped it was Sandy. I had called her earlier in the week after returning to my office. My excuse was her demand that I call her when I was safe. And, of course, she didn't answer, not that I expected she would. I was prepared to leave a voicemail. It explained that I had complied with her wishes. I was safe and sound in my office building in Charlottesville as she had instructed. And I had not met with the old man from Thailand. Then I asked her if there was anything else she needed or wanted from me because I was at her complete disposal, body, and soul. Not that I expected a reply. I assumed she would not. But I could hope, couldn't I?

Unfortunately, the phone call was not from Sandy.

'It's Buddy,' the caller said. 'You have a visitor.'

Buddy was the head guy in charge of office security. He had been with me for a few years. I briefly wondered why he was on duty on a weekend. Probably because he knew his boss was concerned.

'Who's here?' I asked.

'Ilana,' Buddy reported.

A trail of dripping water followed her across the wood floor when she entered my apartment. Her clothes were completely soaked. Seemed she hadn't brought a rain coat with her. And jeans, a sweater and a light blue coat were no match for a steady cold, northeastern rainstorm which greeted her at the airport. I guess she forgot how cold and wet it could be in Virginia in January. Her long black hair fell damp around her face.

She smiled weakly at me.

I gave her a hug and felt her tremble beneath my embrace.

6:35 PM. JOHN

Her wet clothes lay scattered over the bathroom floor where they had fallen after I peeled them off her wet, cold body.

Soaked to the bone, she was so cold she couldn't stop shivering. I turned on the shower. After undressing myself, I carried her into the shower, held her under the steaming hot water, and let the warm water flow softly over her small brown body. In a few minutes, she stopped shivering. Sliding out of my hold, she stood under the shower, nestled inside my embrace as hot water covered her back. When her hand reached to touch me where I liked being touched, I leaned over and kissed her waiting mouth. She had returned, my bundle of island joy. Lifting her, this time with a smile on her face, she wrapped her legs around my waist. Steam rose from the hot water, filling our world with disguised details and soft lines. She kissed my neck and held me tightly, unwilling to let go. I closed my eyes, feeling every soft curve of her body against me: her round breasts, her gentle thighs around my waist, the texture of her shiny black hair, her tongue searching for my lips. She was so beautiful, so pure, my island girl.

Pressing her back against the shower wall, I entered her, and we moved together to the remembered rhythm of her warm Caribbean Sea so very far away.

We ate the food she prepared, but not until after I found some warm clothes for her to wear. One of my big, heavy winter sweaters was the final touch in her evening outfit. It covered three or four layers of clothes she was wearing to stay warm. But it was not until I turned up the thermostat to about 80, only then did she finally look content.

We smiled. We laughed. We didn't talk about anything serious, reminiscing about times from our past. It was fun. It was great being with her again. At some point in our conversation, I mentioned to her that I had not met with Sophon's uncle at the cottage. I thought she would like to know. I said he still wanted to meet me, but I wasn't sure I wanted to meet him.

She smiled.

I didn't ask her why she came or how she knew where I was. I had decided to wait, content for the moment, to have her company. When she went into the bedroom to put away her clothes, unpack her suitcase; as I was cleaning the dishes in the kitchen sink, I heard her cell phone ring in my bedroom down the hall. She took the call as I continued to work, only vaguely aware of what she was saying.

'She wants to talk to you.' Ilana came into the kitchen with her cell phone in her hand.

'Who wants to talk to me?'

Ilana didn't respond, handing me her phone.

'Hi John,' Sandy said.

'Sandy?'

'You invited Ilana to visit you?' she asked.

'No, I had no idea she was coming. Guess she wanted it to be a surprise, kind of like someone else I know.'

'Thank you for not meeting with the man from Thailand,' Sandy replied, ignoring my comment.

'You're welcome.'

'Ilana tells me he still wants to meet with you. Have you decided what you are going to do about him?'

'Why did you call?' I asked, ignoring her question as she had been ignoring mine.

'I called Ilana. I didn't call you. We talk sometimes. We are friends.'

'I see.' It had not occurred to me that they would continue to talk. I guess I assumed their friendship would go on hold after Sandy returned to the States.

'Did you think I would ignore my friend Ilana just because I stopped talking to you?' Sandy confirmed.

'No, I guess not.'

The phone was silent for a moment. Finally, she asked, 'What are you planning to do about Sophon's uncle?'

'I haven't decided.'

'You need to be careful.'

'Do you think I should meet with him?'

'I can't tell you what to do.'

'Okay, but what would you do?'

'I don't know. Just be careful, do not meet with him without taking proper precautions.'

'Okay.'

Our conversation was at an end. With Ilana standing in the room, I had nothing more to say to Sandy. Even though I wanted to tell her things, I couldn't, not when Ilana could hear what I said.

After hanging up the phone, I watched as Ilana washed the dishes I had placed in the dishwasher. She didn't like dishwashers. I grabbed a towel to help.

'What were you talking about with Sandy?' Ilana asked.

'She asked me about the meeting with the old man.'

Ilana didn't react, continuing to wash dishes while I dried.

'What do you think I should do about the old man?' I asked her.

'I have been thinking,' she said as if she had anticipated my question. 'I think you should talk to this man.'

'Why? He is Sophon's great-uncle. He is Nue's uncle. Weren't you the one who warned me about him? Now, you want me to trust this man?'

'You said he is old?'

'I assume he is old. He said he is Sophon's great uncle.'

'Perhaps he is the old wise man in the family. Maybe you can settle this thing with him?'

'Yes, but what if he is just like the others?'

'Will it hurt to talk to him?' she asked.

'I suppose not.'

'You can talk to this old man in a room with bodyguards. You don't need to be afraid of an old man, do you?'

'No, I guess not.'

'Okay then, you should talk to him,' Ilana said without further explanation. She was a mystery sometimes. A mystery I had never been able to solve.

But then, aren't all women mysteries?

MONDAY, JANUARY 11, 3:55 AM. BUDDY

Electrical outages in the middle of the night were not uncommon, but when the auxiliary generator failed to fire, Buddy, my security chief, became concerned.

Lights throughout the office apartment building went black, including all the video screens on his console. He dispatched Derrick, the other night security guard, to go outside and take a look at the generator with a flashlight. In the meantime, Buddy grabbed his flashlight to physically check the interior of the building.

He had just finished canvassing the main office area when the lights came back on. Relieved, he headed towards his station to check the video screens. A quick review of each and every screen showed nothing out of the ordinary. Buddy settled into his chair to review the alarms; be sure they had not tripped.

Everything looked normal, no problems.

Derrick returned with his report. Something mechanical was wrong with the auxiliary generator. Their repair service needed to be called in the morning.

Their coffee machine began to percolate again. After pouring a cup, they settled into their chairs to wait for the morning.

'Why don't you just take another look around?' Buddy was still concerned.

'You don't think we have a problem, do you?' Derrick asked.

'No, just a precaution.'

4:05 AM. JOHN

Submerged deep in a murky nighttime world of elusive dreams, something sticky pressed against my lips, something uncomfortably real.

A hammer blow, hard and heavy against the side of my head, stunned me. Unable to fully comprehend what was happening, a shadow passed before my glazed eyes and picked her up from my bed like she was a small child. Before she could scream, he threw Ilana across the room against a wall, where she fell with a sigh and did not move. The shadow came after me next. I vainly attempted to slide away, rolling and falling off the bed, turning through a semi-dazed world badly distorted by the blow to the side of my head, like I was living in a half-conscious nightmare, somewhere between reality and a dream.

The shadow hit me again, a stunning, paralyzing blow to my head filled with instant pain. Taking hold of my arm, he twisted it behind my back while wrapping tape around it. After painfully pulling my ankle backward, he taped it to my wrist. Vainly trying to regain some control over my mind and body, I screamed as he worked over me, but only a muffled cry escaped the tape over my lips. Clawing at the tape with my free hand, the shadow hit me in the mouth. Next, he took my free hand and taped it to the same ankle as I lay stunned on the floor.

Arched over awkwardly in an excruciating disassociation from reality, I tried vainly to understand my condition through a haze of pain engulfing my mind.

He went to work on Ilana next before she could fully recover from her flight across the room. The shadow taped her mouth and then her hands, twisting her arms behind her back as I half-consciously listened to her muffled screams. Picking her up like a rag doll, he threw her on the bed. Then, oddly... he stopped for a moment as if he was content and wanted to admire his work before continuing.

Removing a cell phone from his jacket, he dialed a preprogrammed number.

After listening silently, he returned the phone to his pocket.

4:15 AM. LUANG

Waiting until the security guard was out of sight, Luang carefully completed his work, reattaching the electrical line before retreating into the shadows.

His original plan had been to enter the building after his accomplice disabled the inhabitants. Then, kill the murderer in his bedroom. But a roving security guard changed his mind and added a dangerous variable that would not be wise to test. He chose instead to wait for another opportunity, one which offered a lower risk of failure.

New instructions were given to his man. The final solution was his to fulfill, his to accomplish with his own hands, seen with his eyes; just as Sophon had requested.

He could wait for now, be patient. A better opportunity would present itself.

One which would be far more satisfying.

4:20 AM. JOHN

Unable to move with my leg and arms taped behind my back, I lay on the bedroom floor like a pretzel, vaguely watching a shadow of a man move across the dark room.

I could hear him more than see him, feel his black presence. He leaned over me. Several ribs were broken, one at a time, each one with a crack, three sharp blows to my side; not much pain, not at first, just a sharp hurt. A kick to my groin brought more pain, instant pain. My eyes closed in tight tears of agony, hurt throbbing through my gut, rising like a wave, rushing through my mind. I cried silently, afraid, knowing I could do nothing to stop him. He dragged me across the bedroom floor in agony, propping my bruised body up in the corner of the room with my leg painfully bent behind me, my wrists taped to my leg behind my back, and my broken ribs racked with pain. Seems he wanted me in the corner sitting, wanted me to see what he planned to do next, hear it at a minimum, know what he was doing, and know I could do nothing to stop him.

He turned on a light by the bed, the nearest one, so I could see him work with his back to me. She lay helpless on the bed with her arms behind her. Rolling Ilana over, he hit her first on the arm, a sharp, quick blow. Her bone snapped. I could hear it snap across the room. She screamed. The tape on her mouth could not disguise her cry.

At no time did he hit her in the face. I guess he wanted her conscious while he worked, wanted her to feel the pain, wanted me to hear her scream. Methodical work, slow and directed. Short jabs as she twisted and turned, trying to get away from his blows. He was patient. He would wait, look down on her, and wait for an opening. Then hit her again, in her ankle, her knee, her groin, all the pressure points, all the places that hurt the most. She screamed and twisted as he worked.

For what seemed an eternity, he jabbed at her small, vulnerable body with precision until she became strangely quiet, whimpering, lying in agony, and silently crying. Then he stopped and looked down at her as if he was wondering if he should inflict more damage.

I looked away in disgust.

When he was done, he turned out the light.

I never saw the blow. Just felt his black fist smash into my head, my eyes quickly filling with blood and tears.

7:50 AM. JOHN

As I wandered aimlessly through a burning land, blackened, burned trees stood like monuments, visible remnants of a once proud forest, the residue of a devastating forest fire.

Ashes covered the ground. Broken branches and fallen trees lay twisted and silent everywhere I looked. No relief, only lifeless agony and death. Shadows swirled through this stark forest like lost screams unheard in the night, searching for me, reaching for me, wincing in pain, twisting to avoid their murky blows. Over time, the cold, lifeless black forest melted into a gray liquid covering my eyes. I tried, but I could not remove the sticky stuff. Finally, after repeated blinking, my world slowly returned to comprehensible images. I could see it again.

Time had passed.

I didn't know how much time, except it was now light outside, the morning, I assumed. I was lying on the floor, my arms and legs still taped, my back arched painfully backward. I looked for him, the shadow who had done this. I was afraid he was still in the room. That's when I saw her, lying quiet, twisted, unmoving beside me. I had no idea how she got there. I was afraid she was dead. I screamed silently inside. Inching over to her body, looking for signs of life, she lay very still. Nothing in her appearance indicated she was alive. Her mouth was only partially covered with gray tape. Her wrists were taped behind her back; her broken arm was twisted at an unnatural angle. I brushed my head against her shoulder, bumping her gently. She moved in response. Eventually, she opened her eyes. Her face attempted a smile, but only pain reflected in her eyes. Her eyes looked so sad. I saw no joy in those eyes, only deep sadness. The tape on her mouth had begun to come off on one corner. She slowly moved her mouth up and down until the tape fell to the floor.

'Are you okay, John?' she asked when she could talk.

I must have looked bad; my face was covered with blood, but I nodded yes. She seemed relieved. Then she moved closer and began to bite the tape off my mouth. While she worked, she whimpered, each movement causing her pain. She continued until most of the tape on my mouth was loose.

I smiled at her. 'Thanks, that feels better.'

'You are welcome.'

'Are you okay?' I asked.

'I am hurting, but I am okay,' she said with a grimace. 'Why don't I try to get the tape off your wrists?' she volunteered.

I twisted on the floor until she could bring her mouth to my wrists. She tried, crying often in pain, but it was no good. The tape would not come loose. Too much tape and it was on too tight.

'Stop,' I finally said. 'I'm going to start calling for help. I know the walls are thick, but eventually, someone will hear us.'

CHARLOTTESVILLE HOSPITAL, 10:55 AM.
JOHN

Her hand was so small, so delicate.

I held her hand as I sat beside her hospital bed, afraid to hold it too tight, afraid of hurting her, each finger so perfect. A near coma had been induced by doctors to relieve her pain, administered by narcotics dripping through a long plastic line connected to an IV bandaged in her arm. Her other arm was encased in a new white cast. At peace now, her eyes were closed, her long black hair spread over a clean white pillow. Doctors had worked on her, but they could do only so much. No serious internal injuries were detected. Black and blue marks indicated where she had been hurt like a person in a car wreck, an accident that caused most of her perfect body to be injured. Thankfully, the intruder had left her face untouched. It was just as beautiful as ever, almost radiant as she rested.

My injuries were not as numerous, but more serious. A concussion, three cracked ribs taped, and stitches in my forehead, fortunately high in the hairline so the scar would not show. Still, I could walk and go home, but I didn't go anywhere. I sat by her hospital bed to be near her.

The police wanted to know what happened.

I didn't know what to tell them. It all happened so fast. I saw nothing which would help identify the man. It was dark most of the time. His back was towards me when the light was on. I wasn't much help.

Buddy, the head of security at the office, came to the hospital with a report. The generator had been disabled first. Power cut to the building next, long enough for an intruder to get in undetected. Buddy said the guy came in through the garage, opened the lock like he had a key. Guess he was an expert. When the lights came back on, Buddy thought everything was fine.

I asked him if anything was taken. He said no. As soon as the intruder was done, the power went out again so the man could escape without being recorded. He must have had some help on the outside.

Buddy had assumed it was a local electrical problem. He did not check on us. It was the middle of the night. He didn't want to disturb our sleep. Buddy said he was sorry...

I told him it was not his fault. No security cameras were installed in my apartment at my request. Nothing he could do. I told him to return to the office to determine what measures were necessary to insure this would never happen again.

He nodded.

I think he was afraid I was going to fire him. I was not. It wasn't his fault.

She moved, slowly whimpering, like she was having a bad dream. No one was in her hospital room at the time except me. I couldn't believe I had allowed this to happen to her. Her hand was so small and vulnerable, so depending.

I silently cried deep inside, where no one could see my tears.

WEDNESDAY, JANUARY 13, 3:10 PM. JOHN

List was long.

In her usual meticulous fashion, Helen, my secretary, had complied a list of names on a several sheets of paper; names and return numbers for everyone who had called, each phone call categorized by date and time.

Sitting in my office, I half-heartedly scanned the list with no real desire to call anyone. Perhaps later to some of my good friends. Others could wait until tomorrow.

Ilana was resting in a chair in the den of my apartment. Doctors had released her from the hospital even though she was still very sore. We survived our first night and the next morning limping around my apartment together, helping each other. She was doing much better by the afternoon. Her pain was beginning to ease. I gave her a few magazines and a glass of water. The TV remote was on a nearby table if she wanted to watch some programs. The door to my apartment was open if she needed anything. Said to call me, please.

She had insisted I go. Said she was not an invalid. She could take care of herself, quit bothering her. Truth was, she was doing remarkably well given the beating she had endured. The cast on her arm was a bother, but everything else appeared to be healing nicely. I, in contrast, was not doing so very well. Every time I moved, my side hurt because my ribs were broken. Doc said not to worry. Ribs eventually heal by themselves after about six weeks. Six weeks? Are you kidding me, Doc? Are you telling me I can't sneeze for six weeks, can't move naturally, and need to walk gently? Any fast movement caused serious pain. He gave me some pills and told me to take them if my pain was bad. I put the bottle in the bathroom closet and ignored it. I was more concerned about her, about taking care of her.

However, her opinion of my help was another matter. Said I was becoming a pest. That was her version, anyway. She was sick of me hanging around her all the time. I went to my office after she kicked me out of the apartment because I had nowhere else to go.

Charlie's name was at the top of Helen's call list, and it appeared several more times on other pages. Seems I owed him a call. But why, I wondered. He already knew what happened. CIA knows everything. Tomorrow, I procrastinated, I will call him in the morning. I was in no mood to deal with Charlie that day.

Sandy's name also appeared on the list more times than Charlie's. I had not talked to her either. Ilana had. They talked while Ilana was in the hospital. Ilana told her some of the gruesome details of her experience. So, I guess I owed Sandy a call. I couldn't put her off forever. Phone was in my hand. All I had to do was dial her number. But truth was I didn't want to talk to her. In fact, I had been deliberately avoiding even thinking about her. My attention was on Ilana. I wanted to make it up to her somehow because of the beating she took. I couldn't stop thinking about what I saw. I couldn't stop seeing him hit her over and over again. It was painful to watch, more painful than being hit myself. Nothing I could do to protect her, nothing but lie on the floor and watch him hurt her. Even in the limited light of the bedroom, I saw his every move. Each blow he delivered was etched in a surreal light, the pain so intense that it seemed immune to the darkness.

I sat back in my chair, wondering what I could do to make Ilana's day a little brighter. Sandy was not my first priority.

Thinking of Sandy seemed to betray what I owed Ilana.

FRIDAY, JANUARY 15, 1:55 PM. JOHN

Friday afternoons at my office are normally slow.

However, this Friday afternoon was anything but normal.

Ilana was somewhere in my apartment, doing, I didn't know what. She had become more mobile and didn't need me like before. In fact, she specifically told me, on more than one occasion, to leave her alone. She informed me she could take care of herself. In addition, she made a unilateral decision to move out of my bedroom and into the guest bedroom. Seems she didn't want to be accidentally touched in the middle of the night. I guess I understood. She was still hurting, black and blue all over.

And then she did something else. Something I really didn't appreciate. She started to eat alone. When I asked her why, she shrugged her shoulders. Said she was hungry. So, she ate. Didn't want to wait for me. Result was, I had to eat alone. Not what I wanted. What I wanted was to eat with her.

'Charlie is on the line,' Helen said through the intercom.

Helen's meticulous list had been ignored. I had procrastinated. It was Friday, and I was reasonably confident I wouldn't get many calls on a Friday afternoon. Friday afternoons are normally delegated to the weekend. Not many business calls come in on a Friday afternoon. After surviving a morning marred by only a few incidental calls, nothing important, I assumed I was home, free to enjoy my weekend. Helen's scrupulous list of return calls could wait until Monday.

Then Charlie called.

I briefly considered asking Helen to tell Charlie I was busy, whatever. But I knew I would have to face Charlie's music sooner or later. So...

'Charlie.'

'John.'

'Yes, it's me.'

'The rumor of your demise is premature again,' he stated without humor.

'Yea, sorry to disappoint you, old pal. I'm still among the living.'

'Look, John, all kidding aside, we need to talk. This problem you have, it's not going away.'

'What problem?'

'You know what problem. Don't play games with me.'

'You aren't talking about the burglar, are you?'

'John, we both know the intruder was not a burglar. Nothing was taken.'

'You know too much.'

'It's my job to know too much.'

'Okay, so let's assume I agree with you,' I sighed. 'He wasn't a burglar. So, what should I do about him?'

'That's the hard part.'

'Yea, that's the hard part, isn't it, Charlie.'

'Has anyone from Nue's family contacted you recently?' Charlie asked.

Now I had a problem. I had not told Charlie about the call I received from Sophon's great-uncle. I should have, but I didn't.'

'I guess we need to talk,' I reluctantly replied

'John, are you holding something back?'

'Let's just say we need to talk.'

'About what?'

'Well, something happened while I was in Michigan. It's a long story, and I'm not sure I want to tell you over the phone.'

'John, you do remember the last time you weren't exactly up-front with me.'

I ignored his comment and asked him if he was busy this weekend. Maybe he would like to drive down from Washington. Sorry, I wasn't in any shape to travel, broken ribs etc. He reluctantly agreed. Said he would come tomorrow.

Before I could hang up, Helen was in my ear again. This time, with a call from Sandy. Seemed I was on a roll now, talking to all the people I should have talked to earlier. Or it may have been more accurate to say they were on a roll, all my friends, all out to get to me on a quiet Friday afternoon. Didn't seem fair.

I tapped the blinking green button on the consol.

'Sandy, thanks for calling. I have been meaning to call, but...'

'You don't have to apologize, John. I know you are busy. I called to see how you and Ilana are doing.'

'We're fine. Ilana is buzzing around the apartment. She is more mobile than I am. My broken ribs are still a problem. But otherwise, I'm fine.'

'Good. I'm glad you're healing. You sound good.'

'I'm okay. You don't need to be concerned.'

'I'm not concerned. I assumed you were okay. I just wish you had called.'

She said it, didn't have to say it, but she did. She said I should have called. I knew it. She knew it and she wanted me to know she knew it. I was guilty as charged.

'I'm sorry.' I said again.

Having accomplished her goal, she ignored my feeble apology, making me feel guilty.

'Can I speak to Ilana?' she asked.

'Sure, I'll have Helen track her down for you.'

'Goodbye, John,' she said quickly like she suddenly didn't want to talk to me anymore.

I buzzed Helen to ask her to find Ilana for Sandy's call. That's when Helen informed me David was on-hold, waiting to speak to me. Seems he didn't mind waiting. He wanted to talk. Helen said she would connect him now and transfer Sandy's call to the apartment for Ilana. I thanked her although I wasn't quite sure why.

'I just got through talking to Charlie,' David said, skipping even the feeblest attempt at a formal greeting. 'What happened to you?'

Typical of my friend David, always right to the point, no delay for polite niceties.

'I'm okay,' I said. 'How are you? How's the weather?'

'John, be serious. Charlie is very concerned. I'm concerned.'

'Why? Do you and Charlie know something I don't?' I replied, becoming somewhat frustrated. I didn't like them ganging up on me.

'Charlie gave me a brief report, John. You know why.'

'Okay, so now you know.'

'Want to give me the details?'

'You sure you want to hear them. They are pretty ugly?'

'John. I'm your friend. Friends talk to each other when they're in trouble. So, talk to me.'

I groaned inside, and I told him about the incident at my apartment...well, not the whole story. I left out most of the really ugly stuff. I didn't want to talk about it. Just told him how some guy got inside and beat us up in the middle of the night. Said it got bad for a while, but everything was okay now. We were healing.

'Charlie also told me about something else that happened while you were in Grand Haven.' David said. 'Something you apparently forgot to tell me. Was it the reason you canceled lunch before leaving town?'

'Yea, I have been meaning to tell you. Sorry. I have just been a little...'

'John, skip the apologies. I don't require an apology. Just tell me what happened.'

I paused. 'An old man called who claimed to be the great uncle of the kid who kidnapped us in Belize. Said he wanted to talk.'

'Did you talk to him?'

'No.'

'What did you do?'

'Put him off by leaving town.'

'Was that wise?'

'David, I don't know what wise looks like anymore.'

We talked for a few more minutes. David said he was glad I was planning to meet with Charlie, asked me to call him after I talked to Charlie. I agreed. Didn't want to, but it was obvious they were not going to leave me alone.

After David's call, I sat at my desk for a few minutes, trying to digest the damage done by the phone calls. Friday afternoon had not gone anything like I had envisioned. I had been looking forward to a peaceful, relaxing weekend, regaining the energy I needed to deal with my problems, but obviously, that didn't happen.

The coffee pot was hot. I poured a cup.

'It' was out to get me again.

'It' didn't have a name, and I didn't know what to call 'it.' But one thing was obvious; 'it' was alive and well. This thing, this problem, this series of tragedies and problems was determined to plague me. And 'it' was not going away. 'It' was like a wave on the waters of time, an ugly heavy wave which had caught me, hung me high on its crest before driving my helpless body under its heavy, swirling surf, holding me under where I was unable to breathe. I wasn't sure I had the mental will or energy to survive its fierce splashing waters. I felt like 'it' was ready to curl up again over my head, a high smooth wall of water rising above me, ready to crash down, driving me deep under its rushing waters to depths in the sea, crushing me against unseen rocks on the seafloor. It was only a matter of time before 'it' got me again; another wave of pain crashing down on me, pulling me under the water in a twisting, crushing journey down to the depths.

I wanted 'it' to go away. In the worst way, I wanted 'it' to leave me alone.

Coffee tasted good. Hot and smooth as I slowly sipped.

Helen buzzed.

'John.'

'Helen.'

'I have a call for you.'

'Nice to hear from you again, Helen,' I replied in jest.

'I don't believe you.'

'Helen, believe me.'

She simply ignored me. The lady was no fun.

'A man named Luang is on the line,' she said. 'Wants to talk to you.'

It seemed everyone was out to get me. I felt like I was in a wrestling event. They were tag teaming me, everyone on the same afternoon. And now Luang, the last opponent to jump into the ring. My biggest nightmare was calling to deliver the knockout punch.

I couldn't believe he was calling, not now. I should have told Helen to tell him to go kill a duck or something, anything, to avoid talking to him. But for some reason, probably because I was tired... or because I wanted to get it over, I took his call.

'John Van Laan,' he began.

As always, very proper; it was easy to recognize his voice, his clipped Thai accent, his patient manner of speaking. I sensed he felt no need to speak quickly. He chose his words wisely. He lived in a world where others were required to wait silently and listen to him before speaking.

'Yes, this is John Van Laan.'

'Thank you for giving me an opportunity to speak with you this afternoon. I hope all is well with you.'

'No, but that's another story.'

'Oh, I am sorry.'

'Are you?' I asked.

My patience was running thin. One tough call after another, all in one afternoon. I decided to confront this old man. He had called me. I didn't call him. I didn't ask for his call. Why not take the opportunity to put him on the defensive?

'Why are you asking, Mr. Van Laan?'

'I'm asking if you sent a man to hurt me and my girlfriend in my apartment a few nights ago.'

'I don't know what you are talking about.'

'I think you do.'

'You must believe me, Mr. Van Laan. The only reason I called was to request a meeting with you as you promised.' He paused, 'You do remember?'

'I remember saying I didn't want to talk to you.'

He didn't immediately respond.

'Answer my question: did you send a man to deliver a message?' I continued. 'Meet with me, or I will hurt you again.'

'I don't know anything about a message.'

'Do you know what your man did? He hurt my girlfriend so bad she had to go to the hospital.'

'I am sorry for your troubles.'

'I'm not sure you are.'

'Please be assured, I do not wish anyone trouble. But in life, we all have weaknesses, places where we are vulnerable, Mr. Van Laan. If unattended, these can become problems.'

'What are you talking about?'

'Nothing more than what I said. We need to attend to our weaknesses to avoid trouble.'

'Are you admitting you sent the man to attack us?'

'John, may I call you John?'

'No.'

'Okay. Mr. Van Laan, please be assured I do not know what you are talking about. I am calling you because I am an old man.' He paused before continuing. 'Unfortunate events have occurred between my family and you. I am seeking an opportunity to resolve these problems before I die. I am asking you to help me find a solution. This is the only reason for my call.'

His answer momentarily slowed me. Was he was telling the truth? Perhaps, but the incident at my apartment surely begged a question. Why else would someone break into my apartment and take nothing? It had to have something to do with this old guy.

Instead of pursuing the present line of questions, I changed the subject by asking, 'How can I possibly help you resolve our mutual problems?'

'That is what I want to discuss.'

'Okay, let's discuss it.'

'This is not a subject to discuss on the phone.'

'I'm not sure I want to discuss it with you except on the phone,' I argued.

'It would be better discussed in a meeting, talk face to face.' He replied.

'No.'

'Do you want this to end?' he asked patiently.

'As far as I am concerned, it's over.'

'I'm sorry, Mr. Van Laan,' he said after a pause. 'I wish it was over, but it is not.'

'Why? I met with your nephew's son, not exactly under the terms I would have chosen, but I met with him and we talked. He could have killed me, but he did not. So, as far as I am concerned, it's over.'

'Sophon does not speak for my family. I do. I am the head of my family. You must speak with me if you...'

'No.'

'Mr. Van Laan, our mutual problems will never end until we talk. Isn't this what you want? I do. I am asking for an opportunity to resolve our problems. It would make an old man happy.'

I considered his words. I didn't want to meet with him, but I also wanted to end it. Probably more than he did.

'It's over. I responded. 'You can die happy.'

'It will never be over unless I say it is over... Do you understand?'

'Are you threatening me?'

'No, I am telling you the truth.'

'Well, I don't want to meet you. And I will not be blackmailed by your goons, not now, not ever.'

'Please reconsider. I will meet with you anywhere and under any terms you suggest. I will come alone. I am an old man, Mr. Van Laan. You have nothing to fear from me?'

'No. Now leave me alone.' I hung up.

SATURDAY, JANUARY 16, 2:05 PM. JOHN

Eating lunch alone was no fun, just like breakfast.

Ilana always seemed to have an excuse to avoid eating with me. She made it sound perfectly reasonable like nothing was wrong. Today, she said she was up early and hungry. She had breakfast, and then she decided to skip lunch.

I assumed she was now bouncing around somewhere in the apartment, doing who knows what. She did say she wanted to talk to me sometime today, but she didn't say about what and she didn't say when. Just kind of waved me off when I asked what was on her mind.

Women...always unpredictable, always a problem.

Charlie was due anytime. Said he would be at my apartment by midafternoon, didn't give me an exact time. He had some work to complete in the morning before he could get on the road. Asked me if it mattered when he came, I said no. Saturday was open. I was busy healing my ribs, nothing more.

I decided to get some work done to fill the time. An ad campaign was spread out on my desk when Ilana arrived in my office unannounced and sat down in a chair on the other side of my desk. No problem, it was Saturday. Normal office protocol was casual on Saturdays. I didn't mind her showing up unannounced.

The white plaster cast on her arm was the only visible evidence of the beating she endured. Her badly bruised body was covered: jeans, a turtleneck, and a sweater. I think she would have worn gloves if she didn't think it would look funny wearing gloves inside. My island girl could never get warm when she was north in the winter.

'John, I have come to tell you I am going home,' she began in her usual, natural tone of voice, nothing that warned me about the importance of what was to be discussed. 'I don't want to be here anymore. This place is cold and cloudy all the time. I am going home where it is sunny and warm.'

'Okay,' I replied, somewhat shocked at this sudden change in plans. 'When are you leaving?'

'Tomorrow morning.'

'Okay.'

'I have more I need to say to you, John, and I am sorry to have to say these things, but I can't help it.'

Now, she had me worried. 'What's wrong?' I asked.

'I don't want to be with you anymore, John Van Laan. I am sorry. I still love you, but I can't be with you. Every time I am with you, something terrible happens. My life was happy before I met you. Now, I have days filled with sorrow and pain. I cannot be with you anymore.' She blurted it out in a big hurry like she wanted to say it quickly before she changed her mind.

I leaned back in my office chair. She looked so small and vulnerable, sitting in the chair on the other side of my desk. I began to stand, wanting to hug her, begging her to stay.

'No, do not get up,' she demanded. 'This is where you belong. This is how I want to remember you when I think about the day I told you I do not want to be with you anymore. I want to think of you sitting behind your desk doing your work.'

'Ilana, I don't...'

'No, John. Do not say something you do not mean.'

'Please do not...'

'Stop talking,' she demanded. 'I want to finish. I have prepared everything I want to say to you. Now, you must listen to me. Then, if you want to talk, I will let you. But now you must be quiet and listen to me.'

I sat in silence as instructed.

She continued. 'You gave me money. I have my checkbook, and I know how much money is in the bank. I have written you a check. I want to give you back your money.' She placed a check on my desk.

I didn't even look at it.

'Ilana, it's your money. You earned it. I don't want it.'

'As you wish,' she said as if she knew how I would respond. 'When I return to Belize, I am going to move out of your house. I will build my own house. If you don't want your money, I will use your money to build a house for me. I do not want to stay in your house anymore. It is a bad place. Bad things happened there. I do not want to live in your house anymore.'

'Okay, but remember some of the good times were had in that house.'

'Yes, but always followed by bad times.'

'Okay, if that's what you want to do. Use the money to build a new house.'

'I am going now,' she started to stand.

'No, sit,' I said. 'Now it is my turn. Now, I want you to listen to me.'

She sat.

'I love you, Ilana, and I'm sorry. I'm sorry for the pain I have caused you. I'm sorry for the way I have been acting since I killed a man. It was not your fault, but it changed me in a way that hurt our relationship.' I paused before continuing, 'But it did not change you. You are still the same beautiful woman I fell in love with. Please don't go.'

She didn't respond, looking down to avoid having me see her tears.

'You gave me back my life,' I continued in her silence. 'I owe you. I owe you everything. Don't you understand? I don't want you out of my life.'

'I am sorry, John. I cannot do this. You live with too much pain and too much sorrow. I wish I could take away your sorrow, but I cannot. I do not have the power. I am sorry, but I must go. I want to be happy again. And I cannot be happy with you. As much as I love you, I cannot live with your pain.'

I had nothing to say to her, nothing to convince her to stay. Every word she spoke was true.

'Ilana, I will worry about you. The men who are after me won't know you are no longer with me. They may think they can get to me through you. And they can. I need to know you are safe.'

'I will be safe when I get home,' she replied, tears forming in her eyes.

'Can I send someone with you?'

'No, I don't need anyone. I will be fine.' She looked up at me with those big brown eyes of hers, trying not to cry.

'Please, I will feel a lot better if one of my guys went with you, at least for a little while?'

She thought for a moment. 'Okay, you can send Todd. He is a nice man. I will let him come with me...if this makes you feel better. But when I am ready to send him home, he must go.'

'I will check with him,' I responded, wondering vaguely why she had chosen him.

She was silent.

I looked at her, wondering what I could say to change her mind. 'Ilana, it doesn't have to end like this... I can...' I was thinking as fast as I could. I was not ready to give up, not just yet.

Security had been increased, four men in the office at all times; regular patrols inside and out. New equipment, new cameras, everything Buddy recommended. I told him he could have anything he wanted. I didn't want a repeat of what happened last Sunday. He was in the process of updating everything, and I was beginning to feel safe again. But if Ilana left, I would be constantly worried about her, more worried than if she was with me. I also knew that when she made up her mind to do something, nothing could stop her. Still, I had to try.

'Don't make promises you cannot keep, John,' she interrupted me. 'It is better this way.'

She turned, hearing footsteps.

Charlie arrived.

She stood to leave.

'Can we talk later?' I asked, seeing the tears in her eyes.

She turned towards Charlie for a moment without saying a word before proceeding out the door to my office, my question still hanging in the air.

Charlie watched her go in silence. He must have heard my question and probably saw the tears in Ilana's eyes.

'Is this a bad time?' he asked. 'I can wait if you want to talk to Ilana first.'

'No, sit down.'

'You sure? I can wait in the lobby?' he offered.

'Sit down Charlie. Let's get this over with.' I was disgusted with what had just happened. I was disgusted with my inability to deal with it. I was just plain disgusted.

'I have one call to make first.' I dialed Buddy's number. 'This will just take a minute.' I asked Buddy to call Todd and ask him to travel with Ilana to Belize. I explained the situation. Buddy said he would check with Todd, but he couldn't promise anything. It was Todd's decision. I thanked Buddy and hung up.

'John, look, I can...' Charlie said as soon as I put my phone down. He looked great, strong like he had been exercising. Chiseled dark brown complexion, short cropped black hair, high cheekbones, and intense dark eyes, handsome in every way. I always admired how Charlie presented himself. We didn't always agree, but I believed we shared a mutual respect. At least I respected him, even if he didn't always respect me.

'So, how's your love life, Charlie?' I asked. 'As you can see, mine is the pits.' I was angry. I'm sure it showed.

'Okay, I guess.'

'Just okay? A good-looking guy like you must have a girlfriend.'

'What are you implying?'

'Implying nothing, just asking.'

'Okay. Just so you don't get the wrong idea, I am seeing someone.'

'A girl, I hope?'

He smiled. He would have no more sympathy for me now. Gloves were off. Good, I thought, I didn't want sympathy.

'A girl. Name is Kathy, works at Langley with me.'

'Smart like you?'

'Smarter, she went to Yale.'

'Good, I wouldn't want to think you were leading some hapless young girl astray.'

'If anyone is leading anyone astray, it's her leading me,' he replied with a smile.

'Good, happy to hear you're a sucker like the rest of us males.'

'Can we talk business now?' he asked. 'All the preliminary unpleasantries done?'

'Sure, business as usual,' I replied. 'Want a beer?'

'Early, isn't it?'

'It's Saturday. Besides, I need a beer if I must put up with you.'

He smiled. 'Heineken, please.'

7:05 PM. JOHN

Charlie didn't leave until after dark.

We drank too much. Or maybe I was the only one who drank too much. I don't remember. I do remember we talked about everything. I was completely open with him. I began by telling him about what happened when I was in Michigan, about the old man who called. Then I told him about the beating at my apartment here in Charlottesville. A couple of beers helped me work through it. It was strange, really, talking about Charlie. It was as if I was talking about something which happened to someone else, like I was telling a story, disassociating myself from realty.

Charlie knew most of the details of the attack in my apartment. He had read the police report. Thankfully, I didn't have to fill in the ugly details.

Late in the afternoon, we scrounged through my refrigerator for a snack. Found some food to eat. Not much. I suggested he stay the night. I was concerned about him driving back to DC after drinking too many beers. He said he was fine. Kathy, his girlfriend, was expecting him. He had to go. I understood. I brewed some coffee for him, gave him some to drink in his car on the road home.

Before he left, we discussed talking again next week after he had an opportunity to think about what I told him. He said he would check into Luang. Then we could decide on next steps.

I called David as I promised after Charlie left. David listened quietly. Said he would talk to Charlie and call me next week. I could hear something happening in the background as we talked, sounded like a party. Said he had to go, had friends over. Phone clicked dead.

Security guards were on duty. Everything was locked down tight. Curtains were drawn so no one could see inside and take a shot. I didn't like the closed-in feeling, but it didn't really matter. There's not much to see outside anyway. It had been a cool and rainy winter day. No reason to look outside. Rain dripped ominously on the deck, monotonous tapping, a constant reminder of winter in the East. Ilana was going home to Belize for good. Home to where it was warm and sunny, home to where the sea was a friend who was always available to bring comfort and joy. I suddenly wanted to go with her. Nothing but problems faced me here.

Perhaps because I had too much to drink... or because I was tired... or both. Suddenly, all I wanted was to be with her in Belize.

She was in the kitchen nibbling some crackers and dip when I went to look for her. For a small woman, she sure could eat.

'Don't start, John,' she said as soon as she saw me.

'I don't want you to go,' I said, ignoring her request.

'John, I have thought about everything, and I am going. This is not where I belong. This is not my home. It is your home.'

'Okay, then I will go with you.'

'For how long?'

'Forever.'

'John, please don't make promises you can't keep.'

'Ilana, I will give it all up. I will.'

'And when men come to kill you, will I die with you the next time? Will they break my other arm?'

'I'm sorry. You know I'm sorry. What do you want me to say?'

She stopped eating and looked at me. 'I know you are sorry,' she said softly. 'I know you want to make it right for me. But you can do nothing.'

'Ilana, it doesn't have to end this way.'

'There is no other way, John. There never was.' Tears formed in her eyes.

'Ilana, please.'

'No, John. Just let me go.'

She started to cry and ran out of the kitchen.

10:55 PM. JOHN

She was almost in bed by the time I finally found the courage to talk to her again.

Her suitcase was in the hall outside the guest bedroom door. A car had been ordered for early morning. Seems she had an early flight. Buddy had left a message telling me everything was in place. Todd was going with her. He was a bachelor. He could get away at a moment's notice, no problem.

After she ran out of the kitchen, I wandered my apartment like a man in search of a mission, but nothing seemed right. Still, I couldn't let it end this way. I had to try.

She was humming to herself when I knocked on her bedroom door.

'You want to come in, John?' she asked.

'May I?'

She didn't respond immediately, so I went in without waiting for an answer. She was sitting on her bed dressed in a big white terrycloth bathrobe. I think it was mine. It covered her small body from head to foot. She smiled shyly when she saw me. The light beside her bed was on. Her eyes looked puffy red from crying.

'Ilana,' I began, not really knowing where this conversation was headed, only aware I needed to convince her to stay.

Her big brown eyes looked at me, and I melted inside, knowing nothing was as important as her.

'Stop, John,' she said. 'We talked this afternoon. We have nothing more to say.'

'Ilana, please let me...'

'No. If you have come to talk, I will ask you to leave.'

'Ilana, please.'

'No... no talk,' she stated emphatically, looking me squarely in the eye.

'So, under what conditions can I stay?'

A sly, mischievous grin came over her face, one I had not seen all week. 'You can stay if you promise not to talk.'

'Okay, I...'

'No talking, promise... Just nod your head.'

I nodded.

'And you must promise to be careful. I am still very sore. No lovemaking, do you promise?'

I nodded again.

She took off the big terrycloth robe. Under it, she wore a pink pajama top cut off at the waist and some white panties. Her body, what I could see of it, was a mass of black and blue marks. Most of the swelling had receded, but the beating she had taken was still visible and ugly.

She quickly crawled under the covers and turned out the light.

I undressed and slipped into the bed beside her, carefully rolling over so my ribs wouldn't hurt, cuddling next to her back, resting lightly against her, not wanting to hurt her. It was quiet. I closed my eyes.

An almost inaudible whimpering whispered through the night air as I lay beside her, mixing with my unspoken desires, creating a lonely chorus of despair.

'Ilana, you do know I...'

'No talking. You promised,' she insisted. 'No.'

I obeyed, listening to her softly cry until, finally, she slept.

Early in the morning, before dawn, I went to my bedroom alone.

SUNDAY JANUARY 17, 6:40 PM. JOHN

I overslept.

By the time I got up, she was gone. She left a note on the counter in the kitchen. It read:

John,

I will always love you,
but I cannot be with you anymore.
I am sorry. Please forgive me.
Ilana
P.S. I came to visit you because Sandy
and I decided someone needed to be with you.
We wanted to make sure you did not do anything stupid.
We decided it should be me.
I will call Sandy and tell her I cannot stay.
I am sorry.

The rain stopped late afternoon. I dried a chair on my kitchen deck sheltered by trees and sat with a glass of wine. It was cool and windy. I dressed in a winter coat and hat.

Through the barren winter trees, I watched the sky turn dark beyond a gray cloud bank near the horizon. As I sipped wine, the moon rose, casting its willowy light over lingering remnants of a rainstorm, clouds changing shape constantly as they raced across a black, star filled night sky before disappearing in the distance.

The energy in the night sky gave me life. My apartment had felt like a tomb all day, silent and empty. It was good to be outside. Charlie would have been mad if he knew where I was, but I wasn't in the mood to care. I needed to be outside. I needed the night sky. I wanted to fly with the clouds, fly far away. My decks have always been the place to go when I want to think, at the end of the day, places of solitude. The view over the valley stretches for miles to mountains in the distance. Civilizations exist below my hillside retreat. The sky, the valley, the trees; they belong to me. I was not to be denied my place of solitude because I was afraid, not that night of all nights, not after losing Ilana forever.

I didn't tell Buddy where I was. He would have gone ballistic had he known. I did it without telling anyone because I needed to be in the company of the elements.

My mind wandered over the events of the week as I sipped wine.

Ilana's note came to me first.

She had been unlucky, visiting me when a man came to hurt us. It could have happened when she was not here, but it didn't. I couldn't blame Ilana for wanting to leave. It was obvious to her that I was a marked man, an anathema, someone evil, someone to be avoided like the plague. Ilana's leaving created a hole, a sick black hole in my gut. I loved her. I did not want to lose her. I did not want her out of my life. But I knew she was right. If she wanted to be happy, she had to leave.

Perhaps it was justice she was gone. I didn't deserve someone like her after what I had done, after killing a man. I did not deserve a woman as beautiful and kind as Ilana. I had thought I wouldn't have to pay for my crime, but apparently, I had not walked away a free man after all. A jury of my peers had come to deliver a belated verdict. A judge had issued the sentence. It was time for me to stand before God and accept my fate. I was sentenced to lose her, to live alone. It was a cruel sentence, but it was justice served.

Good... it was as it should be, I thought. What did I expect? I had no right to feel sorry for myself. I had killed a man. I had made a choice. It was a bad decision which could not be undone. Like a man with a mark on his forehead, I was someone to be avoided, someone ugly, an outcast. I was sentenced to live alone for the rest of my life. No redemption, no way to exonerate my guilt.

It was time to accept my fate.

A bright moon formed effervescent halos behind racing overhead clouds, framing their dark, smoky mass with an almost holy appearance before temporarily appearing again from behind the cloud's existence, shining through the trees, casting long moon shadows over the land which quickly dissolved into gray when a passing cloud again covered the moon.

SUNDAY, JANUARY 24, 7:30 PM

Sunday evenings can be one of the loneliest times of the week.

Sunday evening alone in a big apartment can be even lonelier.

Ilana had been gone one week, one week of pure hell, lonely hell. Before, when we were separated, when I was working in the States, and she was living in Belize, I was lonely then, but not like last week. In the past, I always knew she was on her island waiting for me to return. She didn't like it when I traveled north to work, but she tolerated it. And I could always return to be with her, be with her smiles on her wondrous island, visit my island girl when I needed her. She was my one wonderful constant.

I had lost that, lost her for good.

Sandy had been right, of course. I should have listened to Sandy. Sandy said Belize was where I belonged. Sandy told me Ilana was the woman I needed.

I didn't listen.

And Ilana understood that better than I did. She knew. She had tried to make it work. But in the end, it just didn't. It couldn't work. It never had a chance. It took something as terrible as being beaten half to death to make her finally give up and accept what she had been resisting for so long.

Sixty Minutes was on the TV, something to watch, anything to occupy my tattered brain. But I wasn't really paying attention. I was thinking about Ilana. For most of the week, she had wandered in and out of my consciousness. Even when I was working in my office, she would come to me and I would stop and think about her, wonder what to do about her. It was something unresolved, something that needed attention, something needing a solution.

Many scenarios played in my distressed brain during the week; possible solutions to my dilemma. On one occasion I came close to ordering a plane to fly to Belize and beg her to take me back. Another time I picked up my phone to call her... then hesitated... putting the phone down without dialing. I even penned a few letters which I quickly threw into the wastebasket. Nothing I wrote made any sense.

Still, I wanted her, wanted her in the worst way.

Wanted what I could no longer have.

BANGKOK, THAILAND, MONDAY, JANUARY 18, 4:35 PM. LUANG

Luang sipped his tea on his garden deck, letting his thoughts wander.

It was almost time to return to America. He had been patient.

Sophon had not questioned his uncle after he returned to Bangkok. And Luang had simply avoided introducing the subject of his travels whenever he and the boy were together. Luang did not feel required to tell Sophon where he went or why. Luang was Sophon's elder. In his mind, Sophon had no authority over him. Besides, if Sophon really wanted to know, he only had to ask one of his subordinates. They knew. They would tell him. Or perhaps Sophon never asked because he wasn't really interested. It was possible the young man was too busy with his new job. The work of running the family business was a great responsibility. The boy had taken to the work like he was a natural. The old man was very proud of him.

And although he had the right, Sophon did not ask the old man to move out of the mansion when he returned. By tradition, the old patriarch should have been obligated to move out. Sophon's father had forced Luang out. But apparently Sophon did not feel the need to ask the old man to leave the mansion. The house was big with many rooms. It contained more than enough space to live comfortably, more than enough for an old man and his young single nephew.

Luang was happy Sophon had not forced him to move. He hoped he would be allowed to live in the mansion until he died. He did not want to move again. His garden was here. His room, his bed, his life was in this house. Memories lived with him in this place. Anywhere else would have been a forced exile. He had done this once before. He did not like it then and he was grateful to Sophon for allowing him stay.

Occasionally, Sophon called Luang to ask for advice, and on those occasions, he attempted to give the young man the best advice he could. He hoped it would encourage the boy to seek his counsel in the future.

94

CHARLOTTESVILLE, VIRGINIA, JANUARY 20, WEDNESDAY, 11:40 AM. JOHN

David's call came before lunch.

Seemed he had been talking to Charlie and together they had decided on a plan of action and David was chosen to be the designated bearer of bad news. Apparently, he was the guy best suited to convince me to go along with their plan. Not Charlie, Charlie and I had a history of disagreeing, or should I say, of being disagreeable. So, it was David who called because it was assumed his approach would be far more diplomatic.

'You should meet this guy, what's his name?' David suggested.

'Luang.'

'Yes. You should meet with him as he requested.'

'Why?'

'Just listen, please,' David said. 'When I'm done, you can object. Okay?'

'Yes, your honor.'

'Okay. And cut the 'your-honor' crap.'

'I'm all ears.'

'Okay, this is how we see it. We don't, and you don't know why this guy wants to meet with you. And it's just possible he has something constructive to offer.'

'Something destructive might be more like it,' I argued for no other reason than to be disagreeable.

'True, but we don't know that, do we? And given the lack of evidence to the contrary, we should give him a chance, right? It could be good. If he wants to make peace, you should listen to him,' David theorized.

'Yea, maybe, but we don't know, do we?'

'I think I just said that.'

I didn't respond.

'John, just think about it.' David continued, delivering his prepared statement calmly. 'Let's assume for a minute we hear him out first. Then, if it is determined the conversation is going nowhere... well, that's when we send in Charlie. He comes in the room and lays out a rather negative scenario for the old man.'

'Like what?'

'Charlie has been talking to some guys at the State Department and they are willing to be helpful.'

'What are you suggesting?'

'Let's just say it involves putting this old guy and his whole family on a no visa, no entry, no business in the U.S. list. Charlie has the details. But here's the point, Charlie can describe a pretty bleak picture for the old guy, accuse his family of racketeering, etc. Charlie has plenty of evidence to support his case. Luang will not find this very agreeable. His company, or should I say his family, has made a considerable amount of money in the United States. We don't think he would enjoy the prospect of being excluded from doing business in this country.'

'Okay, what do we ask from him in return.'

'Agree to a truce, or we apply the brakes.'

'So, he agrees, and then he sends an assassin to kill me anyway. What then?'

'Then we shut down his business in the US.'

'But I am dead.'

David didn't respond immediately. Obviously, there was one flaw in their scheme... a minor one, but a pretty important one to me personally.

'Got a better idea?' David finally responded.

'Two.'

'And they are?'

'First, we go to Bangkok and kill them all, the whole family.'

'That might have some rather negative international ramifications.' David responded sarcastically. 'Given they are a very prominent family in Thailand.'

'Yea, but it would take care of my problem.'

'What's your second idea?' David asked.

'I go to Bangkok and confront them. And if they still want to kill me, they kill me, and it's over.'

'That's a lot simpler solution, but not necessarily a good one for you.'

'Yea, I see your point.'

'So, are we agreed? Do we give our plan a chance to work?'

'Let me think about it. But barring some elusive solution, you have not yet considered; I guess I'm willing to give it a try.'

We continued to talk. David asked if I knew when Luang would call again. I told him the truth. I didn't know if he would ever call again. I had been pretty rude to him the last time. After some small talk, I hung up the phone.

It was good to talk to my old friend, David. I always valued his advice. I just didn't like the current subject of our conversation.

Hopefully, better times were ahead, times when we could simply laugh and talk trash.

FEBRUARY 3, WEDNESDAY, 2:55 PM. JOHN

Charlie called later, the same day as David.

I guessed Charlie assumed it was okay to call after David told him I was willing to consider their plan. Charlie and I talked, nothing important, and rehashed what David told me, only in more detail.

Waiting for Luang to call came next. Two weeks passed. I began to wonder if he would ever call.

Business continued in a normal fashion while I waited. I guess you could call it normal, but in reality, it was not even close to normal. I was simply going through the motions, not really interested. I answered calls. I did my work. I prepared reports. A quarterly meeting of the company's board was scheduled in a few weeks. I had to be prepared, but my heart wasn't in it; too much else on my mind, like Ilana. Buddy had been checking on her for me several times in the past weeks, talking to Todd in Belize. His reports were positive. Ilana was making plans for her new house. Seems she had already moved out of my house and into a rental property, some nice condo with two bedrooms overlooking the ocean near town. Todd was living in one bedroom, and Ilana in the other. She had hired an architect and was hard at work designing the house. I was happy for her, and I was seriously envious of Todd.

I thought maybe I should apply for his job. But didn't, because that would have been self-defeating since I was the danger.

And Sandy, I had heard nothing from Sandy recently. But then, I didn't really expect anything. Sandy knew what happened to Ilana. Sandy was not stupid. She was smart enough to stay away.

So that was that. No Sandy, no Ilana. I went from a man who lived with two beautiful women to one who lived with none. It's amazing how life changes in a heartbeat. It was back to business for me. Work was the only activity that kept me from going crazy. I worked, and I waited for a phone call that might never come.

It finally came, but when it did, I wasn't in the mood to talk to him. I don't know why, but I didn't want to talk to the old man.

'Mr. Van Laan.'

'Yes.'

'Thank you for taking my call.'

'It wasn't my idea,' I replied into my phone while sitting in my office chair.

'I'm afraid I do not understand what you said?' Luang replied across a phone line from somewhere far away.

'Never mind.'

'What does this word mean, 'never mind'?'

'It means you do not need to be concerned.'

'Good, I will not be concerned,' Luang said.

'Good.'

'Have you reconsidered my request?'

'What request?' I asked.

'Will you allow me to meet with you so we can talk?'

'Yes, I guess you can come.'

'Thank you, Mr. Van Laan. You will not regret it.'

'Okay.'

'Where would you like to meet?' He paused. 'The location of our meeting should be your choice.'

'We can meet here in my office, Charlottesville, Virginia. Do you know where it is?'

'I do not know, but I will find it. I have the address.'

'And you will come alone, understand?' I stated emphatically.

'Yes, I will plan to come alone,' he reassured me.

'Okay, now when would you like to meet?' I asked, suddenly anxious to get on with it.

'I will call you shortly and give you my itinerary. I am talking to you from Bangkok. I will make plans to travel now that I know you will meet with me.'

'Okay, you can call me personally, or you can talk to my secretary. Her name is Helen.'

'Yes, Helen. I will call Helen as soon as I am able.'

The phone went silent. I don't think either of us knew what to say next.

Finally, Luang said, 'Thank you, Mr. Van Laan. I will see you soon.'

So, the old man was coming after all. It was time to call Charlie and David, and let them know we were on.

Just didn't know exactly when.

6:05 PM. JOHN

Lately I had been making a habit of sneaking onto my back deck in the evening without telling anyone, mostly my security guys because I knew they wouldn't like it.

The sun goes down early in the middle of winter. With a glass of wine and headsets for music, my deck could be a very relaxing place to watch the sunset at the end of the day before returning inside, no harm done. However, I got caught in the act that evening. Not for any foreseeable reason on my part. In fact, before going outside, I had given Helen explicit instructions to go home, and I made it perfectly clear to everyone still working in the office: no more phone calls, please, not until tomorrow. I didn't want to be bothered.

My apartment was empty, mine alone to wander for the evening. After spending some time relaxing on my deck, I was planning to scratch together a meager meal. Then some TV or a book before heading to bed.

Normally, no one ever bothers me once I leave my office unless it is an emergency. And I'm not in the habit of bothering anyone. In fact, I was becoming accustomed to living alone again and I was beginning to like it. I could do what I wanted. Didn't have to worry about what anyone thought, especially anyone of the feminine gender. The freedom was growing on me. I liked being a lonely bachelor again, like old times. Or at least this was how I was playing it in my head.

The reality, of course, was a very different matter. Truth was, it wasn't really that much fun. 'Bleak' might be a better word to describe my solitary lifestyle.

That evening was relatively warm for early February. The sky was mostly clear with only a few wispy clouds near the horizon. There was a nice sunset, nothing spectacular with faded pinks and oranges briefly streaking out from behind some gray clouds before the sun quickly hide behind the mountains and the sky faded into a black, star-filled void. The moon appeared eventually, a sliver of light in a dark sky.

A third glass of wine extended my stay. It was dark, and I was feeling mellow. Work was done for the day and I was content to be alone under a night sky with music playing in my earphones.

So... it was something of a shock to my system when someone burst onto the deck followed closely by a security guard.

'John Van Laan,' this unexpected guest loudly exclaimed, making it impossible to ignore her harsh admonishment over my headsets. 'What in the world are you doing out here?'

In a state of slightly inebriated shock, I turned to see someone who looked a lot like an apparition of Sandy standing over me. Okay, she couldn't really be a ghost, but in the limited light on the deck, she didn't look real, either. A vision, maybe, a beautiful blond figment of my deeply troubled, alcohol-aided imagination; nothing possibly real. However, it quickly occurred to me that visions don't normally make a habit of bawling you out, acting like your mother. Therefore, the possibility of her being real was something I probably shouldn't dismiss. Coupled with this troubling realization came an even more disturbing possibility. I might be in a lot of trouble for being outside alone, but rather than apologize for my obvious lack of suitable behavior, I went on the offensive.

'Maybe I should ask you the same question?' I replied after removing my headset. 'What are you doing here?'

'John,' she exclaimed with exaggerated theatrical exasperation like I should know what she was talking about.

'What?' I asked. 'I live here. What's your excuse?'

'John, you are a sitting duck on this deck.'

'What's your point?'

She stared at me for a moment, probably thinking I was the idiot she always knew I was, before stomping inside.

It was then that it dawned on me that this, our latest unanticipated reunion, was not off to an especially great start.

'Mr. Van Laan,' the security guard said in a low, calm voice. 'We would appreciate it if you would kindly move inside, sir. It is not safe out here.'

I dutifully complied with his request, collecting my wine glass and headsets to go inside, bowed but not yet broken.

7:20 PM. JOHN

When I arrived inside, her suitcase was sitting next to the couch in the living room which she was occupying as one does a seat in an airport lounge waiting for a plane, looking anxiously like she wanted to get up and leave as soon as possible. Casually thrown over her brown and black overnight bag was her dark brown cashmere overcoat. Tight jeans and a light blue sweater completed the package. I had to admit, the lady looked good, very good. My immediate problem was that she also looked like she was preparing to walk out my door at any second.

'So, would you like to go to the Club and get something to eat?' I asked, knowing my refrigerator was mostly devoid of what she considered edible food. My recent eating habits left something to be desired. Sliced sandwich meat, bread, cans of soup, beer, and wine made up my diet. Occasionally, I had a salad. Helen did my grocery shopping and I suspected that if she knew how much food I threw out because I let it spoil, she probably would quit.

'I'm still on California time. I'm not hungry,' she replied.

'Would you like a drink? I have beer and wine.'

'No. I'm trying to decide if I should go home,' she answered with a genuine lack of enthusiasm.

'Why would you do that?'

'Because I don't like spending time with stupid men.'

'Me?' I asked dumbly.

'John, why in the world were you sitting on that deck? Don't you know how dangerous it is out there?'

Nothing I could say was going to get me out of my predicament.

'We were in a panic looking for you,' she continued.

Okay, I was guilty as charged, and I have learned long ago that when you have sinned in the eyes of a woman, it is better to keep your mouth shut rather than give the prosecution more ammunition to put you away.

'I screamed for you at the top of my lungs, but you didn't answer,' she continued.

'I guess my headphones kept me from hearing you,' I replied lamely.

'How loud do you set those things?'

'I like my music loud.'

'I thought you were dead. We all thought something bad had happened to you.'

'I'm sorry. If I had known you were coming, I would have been better prepared.'

'That...' and she paused as if she needed time to gather strength before proceeding. 'That is no excuse.' She bellowed in exasperation. 'You know better than to be sitting on that deck alone. What were you thinking?'

Nothing I could say. I couldn't tell her I didn't care. I assumed that was not an answer which would be well received.

'I'm sorry. I didn't mean to upset you.' I answered lamely.

BANGKOK THAILAND, THURSDAY, FEBRUARY 4, 10:15 AM. LUANG

Sophon worked while he waited for his great-uncle to arrive at his office.

He appreciated the fact that the old man had called in advance and asked to see him. Luang wasn't obligated. He could have arrived without an appointment. Sophon's staff would not have stopped him. Most of them had worked for their great-uncle for many years and still thought of him as their boss. Only a few new employees had been hired since Sophon took possession of the office complex in the mansion. Only several key employees, only those whose loyalty would never have to be questioned. His first hire was a beautiful young secretary. Tall with long black hair, she had gorgeous eyes and was very smart. His next appointment was a young, university-educated accountant. The man came highly recommended. The accounting practices of the family's businesses had been transformed with the use of computers. Daily reports were available, and it was one of these reports that Sophon was reviewing when his great-uncle came into his office.

'Thank you for seeing me,' Luang said after arriving in Sophon's office.

'You do not need to thank me, uncle. You are always welcome here,' the young man replied.

Luang smiled and sat down in a leather chair opposite Sophon's elegantly carved desk.

The desk was enormous by Western standards, but given the size of the room, it didn't appear large. A ballroom might be a better description of Sophon's office space. Paintings encased in gold engraved frames covered the walls: scenes of ancient Bangkok, agricultural settings, hunting parties, and battles; each picture was a story from his family's past. The paintings had been undisturbed. Only the furniture had been rearranged after his great-uncle vacated the premises. Newly purchased items included a personal computer and file cabinets. Ornamental furniture that served no working purpose had been removed to make space for a modern conference table and chairs. All this was necessary because, in the past, the room did not function as a modern working office. Furniture such as Sophon's large ornamental desk was seldom occupied. Instead, tables were for tea, and couches for conversation and picture taking. Plush, cushioned chairs were designated for signing pre-arranged contracts. No real work had ever been accomplished here. The room was for social gatherings. Solicitation might be a better word to describe the designated activity.

The family business had been extremely prosperous for generations. It operated almost completely independent of direction, based solely on practices and customs developed over hundreds of years. The only real work required was the granting of favors to those who came to this room with requests. But when the American company began to compete for the family's core business, money and power no longer flowed easily into the family coffers. Everything had to be earned. Sophon understood this. If he learned anything from observing John Van Laan, he understood what he needed to do when he returned home.

Fortunately, Sophon had been trained for the task. After attending an English university, majoring in business for three years, he became rather bored with school and dropped out. However, the knowledge he gained at the university was now being applied to the family business. His office had been rearranged into work areas. Computers tables now sat where ceremonial food and drink had once been served. Telephones and computer screens were installed. His new secretary occupied a desk on one side of the room. Sophon could summon her at any time. He sat behind his big desk and worked. His first job was to determine the extent of the problem: how much core business had the American competitor taken, and how much of the marketing and sale of the colored gemstones, mostly sapphires? To date, the information he had pieced together with the help of his accountants and computers was pessimistic.

Luang took a moment to survey the room before speaking. Sophon's father had made no changes. When Luang returned to this office after his nephew's death, the old man had simply worked as he had in the past. Now, everything was different. The old patriarch was both pleased and downhearted by what he saw. He knew Sophon was doing what needed to be done. He only regretted the necessity. He wished everything could return to as it was in the past. Maybe it could, he wondered, maybe after he completed his task.

'I have come to tell you I am returning to America to visit Mr. Van Laan,' Luang said.

'When will you be leaving?' Sophon replied.

'My travel arrangements are being made. I will have my itinerary sent to you when it is completed.'

'How many men will you take with you?'

'The men I need are already in place where I am going.'

"Will they go with you when you meet with Mr. Van Laan?'

'No, only my manservant will accompany me.'

'Is that wise?' Sophon asked.

'I can accomplish what I need to do without help. If I do not succeed... if I don't return, it is of no consequence. I am an old man. I have done and seen many things in my life.'

He paused.

'If this is my time to die, then it is my time.'

CHARLOTTESVILLE, WEDNESDAY, FEBRUARY 3, 11:30 PM, JOHN

When things finally calmed down from what I considered a relatively innocent incident, it was late in the evening.

My explanation, or should I say my feeble attempt to justify my less-than-stellar behavior, did not fly with her. She had used other words with great emphasis to describe my errant behavior, words not worth repeating. Let's just say she was not happy with me. Eventually, I gave in and agreed with her, which is what I should have done in the first place, but I guessed I'm just wasn't that smart.

Anyway, I was getting hungry by this time. And although I had asked her several times about going to my club or to a restaurant for dinner, she had declined my invitations. It seemed she felt safer in my apartment. Apparently, she and Buddy had been talking. Rather extensive distant conversations had been conducted over the phone prior to her arrival. Conversations which concerned new security arrangements. Buddy gave her an update on the newly installed equipment. He assured her she would be safe inside. However, outside was apparently a different matter. Outside, he said he could not guarantee anyone's safety. Once she was satisfied with the new arrangements, she decided to visit.

Now, Buddy never mentioned any of this to me. Buddy and I were destined to have a talk in the near future. The subject of our meeting would be about who was working for whom. Because it would have been nice of him to tell me she was coming. It would have saved me a lot of grief. Now, that didn't mean I wasn't happy to see her. That wasn't the problem. Fact was, I was ecstatic. It just would have been great if he had given me some warning.

Okay, water over the dam. Damage was done. My former girlfriend and I were not off to a passion-filled reunion. When she finally calmed down enough to have a civil conversation, the first thing she asked, was not about food. She asked about Ilana. More specifically, she wanted to hear my version of what happened the night Ilana was badly hurt. She said she had talked to Ilana, but she couldn't bring herself to ask Ilana for the painful details. Sandy was concerned that reliving her nightmare by talking about it would be painful for Ilana. Sandy had waited instead to ask me. Now, she wanted to know all the lurid specifics.

I cautioned her. Asked if she really wanted to hear the ugly details.

She said she did.

I warned her. Said it was not pretty.

Just tell me, she demanded, everything.

I did, told her the truth, and didn't spare her anything until she told me to stop. Seems she really wasn't that anxious to know all the gruesome stuff after all. I didn't blame her.

Next, she asked about the old man. Wanted to know if the break-in was related to the old man's request to see me? I told her the truth. Said I didn't know for sure, but I thought it was.

The next item on her agenda was to ask me why Ilana had gone home, my version again. Seemed she wanted to know everything from every angle. Typical for her.

Again, I told her the truth. Said Ilana decided to leave because she didn't want to be hurt again. I asked Ilana to stay, but I could not prevent her from leaving. Added that I didn't blame her.

By this time, we both had a couple of drinks, and I was even hungrier than before. I asked her if people were still taking nourishment in La La land because out here on the East Coast, folks need to eat to live. She didn't bother to bless my comment with a reply; she simply went into the kitchen without further comment.

Supplies looked rather bleak in the refrigerator when she opened the door. Nothing much inside. Helen was due to go grocery shopping in the morning. Sandy found a can of clam chowder in the pantry. A few stale vegetables and lettuce made a salad. Some frozen corn and sliced turkey were added to the soup, and we had a meal. It was great as far as I was concerned. When it comes to food, I'm more interested in quantity than quality.

While we ate, I asked her if she intended to stay. Her luggage had not moved. It was still in the living room where I first saw it.

'Well, assuming I won't have to witness any more suicidal acts of male stupidity,' she replied. 'I'll consider staying.'

'Have you witnessed any suicidal acts recently?' I asked.

'Not in the last couple of hours.'

'So, does that mean you will stay?'

'If I thought you could live on your own, I would probably leave. But it appears you need constant supervision. So, I guess I will have to stay. I should have come as soon as Ilana told me she was leaving. Unfortunately, I had a few things which needed to be done at home first.'

'Stuff more important than me?' I asked stupidly.

'John, I don't think you want me to make any comparisons right now. You are not very high on my chart, especially in the brainpower department.'

'Do I have some other area where I come highly recommended?'

'What? Like in the prized weenie area?' she inquired.

'Yea, something like that.'

'Not recommended as far as I know.'

'You sure?'

'John, can we talk about something else?'

'Like what?'

'Like, what are you going to do about this Luang guy?'

Our evening deteriorated after this into a long discussion about what David and Charlie thought I should do. I admitted that Luang had called today. So, I guessed a meeting could happen. She listened carefully, had a lot of questions. I asked her what she thought I should do. She wasn't sure. The woman was smart and cautious by nature. Said she would have to think about it first.

By the time we were finished, I was very tired. One too many glasses of wine were ganging up on me. It was time to head for the sack. Unfortunately, her luggage had not moved any closer to my bedroom, which was where I wanted it, where I wanted her. But I didn't dare ask. I didn't think the timing was right. It seemed enough to have her in my apartment. Probably best to let things take their course. Not push it. She knew where my bedroom was. And she knew where the spare bedroom was. It was her choice.

While I was having trouble keeping my eyes open, she was still looking perky. I guess she was on California time. Nothing I could do about that. Told her I had to get some shuteye. I was going to bed.

It was odd, in a way, getting ready for bed, knowing she was in my apartment. I wanted her, wanted her lovely body next to mine, but I did what I had to do. I got into bed alone, turned out the light, and listened for sounds in the night, wondering what she was doing.

And despite longing for her, I quickly fell to sleep.

THURSDAY, FEBRUARY 4, 12:05 PM. JOHN

'You are a fool. You know that?' Sandy said as soon she saw me enter my kitchen.

Apparently, she had been waiting with guns loaded, must have thought about things since we talked last night and was now ready to fire both barrels.

I had gone into my apartment at lunchtime to check on her. She wasn't up in the morning, but then I didn't expect to see her. She was on Pacific Coast Time. It would take her a few days to adjust to living in Eastern Standard Time.

Besides, the woman never did anything impulsively. She moved through life in a contented sort of contemplative way, assuming moving too fast was a sure way to make mistakes. She always wanted to think about everything first and take some time to let it percolate through her brain before deciding on a proper course of action. It gave her an edge, a self-assured view of the world. She could be infuriating because most of the time, or should I say, every time I had the unfortunate opportunity to mentally challenge her, she was right. So, when she started in on me, I knew I was in trouble.

'Okay, I'm a fool,' I agreed. 'Just tell me which one of my many faults you talking about?'

'You let her go away.'

'I assume we are talking about Ilana.'

'Yes.'

'She left on her own accord. I didn't let her go.'

'Oh John, you could have stopped her, and you know it.'

'Sandy, it's complicated. Besides, it's dangerous living with me. Maybe I thought it was better for her to go.'

'I don't believe you.'

'Does it matter?'

'Yes.'

'Well, for the record, it was her decision to go, not mine. I tried to stop her, but she went anyway. I even offered to move to Belize to live with her. She didn't want me. Said I was the problem, the reason she was leaving. So now, can we drop it?'

Sandy had been drinking coffee and munching on some crackers covered with a cheese spread when I entered the kitchen. I wondered where she had found the cheese spread. I didn't know there was any cheese spread in my kitchen.

Her blond hair looked slightly disheveled, like she just got out of bed. She wore the old blue sweatshirt with a big yellow, University of Michigan, 'M' on the front. The one I had given her in Grand Haven. Beneath the sweatshirt was jeans and some big wool socks which was understandable because I seldom turned the heat up in my apartment during the day when I was in my office working.

'Would you like me to turn up the heat?' I asked. 'You look cold.'

'That would be nice,' she responded. 'You know, John. If you were in Belize, where you belong, you wouldn't have to deal with thermostats.'

'I told you I offered to go there, but Ilana didn't want me.'

'What are you doing here, John?' Sandy continued, ignoring my comment. 'You have money, or at least I assume you have enough money, so you don't have to work anymore. Why don't you give up this fight and enjoy the rest of your life?'

'I don't know.'

'Not enough money?' she asked. 'Never enough money?' she queried.

'Sandy, it's not about money.'

'What then?'

'Can we talk about this later?' I asked, looking for any way to escape her wrath.

She didn't reply, just continued to munch crackers as she watched me exit my apartment on an empty stomach.

6:10 PM. JOHN

Not one word of pleasant social greeting escaped her full red lips when I reappeared in the kitchen that evening after work.

Okay, I assumed she would still be mad at me; nothing had changed since I left her at lunchtime. Except this time, I was prepared. Fact was she had been on my mind all afternoon. Even though I didn't want to think about her and I had enough work to avoid thinking about her, that wasn't possible, not completely. Sandy's well-directed criticism kept looming through my mental landscape like sinking sand in a desert. No way could I avoid thinking about that woman and how to deal with her pointed criticism. Slowly, carefully, a defensive plan of action began to take shape in my mind and I was determined to be ready this time. In fact, I was actually anxious to see her, to set her straight.

However, as soon as I opened the door to my apartment, my mental resolve immediately began to dissolve. It seems she was prepared, better prepared for me than I was for her. Wonderful aromas waffled through my apartment like the smell of roast beef cooking in the oven and a freshly baked apple pie cooling on the counter. The problem was I was completely vulnerable, hungry, actually starved by this time; not just hungry, real hungry. I didn't have any lunch. It had seemed more prudent at the time to miss lunch rather than face Sandy's gut-wrenching interrogation techniques. This meant I was famished by the time I returned to my apartment, and as soon as the wonderful scent of cooking food hit my nostrils, my desire to deal with Sandy immediately vanished, replaced by an overwhelming desire to fill my tummy.

But... Isn't giving in weak?

It was time to be a man and face up to my masculine responsibilities.

However, she had devised a multi-layered attack. First came food, and second was an obvious change in appearance. Instead of a baggy old sweatshirt and no makeup, she had combed her hair and painted her full red lips. Complimenting the presentation was a tight pink top that adorned her slim body, nicely showing off a set of fully formed breasts accompanied by skin-tight jeans. I was in trouble from the moment I saw her. Wool socks were the only item of her feminine attire that didn't perfectly fit her carefully prepared, seductive appearance. The socks looked like they belonged to me, too large for her small feet. But my kitchen had a cool tile floor, warm socks were required. And the truth was, it was oh so easy to ignore her socks because the rest of the package was, well... overwhelming seductive.

Not a good situation.

Not for me.

I was fully aware I was weakening.

Warm food, round breasts... I was in trouble, deep trouble. I was going to lose. She must have assumed I would be on the offensive when I returned, and she had prepared. A glass of wine on the counter was the final addition to her offense.

Cooly informing me that dinner was almost ready, her timing was perfect. Apparently, someone had warned her I was returning to my apartment. I concluded a spy resided in my staff, Helen or Buddy. I made a mental note to deal with these two subversives in the morning.

'The wine is for you, John,' she said with a sly smile.

No verbal guns loaded this time, just warm food and a tight pink top. That's the trouble with women. They have too many weapons in their arsenal. Men have only one: logic. And logic alone is helpless when it comes to dealing with women.

'Thanks.' I sipped some wine while taking a few deep breaths in an attempt to regain my initial resolve. 'So, just what are you doing here?' I began, verbally shadow jabbing while fighting with every fiber of mental toughness I possessed to ignore my baser instincts.

'You need someone to look after you. Isn't that obvious,' she hit back without missing a heartbeat?

'I thought I was doing okay on my own,' I dodged to slip her punch, but her jab had hit the mark. My brain reeled, trying to stay focused.

She looked up from the stove. 'What? Eating cereal and TV dinners, I saw what you had in this kitchen,' she let fly. 'And dirty laundry everywhere? Has this apartment been cleaned since Ilana left?' A well-placed counterpunch from her, a direct hit to my jaw.

I staggered into my corner, still not ready to throw in the towel, but my legs were shaky. 'Okay, so you have me in the maintenance department. I am not very good at housework. But you didn't come here to be my maid, did you?' I went for a body blow.

'You need one.'

'Granted, I need one. But I can hire a maid.'

'Not as cheap as me.'

Our combative conversation was getting me nowhere fast. She was working me over good. It was time for a more aggressive tactic. I lined up a roundhouse, right? 'Okay, maid service it is. Please serve me dinner in the dining room. I'm going to wash up.'

One plate of steaming hot food was set on the dining room table when I returned. And for one brief moment in time, I actually contemplated eating alone to make a point. But I couldn't quite pull it off. She had won again. I was on the mat for the count with only one option available, begging for mercy.

'Sandy, please sit down and eat with me. We need to talk,' I pleaded.

'I'm just the maid, remember. Help doesn't eat with their employers.'

'Is that right? So, are there any other duties besides cooking and washing you are willing to perform around here?'

'Like what, boss?'

'Like sexual favors.'

'Oh, so you want to play it kinky. How fun. Should I get my French maid outfit?'

'Sandy, enough... Please get a plate of food and sit down.'

By the time she came into the dining room with her food, I had devoured half the dinner on my plate. I knew it was not good manners to eat before the hostess, but I was too hungry to worry about social constraints. Besides, the food in my tummy gave me renewed strength to mount a new challenge.

'So, why are you really here?' I asked without looking up from my plate.

'Ilana had to leave. It was my turn to take care of you,' she replied, as if her coming here was nothing out of the ordinary.

Her comment stopped me dead in my tracks. 'Do you really think I need taking care of?' I asked, somewhat flabbergasted she would be so bold as to make this statement.

'Is that a rhetorical question?' she asked without looking up. 'Besides, I know Ilana told you she came for the same express purpose.'

'Well, for one, Ilana is not coming back. So, if you are serious, you are here for good?'

She smiled.

I thought I had finally scored a punch, but she had a comeback prepared, like always.

'As long as you need a maid,' she replied.

8:05 PM. JOHN

My tummy was stuffed.

Roast beef, red skin potatoes, corn on the cob from somewhere south and warm apple pie a la mode. The woman knew my weaknesses. But then it wasn't difficult for her. We grew up in the same city. She knew what a Dutch boy from the Midwest likes.

She knew it, and she used it like a weapon.

We didn't talk during the meal and I guess I should have been content to simply enjoy the meal without further conflict. But I felt like I needed to say something. I just didn't know what ... or what not to say. Everything I had planned to tell her seemed wrong. So, I shut up and ate my food. After dinner, she cleared the table in silence. I helped by bringing dishes to the kitchen, where she motioned me out of her way.

Retreating awkwardly to my den, I opened a bottle of single malt Scotch which seemed appropriate behavior for a lord of the manor. If I had to have a maid, I thought I might as well start acting like I deserved one. Anyway, a sip or two of Scotch fortified my mental resolve and I was now prepared for her. The only problem was, she was still in the kitchen. It was time to summon my maid for an employee interview.

'Sandy, do you think you and I could talk now?' I asked as she was finishing in the kitchen.

'I don't know. I'm pretty tired. Could we do this some other time?'

'Oh, come on, you're on Pacific Coast time. You can't be that tired.'

'Maybe you didn't notice, but this place is a lot cleaner than it was a few hours ago.'

'Sorry, I should have thanked you.'

'No need, one of my duties as your maid, right?'

'Sandy!'

'Okay, give me a minute.'

I returned to the den to pour another Scotch. She came in a few minutes with a glass of wine. Without saying a word, she sat down and took a sip from her glass, her silence signifying, I assumed, the ball was in my court. I hesitated for a moment. Nothing I had planned to say seemed right. I finally gave in and went to the heart of the issue. Let the chips fall where they may.

'Ilana isn't coming back. You know that?' I began.

'No, I don't know that.'

'Haven't you talked to her recently?'

'Yes.'

'Well, then, you know.'

'I know she is very unhappy.'

'But you also know it's over between us. She told you, right?'

'She said many things,' Sandy explained. 'Mostly I listened, but I didn't hear anything which indicated what she planned to do in the future... I felt sorry for her. It must have been terrible what happened to her.'

'It was.'

Sandy paused.

'You need to understand something,' I continued. 'Ilana isn't returning. We live in different worlds. I can't live in hers, and she can no longer live in my world.'

'That's a choice you made.'

'It's also the choice she has made.'

'Maybe,' Sandy replied like she knew more than I did.

She was quiet. I waited, assuming she was contemplating her next move, and that's when she asked the one question I had hoped would never come up. 'Why did you start a relationship with me when you already had one with Ilana?'

I looked at her, pleading with my eyes for her to take back the question. But she said nothing, sitting quietly, waiting patiently for my answer.

'It happened,' I rambled. 'After the accident in Grand Haven when I was almost killed. You remember. You know. You were there, you know what happened...' I paused, hoping this was enough information, enough to get me off the hook.

She said nothing, apparently wanting more from me.

I continued. 'I killed a man, Sandy. I regret it. I wish it didn't happen. But it did. He was on my mind all the time... I was in a bad place when I met you, and well...' I didn't know what else to say because I couldn't explain to her what I could not explain to myself.

'Didn't you owe her your loyalty?' Sandy asked the loaded question, the one question that could sink our relationship forever.

'I did... I do,' I answered as honestly as possible.

'So then, why did you start up with me?'

'I don't know. It happened.'

'Things don't just happen.'

Sandy was not going to let up. This much was obvious. I had no defense. I was doomed to fail. So, I said the only words that came into my weakened brain.

'I love you both... And I will not... I cannot apologize for loving you. If I am guilty in your eyes, then I am guilty. But the truth is, I love you both. If that's wrong, then it's wrong.'

She stood up.

I watched her walk away. I could have followed, begged her to see it my way, tried to convince her. I did not. I took another sip of whiskey as she exited the room.

The smooth, strong liquid magic slid easily down my throat, warmed my body, and calmed my nerves as much as possible. Not enough. I was frustrated with Sandy. I was frustrated with myself, but there was nothing I could do. It had happened. I met her at a time in my life when everything was a mess. Death and trouble surrounded me like a fog, a deeply irrational fog where nothing made sense. Everything existed in a gray, undefined mist. I was lost, completely unable to understand how I had become the man I never wished to be, a man who shot another man and killed another man. I didn't want to be that man.

I was running from that man at the time. I was running from the person I had become. I ran to her. I ran backward to the boy I was when I knew her and loved her as a teenager. Love had been my only relief, my only reprieve from a very real nightmare that my life had become.

She was the only place on earth where I did not see death.

CHARLOTTESVILLE, FRIDAY, FEBRUARY 19, 5:05 PM. JOHN

Thankfully, the quarterly board meeting for my company was over, and I was home safely to my office in Charlottesville.

I was exhausted.

New York City's highly orchestrated, mass-hysteria had once more been the scene of a quarterly meeting of my board of directors, mostly because I had no desire to travel overseas. I flew to New York alone, meaning Sandy did not accompany me. Two of my security guys and I flew into the city the day of the meeting and flew out that night, didn't stay like in the past; assuming it would be wise to avoid staying any longer than necessary.

The meeting was time-consuming, and traffic was a nightmare, as usual. Somehow, I survived my latest visit to the Big Apple. All board meetings are different. This particular meeting didn't have any really outstanding issues. Instead, the members concentrated on details. Every aspect of the company's operations was questioned. This put me on the defensive. I had to answer questions that normally weren't asked at these meetings. However, all in all, the meeting went well, and I think everyone felt good about the company after a thorough examination was completed.

And yet as the meeting progressed, I had this uncomfortable feeling that a number of really important items had been left off the agenda. For instance, the details of my unhappy kidnapping in Belize were not discussed. I'm sure the board members would have been very interested in hearing about what happened there. But telling them would have raised too many difficult questions, questions I didn't want to answer.

And most of the board members didn't know the real story of how Sophon's father died; the truth about why he was no longer a member of the board anymore. My killing of him had been covered up by the CIA, and that was the reason I could never tell them about what happened in Belize. Although it was uncomfortable keeping all this important information from them, my hands were tied.

The other issue which could have been discussed was my impending meeting with Luang. I had no doubt the board would have been very interested in hearing about this old man. However, Luang had not yet called with his itinerary. It was possible he wasn't coming. In my mind, this made it easy to avoid bringing up his name to the board. But at the same time, the delay was very disconcerting. I wondered what he was planning.

But then I wondered why.

What would a meeting with this old man accomplish? His nephew had been killed by a bullet from a gun I fired. How could I justify this to him? Still, I sensed I needed to talk to the old man. Duty bound to try to resolve our conflict.

Then there was the matter of the beautiful blond girl who lived in my apartment. Even though her living arrangements were not a required item for the board's agenda, they sure were bugging me. Her luggage was currently stored in a closet in the guest bedroom where she slept. She had made absolutely no effort to move into my bedroom, not even on a temporary one-night-stand basis. The lady had shown me no mercy. Apparently, she didn't see the need.

Now, that was frustrating, being so close to her and yet so far. I wondered if she had any idea what it was like living with a gorgeous tall blond who was acting more like my maid than my girlfriend? It was tormenting. She was torturing me. I assumed out of some sort of misguided devotion to her friend Ilana.

'Helen,' I said into my intercom.

'Yes, boss.'

'No more calls today, okay?'

'As you wish, boss,' Helen replied.

'And go home.'

'Sure boss.'

I roamed over to the bar in my office, the one hidden behind dark, plate glass panels. After pouring some whiskey into a glass, I took my drink to a nearby couch and sat down. Even though it was late on Friday afternoon, I decided to remain in my office, where it was more peaceful than my apartment lately. A certain beautiful blond woman lived in my apartment, and she was consuming me with her overt sexual energy. Sandy was sleeping in the guest bedroom, and I was sleeping in my bedroom. This was not the arrangement I desired. But I was guilty of betraying Ilana in Sandy's eyes. And I assumed Sandy's mission was to force me to return to Ilana.

Sandy, my dear Sandy... what was I going to do about Sandy?

After a few sips of whiskey, I closed my weary eyes to rest when the intercom buzzed. I remembered telling Helen I didn't want to be disturbed. So... why, I wondered, was she still in the office and why was she bothering me? I decided to ignore her, but Helen was never one to be ignored.

She knocked on my office door before entering without an invitation. 'Sorry, boss,' she said, even though I was pretty sure she wasn't sorry. 'It's Ilana on the phone. I thought you would want to talk to her.'

I stood without replying to retrieve my office phone. Apparently, Ilana's priorities were more important than mine from Helen's perspective. I understood. Helen and Ilana were friends. I was only Helen's boss, not nearly as important. Friendships are stronger than economic security. My door clicked shut.

'Hello.'

'John,' Ilana's voice came through the receiver.

For a moment, I thought something might be very wrong. Why else would she be calling?

'You okay?'

'Yes, I'm fine.'

'No problems?'

'No problems. I just wanted to talk to you. We have not talked for a long time.'

'Okay.'

'I have been working on plans for my new house. I bought some land on the sea to build the house. It is near my brother's house on the other side of town. I am very happy. We start building next week.'

'Sounds great.'

'I think you will like the house. It is a nice house.'

'Great.'

After a pause, she asked, 'How are you, John Van Laan?'

'Fine, I guess. I just got back from New York after a board meeting.'

'Did everything go well at your board meeting?'

'Yes,' I said, still puzzled by her phone call. 'You called just to talk?'

'Yes.'

'That's it. No problems, just wanted to talk?'

'Yes.'

'Nothing has changed?'

'No, why do you ask?'

'I don't know.'

'I'm not coming back to you, John. If that is what you are asking.'

'No, just wondering why you called.'

'Maybe I shouldn't have called.'

'Look, I'm sorry. I guess I'm tired. I'm glad you called. You can call anytime.'

'Thank you,' she hesitated before asking, 'Is Sandy still staying with you?'

So that was it. Ilana was checking on me.

'Yes, Sandy is here looking after me,' I replied. 'You don't need to worry. Would you like to talk to her?'

'Yes.'

'Okay, I'll ask Helen to transfer your call. Stay on the line.'

SATURDAY, FEBRUARY 20, 6:10 P.M. JOHN

No usual chatty chatter.

Dinner with Sandy Friday night was subdued. She was mostly silent. Perhaps she had something on her mind, but I didn't know what and didn't push her, couldn't push her. I had learned that lesson from experience.

I did wonder if her silence had anything to do with the telephone call from Ilana. But because I didn't ask, I didn't know. She went to her bedroom directly after dinner, said she wanted to read. So that was that.

Saturday morning was spent in my office after an early breakfast. Work had accumulated during the week of the board meeting. Saturday was an opportunity to get some paperwork done without interruption. By the time I returned to my apartment it was late in the afternoon. Sandy was busy at the time with something in her room.

She had been on my mind during the day. Couldn't help wondering why she had been so silent at dinner last night. That wasn't like her. I wondered if it was because she needed to go out. She had been cooped up in my apartment too long. I knocked on her door and asked her if she would like to go to the club for dinner. I told her I would have a couple of bodyguards come with us. I assumed she would turn me down and not feel safe outside of the apartment. I was pleasantly surprised when she smiled and said, 'Sure, sounds good.'

The engine of my Ferrari started sweet and pure as soon as I turned the key. I was worried it wouldn't. It had been several months since the car had been on the road, but it started fine, the dashboard exhibiting no flashing lights indicating a problem. Sandy got in, and we exited the garage. A brown Ford Taurus driven by our bodyguards picked us up in the office parking lot and followed us onto the two-lane road, which meandered down a hill towards the city. I told Sandy the car behind us was our bodyguards. She didn't need to worry. She nodded approval.

Our drive around the beltway was relaxed. I didn't drive fast, I didn't want to lose the guys in the Ford. Sandy seemed content. All in all, it felt good to be out of the apartment for a change.

The Country Club, where I am a member, is a few miles out of town on the other side of the city on a two-lane road that isn't heavily traveled. When a car turned out of a side street in front of me, I slowed without taking too much notice. Another car caught us about the same time, falling in behind our security escort. Apart from the fact that I had to slow down for the car in front, nothing appeared to be out of the ordinary. It was only when the car behind pulled into the left lane to pass our bodyguards on a curvy section of the road only then did it occurred to me that something in all this might not be quite right. The car slowed as it pulled alongside the

Ford and, without warning, turned hard right, hitting the Ford with a loud metallic bang. Tires screeched. The Ford veered off the road, disappearing into a deep ditch in a cloud of dust.

Hearing the bang, Sandy turned to see what was happening. I witnessed the whole thing in my rearview mirror; I didn't need to turn to look. Jamming the accelerator to the floor, the Ferrari leaped into the left lane around a right turn. Praying I wouldn't see a car coming in the opposite direction, I needed to move. I was caught in a box, two cars, one behind, one ahead; I had to get out and fast. My only hope was to get past the car in front and do it before he had time to react.

He saw me coming, hit his accelerator, and turned left to cut me off. I braked hard and veered to the right behind him, downshifting and accelerating. He reacted, turning into me, but not until I was already beside him. I eased towards the shoulder, never taking my foot off the gas, driving through the gravel, accelerating around him before he could hit me. Several shots sounded, one hitting the rear of the Ferrari with a low thud I felt in my seat. I never let up on the gas as more shots were fired. The two cars behind us were not nearly as fast as my Italian speed machine. They disappeared quickly in my rear-view mirror after several curves in the road. Arriving at my Club, I slid to a stop near the front door.

We ran for the door past a couple of startled valets who must have thought we were nuts.

Inside the front lobby I broke the no cell phone rule of the Club and called Buddy. He had already been in communication with his guys in the other car. Their automobile was badly damaged, stuck in a ravine. The guys were unhurt and the cops had been called. They were on the way. I told Buddy where we were.

He said to stay at the Club.

He would meet us there.

8:25 PM. JOHN

Two bowls of tomato soup and a few crackers with cheese were dinner.

Nothing like the meal I had planned for the evening. Dining at my club would have been far more elaborate and enjoyable, but after an exhausting hour of interrogation from the local law enforcers, our appetites were nonexistent. We headed back to the apartment as soon as the cops gave us our freedom, all of which made Buddy happy. He thought it would be wise to return as soon as possible to that place where our environment was closely monitored by his guys.

'So, this is how it's going to be, living with you,' Sandy said as she cleaned up after dinner.

'Never a dull moment.'

'Aren't you getting sick of it?'

'What do you think?' I exclaimed. 'Apart from the adrenalin rush which comes from thinking you are going to die, it's not much fun.'

I took a sip of wine to calm down. I was starting to relax, but apparently not enough to block an emotional reaction to her statement. The dread panic, which I couldn't control, came out of nowhere and washed over my body in waves, penetrating every fiber of my being. No end to this mess appeared in sight. No end except the ultimate end to everything: a sudden, painful death.

'Yes, of course, it's wearing me down,' I continued after pausing to allow the panic attack to pass, enough time to make a concerted attempt to regain my composure. I didn't want her to see me scared. I didn't want her to meet the weak man who lived inside of me.

'You can leave, you know. You can quit the business,' she countered

'Not sure I can. Too many people depend on me.'

'So, what are you going to do?'

'I don't know, Sandy. What should I do?'

'There must be a better way.'

I sighed. 'Tell me. I'm all ears.'

She turned the water off in the sink and walked out of the kitchen, leaving behind the dirty dishes in the sink; she walked away without saying another word. That wasn't like her. I took her glass of wine and followed her into the living room.

The drapes over the big sliders were closed for security. Even though the room was big, it felt small, closed in. Outside, it was already dark, but that didn't matter. We couldn't see what was outside. We lived in big, well-lit rooms. We were safe, but the atmosphere was confining, not being able to go anywhere.

'This is no life for you. You must know that by now,' I said, putting her wine glass on a table next to where she sat.

'I know.'

'Are you returning to California soon?'

'No.'

'Why not?'

'Because Ilana isn't coming back,' she replied.

'I know. I told you.'

Sandy ignored me. Apparently, she had heard it from Ilana. What I said to her didn't count.

'I think she is falling in love with Todd,' Sandy continued after a pause.

'What did you say?'

'I said I think Ilana is falling in love with Todd.'

'Why do you say that?'

'Oh, just some things she said about him. You know, woman's intuition.'

This tidbit of new information wandered around in my damaged brain for a few seconds before eliciting a worthy response. I felt happy for Ilana, but at the same time, something had been lost.

'So, how does that make you feel?' she asked, going directly to the heart of the matter as was her normal course of action.

'How should I feel?' I countered, angry she dared to ask.

'She was your lover, wasn't she?'

'Look, we tried. It didn't work. Events beyond our control took over.'

I paused before continuing, 'Maybe things deteriorated because we came from different worlds. Maybe it was never meant to be. Or maybe it happened when I killed a man. Maybe it was a lot of things. I make mistakes, okay? I'm human.'

'That's it. That's all you have to say.'

'I guess I'm happy for her.'
'You guess?'
'I am.'
Sandy was being direct with me. I decided to do the same with her.
'So, does this change things for you and me?' I asked.
She took a moment before answering. 'Should it?'
'It could.'
'John, she loved you. She took care of you. How could let this happen?'
'I didn't force her to go.'
'You know what I mean.'
'No, I don't.'

NEW YORK, NY, 8:30 PM. LUANG

Luang walked slowly through the airport lounge and down a long, crowded hallway, followed by his manservant.

It had been a long and exhausting trip, Bangkok to Japan, Japan to LA, LA to New York, and it wasn't over. One more short flight from New York to Charlottesville on a small commuter airline, and then he could rest.

He was not overly concerned about resting. Rest could come later when his work was completed. Now, he needed to remain focused, alert, and attentive until he had completed his task. He ignored his tired old body, ignored the hordes of travelers who walked with him down the crowded, lonely hallway, and ignored his growing desire to see an end to his duties, to finally retire from his life's work. Only after one more task remained to be performed.

This was the way it had always been for him, always duty first. It was a discipline he had been taught from the time he was a small boy. And it was never done, this need for discipline, this need to always be constantly vigil and understand he had been born for one purpose and one purpose alone, and that was to serve his family and his country. It was the creed he lived by. It was the reason he walked this crowded lonely hall filled with people.

His manservant followed a step behind the old man, pulling a suitcase, also mindful of his duty. His duty that day was to care for this old man, this man who had treated his humble family with respect and kindness.

CHARLOTTESVILLE, VIRGINIA, 8:31 PM.
JOHN

'This time, tell the truth, John. Why did you start up with me when you still had her in your life?' Sandy asked.

Our after-dinner conversation had not been that unpleasant, but it quickly deteriorated when Sandy interjected this indelicate question into the discussion for no logical reason, none I could think of. She just wouldn't let the issue die. Apparently, I had not previously answered it to her satisfaction, and she wanted a proper answer.

'Sandy, we have been over this before,' I replied.

'Just answer my question.'

'Why, what for?' I paused to gather my thoughts, 'Okay, how about this... I may not have known it at the time, but it was over between Ilana and me before I met you. It died the night I killed a man.'

'Did she feel the same way?'

'I don't know, probably not.'

'Did you talk to her about it?'

'Not directly.'

'Why not?'

'Because it was too painful.'

'That's not the real reason, is it?'

'Okay, I don't know why we didn't talk about it,' I answered, getting mad. 'I couldn't read her mind any more than I can read yours. Most of the time, I don't have a clue about what you're thinking.'

'We aren't talking about me.'

'Sandy, where is this headed?'

'John, you know where this is headed. You betrayed her. When you went out with me, you betrayed her. You had no right.'

'Why... do you think I stopped loving her when I met you? I didn't and I still love her, still want to be with her, want her in the worst way.'

'Then why did you let her go away?'

'Because it couldn't work for us after I killed a man. Because every time I saw her, I thought about the night when it happened. And maybe because every time she looked at me, she saw a killer. I wasn't the same guy after it happened, and she wasn't the same woman. We still loved each other, we still cared for each other, but our relationship wasn't the same.'

Sandy eyed me, obviously not buying a word I said.

'And then she got beat up, almost killed,' I continued. 'She left because she doesn't want to go through that again, and I don't blame her.'

This stopped Sandy's uninhibited assault on me for a few brief seconds and gave her something to think about, but not for long.

'I understand,' she said. 'But people heal, John. She had a bad experience, but time heals. You didn't give her time to heal.'

'Do you really think you ever get over some things?' I asked. 'Do you think she and I could ever be the same after what has happened to us?'

'Not completely, but enough so the two of you could learn to live together again.'

Sandy had an answer for everything; she always did, never undeterred, and never giving in. It was one of the things I loved about her: her courage, her strength. She was great. But this time, she was wrong.

'It can't work, Sandy. We come from different worlds. I have my work here, and she has her island.'

'You owe her, John. She loved you freely. She gave you back your life, and you walked away from her.'

'No, I told you. I didn't walk away from her. And I will never stop loving her. She knows that.'

'But you let her go.'

'She left on her own, Sandy. I tried to make her stay.'

'But it was too late, wasn't it, John.'

'What do you mean?'

'I mean, you began to reject her before we met. It was you who walked away from her, not the other way around.'

'You have lost me.'

'John, she loves you.'

'I told you; it was her decision to leave. She doesn't want to live with the pain that comes from hanging around with me. The night she got beat up forced her to make the decision she always knew she needed to make. I asked her to stay. I even volunteered to return to Belize and live with her. But she doesn't want to be with me anymore because I am the problem. I am the source of pain. If I went with her, the pain would follow. She knows that.'

'I don't believe you.'

'Well, believe me. She made the right decision, Sandy. And it is the same decision you should make.'

After this remark, Sandy immediately stood and went to her bedroom. Apparently, she had had enough of me and my disjointed logic for one night. She didn't want to talk to me anymore. Didn't find what I said agreeable. I understood. Our church, the society Sandy and I shared, would never condone what I did. We were products of our culture, our religion. She was right to question me. My relationship with her had consequences. Maybe not immediately, but eventually, it was bound to be a problem. I couldn't escape my fate. Our religion makes you pay for your crimes. And I was paying for mine. If for no other reason than because love demands loyalty.

I took a sip of wine, feeling mentally buried in my personal putrid mess, a mess I had created.

Monica's smile came to me at this moment.

I thought about how I had loved her and lost her. I wanted her and still wanted her. If she had not died, I would not be in this mess. I would be with Monica, and Sandy would only be a memory from my teenage years. And Ilana, my free-spirited island girl, would be a woman I had never met.

Monica, my wonderful, red-haired lover. I loved Monica, but Monica had died. Life had dealt me a blow. Life had taken her from me. And because Monica was dead, I met and loved Ilana. Monica's death had opened a door for Ilana to enter my life. Did I regret my time with Ilana? No, I loved Ilana and I would never regret the time I spent with my beautiful island woman.

And Sandy, was I wrong to love her?

MONDAY, FEBRUARY 22, 1:15 PM. JOHN

Helen buzzed me shortly after lunch.

'A little old man is in the lobby, some foreigner,' Helen reported. 'He says you know him.'

'What's his name?' I asked casually.

A report from Australia had recently arrived on my desk. Without reading the report in detail, the initial numbers indicated a very good mining year. The Aussies were working in some rich areas in the mountains. The number of gemstones, the size and quality of the sapphires, all the indicators were unusually high. I was happy for them. They deserved it. The quality of their stones was not always great, but the quantity was worth the effort. Plus, their mines could always be relied on to deliver as promised. So, good for them.

'Luang Nue,' Helen replied. 'Do you know anyone by this name?'

An alarm bell immediately clanged in my head, an adrenalin-pulsating alarm.

'Okay, Helen, listen carefully. Do not appear excited. Just calmly do exactly what I tell you. Understand?'

'Yes,' she replied, the tone of her voice assuring me she understood the importance of what I was saying.

'Tell Luang Nue to wait in the lobby. Tell him I will see him shortly. Under no circumstances are you to let him anywhere near my office until I am ready. Do you understand?'

'Yes.'

I hung up my phone and immediately called Buddy.

'Yes, boss.'

'Please send one of your men immediately to my apartment to check on Sandy. Make sure she is okay. Call me as soon as he reports back to you.'

'Do we have a situation?' he asked.

'Yes, now please just do as I ask.'

'Okay.' he hung up.

I got up from my desk and locked my office door. After a few impatient minutes, Buddy called back.

'Is Sandy okay?'

'I have sent a man to check on her.'

'Okay, as soon as you know Sandy is okay, go to the lobby. A gentleman by the name of Luang Nue should be sitting there. Helen can point him out to you. Pat him down. Make sure he has no weapons in his possession. Then call me.'

A few scenarios were screaming through my disturbed brain while I waited. Of all the possibilities I had considered, I never assumed the old man would simply show up one day without calling first. I was not prepared. Charlie was not here. Nothing was as it should be.

Eventually Buddy called. Everything accomplished. The visitor had no concealed weapons. And Sandy was fine. I asked Buddy if he thought the man looked dangerous.

'Not really, he's short and old.'

GRAND HAVEN, MICHIGAN, 1:20 PM.
PHILLIP PALMER

Snow fell softly outside the windows of Phillip Palmer's office as his mind wandered once again through the fantasy land he had created to replace his sad existence.

Phillip's telephone number had been included in the material Sophon offered to Luang before Luang traveled to the USA. Sophon had explained to Luang that Phillip was an excellent source of information about John Van Laan, a veritable encyclopedia about one human being. Sophon also gave Luang a complete rundown of Phillip's weaknesses, everything his great uncle would need to access Phillip's mind, explaining that what Phillip wanted was to gain control of John's company.

Phillip had been very helpful.

During a series of phone calls, Phillip had offered Luang valuable information and intelligence about how John acted in certain circumstances, his habits, where to find him, and anything and everything Luang could use to accomplish his goal. In return, Luang promised Phillip certain favors and said he would use his influence to pressure Sophon into helping Philip achieve his goal. However, Luang failed to mention one important fact. He failed to tell Phillip he might be in no position to help anyone after he had killed John. Truth was, Luang feared he might not survive his attempt to kill John. And even if he did survive, he knew he possessed only limited influence over Sophon's decision. Sophon would choose the person to run the American operation. It was Sophon's decision to make, no one else.

However, even if Phillip was aware of this unfortunate reality, it may have not mattered to him. Phillip lived in dreams. Illusions were his life, lies which created his version of reality. Sometimes his wishes came true, but most of the time they did not because they were little more than figments of his imagination. To Phillip, one dream was a good as another, one promise as a good as another. So, Phillip helped Luang any way he could.

Well, any way short of committing a felony.

Phillip suggested Luang meet with John at his cottage and said it would be ideal. The location offered an excellent opportunity to escape before a body was found. But when John left town to avoid Luang, Luang was frustrated but not defeated. He understood the value of patience. He told Phillip that his task might take months. It didn't matter how long it took. Nothing mattered except his ultimate success.

Now, as Luang waited patiently in John's office in Charlottesville, Virginia, Phillip was waiting anxiously in his office in Grand Haven, Michigan, waiting for a phone call for Luang, a call he had long dreamed about, a call which he thought would change his life forever; turn his dreams into reality. No one could blame him for being anxious and cautious, but he was anxious because this time was different. Phillip knew how it would happen this time. Phillip had asked because he was curious, and Luang had obliged by telling him how he planned to kill John.

Phillip loved it.

It was perfection.

Luang had a knife, a small, thin knife made of hard ceramic material. No metal detector could discover it. The knife was hidden inside the sleeve of his tunic, next to Luang's forearm. Even though the old man looked innocent, in reality, he was lethal. Martial arts had been his obsession from the time he was a boy. The discipline had helped him develop into a strong young man. His skills had saved him many times during his life. It was dangerous to be rich and powerful. Enemies came with privilege. Even when one is careful to avoid creating enemies, they are often a problem for a rich man.

Luang had used the knife many times in the past to defend himself. Kill, when necessary, quickly and cleanly. He knew where to cut. He knew how deep the wound must be.

After he killed John, Luang was prepared to accept the consequences. He knew he was old and slow. Most likely, he would be caught when attempting an escape. However, if he was arrested, he had a recourse. He would claim diplomatic immunity. He had the proper passport. He could not be denied. But the passport would prove helpful only if he survived. And it was highly possible he might die while trying to escape. However, he was an old man. He was prepared to die in peace, knowing his nephew's death had been avenged.

Phillip had listened in utter fascination as Luang explained how John would die, where his throat would be cut. How much blood would bleed from the wound, how long the victim would live before he died, not long enough for anyone to save him. Phillip knew it all.

He also knew when Luang planned to visit John.

He knew it was today, perhaps even now.

In his mind's eye, Phillip watched John slowly bleed to death.

CHARLOTTESVILLE, VIRGINIA, 1:25 PM.
SANDY

Sandy called Buddy moments after a security guard rushed into John's apartment and parked his butt on a sofa near where she was reading.

She asked the guard what he was doing.'

The man simply said he had his orders.

'What orders?' she asked.

'I was told to come here and make sure you are alright,' the bodyguard replied.

'Who sent you?'

'Buddy.'

Sandy called Buddy, and Buddy explained.

'What is John doing about this visitor?' she asked Buddy.

'I don't know. I patted the guy down. No weapons. He's old and looks innocent enough.'

'Where is this old man now?' Sandy asked.

'He's in the lobby.'

'Is his name Luang?'

'Yes.'

'Where are you?'

'I'm watching him on a monitor.'

'Is Helen at her desk?'

'Yes.'

Sandy hung up and immediately called Helen's extension. The number was busy. She waited half a minute or what seemed like half a minute and called again.

'Helen.'

'Yes, Sandy. What can I do for you?'

'Is that Luang Nue still in the lobby?'

'No, I ushered him into John's office.'

'Is anyone with John?'

'Not to my knowledge.'

Sandy slammed the phone down, immediately dialing John's number.

No one answered.

1:30 PM. JOHN

He wore a black suit.

Not exactly styled like suits worn by American businessmen, although similar, but more finely tailored with a high collar. Even though he was short, he stood tall, looked tall, shoulders back, very proper, walking straight and steady towards my desk. His suit fit well, tight across the shoulders, relaxed in the sleeves and pant legs. A black silk shirt closed at the neck and highly polished shoes complimented his austere appearance. He was the epidemy of a very proper, Oriental gentleman. The grey-haired old man made a very impressive entrance.

I, on the other hand, was dressed in my usual, casual. winter attire; a soft collared long sleeved dark brown shirt under a dark blue, cashmere sweater and tan cotton pants. Comfort was more important to me than image. My words and deeds were my signature. My office was my first impression.

However, Luang didn't look too impressed with what he saw. He appeared to be completely unaware of anything around him except me. His eyes never wavered, intently watching me. It was disconcerting the way his thin black eyes stayed so focused on me.

When he came near my desk, I motioned toward a chair on the other side. It was only then that he took his eyes off me and looked around of my office; taking attention to the leather upholstered couches and chairs surrounding an old driftwood log, glass-topped coffee table.

Turning toward me without any formal greeting, like a bow or an offer to shake my hand, he said my name, 'Mr. Van Laan,' in a quiet, controlled fashion, pronouncing each syllable slowly and clearly. It was easy to understand him even though he spoke with a Thai accent.

'Yes.'

'Perhaps we could sit where it is more comfortable. This doesn't need to be an unpleasant conversation.'

'Let's sit here at my desk,' I replied, still not completely comfortable with the idea of him showing up without an invitation.

Looking around again as if to express his disappointment at my refusing his request, making it appear as if I wasn't being a good host.

I waited for him to sit down. This was not his meeting, after all. I had not invited him. He had come on his own. I decided he needed to do as I asked. He didn't comply immediately. Standing at my desk looking intently at me, it was hard not to blink, but I didn't waver, waiting patiently. Finally, he sat. I followed his lead.

'I have wanted to meet you for a long time,' he began.

'Why?'

'You have accomplished much in a very short time.' His eyes once more swept my office. 'Nue told me many stories about you before he died.'

I was surprised he brought up his Nue's name so quickly. I assumed it would be mentioned eventually, but not immediately.

'I understand Nue was your nephew,' I countered, thinking if he wanted to discuss Nue's death, let's get to it.

'I had no a son of my own. My brother's son, Nue, was like a son to me,' he explained.

'I see. You must have been saddened by his death.'

Luang looked directly into my eyes once again as if he was trying to bore inside my head.

'Yes, I was very sad, but I was also not surprised.'

'Why?'

'I did not always agree with my nephew's methods, too harsh.' He paused as if reflecting on what happened to his nephew. 'In life, sometimes we must accept the consequences of our actions. Don't you agree?'

I didn't know what to say to his comment. I didn't think it would be wise to ask if he thought I was justified in killing his nephew. I couldn't imagine him agreeing. But still, his statement begged the question.

'You seem mystified by my words,' Luang said in my silence. 'Do you not think this is true?'

'What?'

'That a man must live with the consequences of his actions.'

'Perhaps,' I answered cautiously.

'A very clever answer.'

'I don't mean to sound clever.'

'Do you think Nue deserved to die?' Luang asked.

'No.'

'But you killed him.'

'Why are you here?' I suddenly became frustrated with the old man.

'I wanted to meet you. Your company and you personally have had a great influence on me and my family. I thought it was time we talked.'

'Why didn't you call for an appointment?'

'Because I was afraid you would not agree to see me. Remember, the last time I called and asked for a meeting, you left town to avoid meeting with me.'

'Do you know what happened to me Saturday evening?' I countered.

'No. I do not know what you are asking.'

'Some men tried to kill me.'

'I am sorry to hear this,' his voice displayed no emotion.

'You're showing up here today doesn't have anything to do with what happened Saturday, does it?'

'What are you asking?'

'I'm asking if you sent some men as a show of force before meeting with me? Cooperate, or I will have you killed. Something like that?'

'I do not know what a 'show of force' means.'

'I think you do. And to demonstrate that I will not be intimidated... This meeting is over.'

'But Mr. Van Laan, we have only begun to talk.'

'Call for an appointment next time you want to meet with me. And don't send your goons to try to soften me up first. Do you understand? One more episode like last Saturday, and I will never meet with you.'

He had nothing to say. We both knew it was true.

'Yes, I promise to call to ask for an appointment. Please forgive my manners.'

He stood.

I remained sitting at my desk opposite him. He stared at me, taking his time as if he was trying to decide something.

'May we shake hands and agree to meet again?' he asked.

'No, the door is open. Please just leave.'

I dialed Buddy's number. Something about the tone of Luang's voice was bothering me. 'Buddy, I have a gentleman in my office. Please escort him from the building.'

'You do not need to ask you man to come, Mr. Van Laan. I am leaving.' Working his knife from his sleeve into his left hand, he slowly began to walk around my desk with his right hand held out, seemingly intent on shaking my hand.

Buddy arrived at that moment and headed straight for him.

'I do not want to shake your hand. Just leave,' I said as forcefully as possible, without taking a step towards him.

He looked at Buddy.

Buddy had his hand on a gun in his holster with his jacket open.

Luang turned again towards me, momentarily frozen.

Shrugging his shoulders in defeat, he walked away with Buddy following him out the door.

1:40 PM. JOHN

She was in my office in a flash as soon as Luang and Buddy were out the door, entering through the disguised library door directly from my apartment.

Standing quite still with her back to me, Sandy stared in the direction of the open oak doors of my office. I assumed she was waiting, wanting to be certain the old man had actually exited the building without blowing us up first. When she was sufficiently confident danger had passed, she began. Without waiting to cross the room before engaging in her tirade, she let loose with both cannons, sweeping across the room like a fighter jet on a strafing run.

'You let that guy into your office alone without anybody here to protect you? Do you have a death wish?'

'I had Buddy check him...'

'Are you crazy? You know he wants you dead,' she continued without letting me finish my sentence. 'What other reason could he possibly have for coming here? Didn't you learn anything from our road trip the other night when we were almost killed?'

She then paused before letting loose her final volley, 'Do you have a learning disability, John?'

I simply sat at my desk chair with my mouth shut. I knew it would do no good to argue with her. Hopefully, she would calm down after a few minutes of raking me with her wing guns, causing only minor damage.

'John, I'm talking to you,' she said after landing in front of my desk. 'Are you listening to me?'

'I have heard every word you said. You are very difficult to ignore.'

She stood there looking at me. It was the second time that afternoon I thought if looks could kill, I would be dead.

'John, I don't want to lose you. Don't you understand? I'm here because...' She paused mid-sentence. 'Why did you let the old man into your office anyway? Just answer my question?'

Assuming any answer I might offer would probably get me into some kind of trouble, I tried to deflect her. 'He's gone. No harm was done. Can we give it a rest?'

Apparently, this was not a proper response. She stood very still, looking down at me as if she was trying to decide if it would be better to kill me herself rather than give the old man the satisfaction. Fortunately for me, she decided to let me live. Turning, she walked away. As I watched her go, I was not too concerned. It seemed like a good idea to let her calm down before continuing our discussion.

But if I had known what she was thinking, I would have never let her out of my sight.

GRAND HAVEN, MICHIGAN, 4:00 PM.
PHILLIP

It was around four in the afternoon when it became obvious, the call Phillip had been waiting for was not coming, not today.

He was not discouraged. Phillip could think of any number of reasons why Luang had not called. For one, it was possible the old man had been arrested after killing John. In this case a call would be a long time coming. And it would not be Luang who called. Someone in Thailand would eventually tell him what he wanted to know. But only after a few days.

Or possibly the old man was on the run from the police with no opportunity to call.

Or, and Phillip did want to think this, it was also possible nothing happened, no reason to call, nothing to report.

Phillip quickly discarded this last errant thought. Instead concentrating on positive reasons for his silent phone, such as Luang had decided not to call. The old man was not always communicative when it did not suit his purpose.

So what, Phillip thought, it didn't matter. It only mattered that the deed was done, finally done. John Van Laan was dead.

Phillip decided to stop thinking the old man would call, stop looking at his phone every fifteen seconds. Instead he stared at the ceiling wondering who he could call. If Luang was unwilling or unable to talk to him, then who could tell him what he wanted... needed to know?

He could try Sophon.

But after Sophon had returned to Thailand from Belize, Phillip had not talked to the young man. Not for the lack of trying, Phillip had tried, but Sophon had simply cut him off cold. All of Phillip's calls had gone unanswered. Phillip could try to talk to Sophon again, but he knew it was useless.

Useless... as much as he hoped the deed was done... somehow, in his gut, Phillip knew nothing had happened in Charlottesville that day. If it was what he wished for, if the deed was done, if John Van Laan was dead, he would know it. He would feel it. The universe would feel different somehow. The sun would be shining. Phillip would be smiling. Life would be good.

Instead, on this cold, cloudy February afternoon in Western Michigan, gray clouds rolled off the big lake, spreading a light dusting of light snow to fall intermittently across the land.

And in his bones he knew he lived in a world still inhabited by one, John Van Laan.

CHARLOTTESVILLE, 7:10 PM. JOHN

What was left of my afternoon slipped away with my head deliberately buried in work.

Every report I could find, I read. Every phone call that came in, I answered. I talked with every caller for as long as he or she desired. Now, this may have felt strange to some of the callers because if they knew me at all, they knew I usually spent as little time as necessary on the phone. Brief-to-the-point telephone conversations were my M.O., with very little chit-chat. But not this afternoon; this afternoon, I was graciously attentive. But what I didn't tell them was why, why all the attention. I didn't tell them my misguided behavior was nothing more than a feeble attempt to avoid thinking about an old man. Everything about my meeting with Luang had been upsetting: the way he arrived, the look on his face, his calm demeanor, the style of his dress. Especially irritating was the fact he had the arrogance to arrive without calling first.

And then there was the matter of his questions. His questions were particularly upsetting. In fact, nothing about our conversation was satisfying. Instead of bringing some resolution to the matter of his nephew's death as I had hoped, our short meeting had been a complete washout. If anything, it had only made the situation worse. It quickly became painfully clear that the issue of his nephew's death was the most important item on his agenda. And this was the one area where I could not help him. As much as I wished to find a peaceful solution, I couldn't. I couldn't change what happened. I couldn't change the fact that I had killed his nephew.

'Do you think Nue deserved to die?' he had asked.

His question had been running through the back caverns of my head like a broken record all afternoon ever since, and it was the one question I couldn't answer, not to his satisfaction. In fact, it was the one question I couldn't answer for myself. Truth was, I had studiously avoided thinking about this question ever since his nephew's death... except, of course, when Sophon had badgered me with the question for hours. But since that horrible night, I have tried to put it out of my mind.

Finally, when my work was not enough to escape my frustration, I went to find her. Although... I knew we had some unfinished business, I didn't think it was serious. In fact, I had spent very little time thinking about Sandy. I assumed she would get over her minor annoyance with me. Given time to calm down, she would be fine.

Luang had been the object of my concern, not her. I didn't know what to do about him. I had waited for weeks for him to call. I had hoped a meeting with him would help us resolve the unfinished business between me and his family. I had hoped to put an end to the matter, but apparently, the old man had other intentions.

And worse yet, when the old man finally came, I was woefully unprepared. And I got mad... which was no help. Probably happened because he showed up unannounced. I had no time to prepare. Truth was, the whole sad deal was a round robin, mind-fuck going nowhere fast. To complicate the situation, Charlie was not with me as planned. He could have helped by putting pressure on the old guy, but he was in DC.

The meeting had accomplished nothing as a result, nothing except for one thing. Now, I was convinced more than ever that I had every reason to be concerned again. This problem wasn't going away. And the more I thought about it, the more persuaded I became in the hopelessness of my situation, no way to fix this ugly mess, none I could think of.

Under a cloud of sad discontent, I went to my apartment to find her, hoping for some relief, some comfort, but when I found her, she was packing.

'What are you doing?' I asked, even though it was pretty obvious what she was doing. 'You moving into my room?' I lamely asked, hoping something positive might come from a scene that looked exceedingly grim.

'No, I'm going home.'

'A short visit?'

'For good,' she replied with no smile attached.

I was momentarily caught off guard, didn't know what to say.

She sighed, stopped packing, and sat down on the bed. 'John, if you are going to die, I prefer you do it when I'm not around.'

'That's a little mellow dramatic, don't you...?'

'You're either stupid, or you have a death wish,' she interrupted without allowing me the courtesy of finishing my sentence.

'That old guy, he was not...'

'You don't know that.' she snarled.

'Come on.' I replied, vaguely aware I should not have been arguing. I should have been agreeing with her instead, begging her to stay. But I wasn't in the mood. I was upset with my meeting with Luang and the last thing I needed from her was a confrontation. What I really wanted, badly wanted, was sympathy. I wanted understanding. I wanted some love. But apparently, understanding and love were not what she was offering. Okay, I understood why she was angry. But didn't I also have a right to be angry? I was having a bad day, wasn't I? And it was getting worse by the minute.

'He couldn't harm a fly,' I tried to get a smile out of her.

'Do you know that for a fact?'

'He looked harmless.'

'Isn't he the guy who sent those goons after us the other night? The men who tried to kill us?' she argued.

'I suppose.'

'Why do you think he came here?'

'He wanted to talk.'

'John, you are just plain stupid, and I'm not going stay here and watch you die.'

'I'm not going to die.'

'John, you are going to die.'

'Sandy, come on.'

'No, you listen. You are going to die, and I don't want to be here when it happens. I don't want to see the blood. I don't want to see the mess... When it happens, I want to read about it in the newspaper. I want to read about it while sitting on my deck in San Francisco, sipping coffee in the morning. I don't want to be here to witness your lifeless body lying in a casket.'

'Sandy.'

'No, John. I don't...' She stopped talking, yelling really, and turned her back to me.

I touched her shoulder, but she pulled away with tears running down her face.

'You don't get it, do you?'

I didn't know what to say.

'Please leave.'

'Sandy...'

'Just leave,' she yelled and went into the bathroom, closing the door with a slam.

9:40 PM. JOHN

I sulked back to my office.

Didn't know what else to do except to give her some space to calm down.

Pouring a glass of whiskey, I sat down behind my desk and stared at the closed, confining curtains covering my office windows. The sweet liquid slid down my throat easily, calming my nerves. A mining report from Montana on my desk caught my eye. I read it while sipping my drink, anything to take my mind off my troubles.

When I went looking for her later that night, she was gone. No suitcase inside her bedroom, no brown and black bag, no nothing; everything was gone. Only the scent of her perfume lingered in the guest bathroom and it seemed almost indecent to smell her perfume, to imagine her putting on her makeup. It is wrong. It was like I was invading her private space. This bathroom was her space. I made a mental note to ask Helen to have someone clean the bathroom in the morning. In the meantime, I needed to get out and allow her fragrance some privacy.

A bottle of wine in the pantry was open, and a plastic cork held dreams inside. Releasing the cork, I poured the dream-inducing, soft red liquid into a glass. Putting on a winter coat, I carefully parted the curtains over the sliders and escaped to an outside deck in isolation.

With no one again living in my apartment, I was once more free to engage in playful fantasies of invisibility. It was winter, and the deck was dark. I reasoned a shooter would have no reason to be out there in the dark.

It was a warm night for winter with a southern breeze holding the temperature to a tolerable level, tolerable if you wore a coat and hat and gloves to keep warm. I sipped my wine, feeling free again. She was gone and I could do as I wished. I could sit out here as long as I wanted and no one would yell at me. Sandy, my surrogate mother was gone. I could do what I wanted again.

I could die out here if I wanted.

It soon became cold and quiet as I rested with my valley existing in the distance under a winter's night. Stars transformed the clear, cold black sky into an infinite number of sparkling worlds, hopeful worlds perhaps where life was more than one difficult crisis after another. Worlds where peace and grace replaced the hectic, frantic rush to death that seemed to occupy my life.

I rested and listened. <u>But I</u> heard no tree frogs chirping on this winter night to keep me company, nothing but the whisper of the wind through leafless tree branches. The whisper of the wind and a lingering sense I was not alone... that this was all wrong, I should not be sitting out here alone. She was talking to me. In my mind's eye, I saw Sandy standing behind me, asking me if I had a death wish... asking me if I was just plain stupid.

It wasn't the same as before. It was no good. I couldn't sit out here in peace anymore. Resigned to my fate, I went inside, closing the sliders behind me, feeling the warm air inside, knowing I was safe and secure...

Alone and afraid.

GRAND HAVEN, MICHIGAN, WEDNESDAY, MARCH 10, 11:00 AM. PHILLIP

Phillip finally got his call from Luang.

He had almost given up when it came. It had been several weeks and just when he managed to put it out of his mind, it came. Unfortunately, it wasn't the call he desired. It didn't tell him the news he had been hoping to hear. But then, he already knew what happened. So, the call did not make him unhappy. He was simply gratified to know the old man was still talking to him.

Before receiving the call, he had tried every channel he could think of to learn what happened when Luang visited John. No one knew anything, no one in Bangkok, no one anywhere. It seemed Luang had built a barrier of silence between him and the world. He had studiously avoided calling anyone since arriving in the US. But from what Phillip learned, this was the normal operating procedure for Luang. No one expected to hear from the old man. Whatever Luang was doing, it wouldn't become common knowledge until it was over.

In frustration Phillip devised a phony excuse to call John's company. He asked to talk to John Van Laan. The receptionist initially was no help, but after some pointed questioning, she managed to tell Phillip that John was in that day, just not available to take a call.

That's when Phillip knew the truth.

GRAND HAVEN, MICHIGAN, 11:50 AM.
JOHN

It was time for lunch.

I briefly considered going to the kitchen of my cottage and scrounging around for something to eat. But I wasn't really hungry. So why bother? Why the necessity for three meals a day? Why the ritual? Why eat when you aren't hungry? Or, more importantly, why eat at all when you have no one to share your meal?

I could have asked Buddy to join me. He was outside someplace, said he wanted to do some recon. I think 'recon' was the word he used; meaning he wanted to check out the place, look for weaknesses.

Why, I wondered. Why bother when all he saw was weaknesses. My cottage on Lake Michigan was nothing like my office in Charlottesville. The office had cameras, security zones monitored by laser beams. It had three bodyguards on duty at all times and the best gadgetry money could buy. In contrast, my cottage on the shore of a big lake had nothing, nothing but a home security system and Buddy.

Buddy came inside after a while and immediately asked if he could have the security system upgraded. I told him to have at it, have a good time. Buy all the fun gadgets his heart desired. He immediately went into the spare bedroom with his phone glued to his ear.

So, Buddy was busy and I wasn't hungry. So, no lunch. Instead, I sat in a chair behind my desk and stared outside the big sliders which overlooked the lake.

Most of the winter snow on the lakeshore was gone by this time. Only a few isolated patches of the white stuff were still visible in the sand dunes, ugly brown remnants of winter storms. The lake, Lake Michigan, looked cold. A dull-green water world on this day, the lake was filled with protruding ice dunes near the shore, dominating the scene beyond my sliding glass windows. Rising ten to fifteen feet above the water, the dunes had been formed by angry winter storms. Beach sand now tarnished their once pristine white surfaces, making them appear to look old and tired and dirty. Rivulets of clear open water separated the dunes from the beach. Chunks of melting ice floated in the rolling waves beyond the dunes, slowly disintegrating in above-freezing temperatures. Winter was withdrawing from the shoreline, but not without a fight, not without sounds of ugly, loud regret as wave-driven ice crashed against the dunes.

Monotonous days of gray clouds and fierce winds were forecast for the next few weeks. The harsh, cold winter was not giving up its death grip on the land without a fight. The dull green water beyond the dunes, driven by damp-cold winds, was a mad white-capped fury of spraying water and ice crashing spectacularly over the dunes. Anyone attempting to walk the beach in these conditions was soon driven indoors by the cruel wind against their barren skin, eyes watering, checks aching, and heads turned down.

I had not yet attempted to go outside. I knew what it felt like from experience. Instead, I worked in a makeshift office near the front windows where I could see the lake. A chair, an old table, an internet connection through the local cable provider, and a fax machine tied into the phone line and my computer: this was all the equipment I required. And I had Helen. She was available by phone if I needed her assistance. Truth was, the whole world was available by phone if I needed it. But I didn't need it. And I didn't really want to talk to anyone. I made only a few calls, as few as necessary, only the phone calls required by my job. Truth was, I was becoming quite reclusive. That's why I traveled to Grand Haven. I wanted solitude.

But now that I was here, I wondered why.

Buddy came with me because I needed someone to keep me safe and secure.

Ever since Sandy left, I had been a good boy. I did everything I needed to do to be safe. I never went outside without a bodyguard, I never opened the drapes at my apartment, and I never did anything that could be considered dangerous. I did only what I thought Sandy would want me to do.

Work occupied my time until the day was done. Then I went to my apartment to eat and sleep. In the morning I got up and did it again, the same routine; one monotonous day after another. I began to wonder if I was doing all this to prove to Sandy I could be trusted, that I was a good guy after all, not the stupid guy with a death wish she accused me of being.

I was doing what I should, what I thought she would want me to do. But why, I wondered. No one knew what I was doing. Sandy didn't know. And why did I travel to my cottage? I knew it would be like in March, especially early March, when it is cold and cloudy most of the time.

But I also knew I needed to get out of my office.

I couldn't stand being interred in that warm womb for one more day.

7:45 PM. JOHN

I never heard a sound.

One second an empty room. The next second, I look up and he is standing in front of me.

I had been reading a book disturbed only by the sound of a storm outside and vague noises coming from a TV in the guest room of the cottage, lingering mostly unnoticed in the background, evidence Buddy was watching the tube in his room. We had driven into Grand Haven in the evening to have dinner. I took him to my favorite pizza place where they make a special thin crusted pizza dripping in olive oil which was like no other pizza on earth. Pepperoni and mushroom pizza which I loved along with a couple of beers to wash the oily stuff down and life was good again. Good for a short time, anyway. Gastric rebellion was a possibility later.

We talked sparingly at dinner. Buddy told me about the improvements to the security system he was planning. I listened half-heartedly, not really interested. He knew his job. He was good at it. I thanked him and enjoyed my pizza.

It is easy to have a conversation with some people, often because you share common experiences. But with others, it is difficult no matter what the circumstances. Buddy and I were an example of a difficult relationship. Even though we shared a common hometown and work place, we still found it difficult to communicate. This wasn't because I didn't like Buddy. He was a big friendly guy with an easy smile, a great guy really. I assumed this was why he was called Buddy. He was everyone's buddy.

But apparently it takes more than sharing common experiences to have a meaningful conversation. Perhaps because real communication requires more, like having a common view of the world and comes with sharing an intense curiosity to understand life.

I'm never really sure what it takes, but I do recognize it when it happens, happy when it is happening and always uncomfortable when it isn't happening. And it wasn't happening with Buddy that evening. Still, as I said before, I liked him and I was happy to have him with me. I felt secure with him doing his job. In addition, he never forced me to talk when I wasn't in the mood, he left me alone and I liked him for that.

After Sandy moved out, I sort of got used to being alone again and I decided it wasn't all that bad. I didn't have to talk to anyone if I didn't want to. And most of the time, this is exactly what I did. I talked to very few people because I wasn't in the mood to talk to anyone. So, being alone was fine with me. At least, this is what I told myself, even though I wasn't really sure it was even close to being true.

A book by Jim Harrison I found at the cottage had been helping me through the evenings. I had begun to read the book the last time I was at the lake, but I did not finish it. This time I decided to read it to the end.

A glass of wine sat half empty on a table next to a big leather armchair where I was comfortably reading. Normally the chair was turned towards the lake. Not tonight, tonight the chair faced inside because I had nothing to look at outside. Everything outside was dark and disturbing. A storm was whipping across the lake from the northwest. Raindrops were pelting the windows, occasionally overwhelming the sound of the wind whistling through barren winter trees. Sporadically the wind increased in intensity, sounding like a freight train as my cottage shivered ever so slightly, like it was freezing in the storm.

Only one solitary light over my chair illuminated the dimly lit scene. So, when I looked up and saw him, it was as if a shadowy figure of a man dressed in a long black winter coat, black pants and shoes had suddenly materialized out of the darkness.

He stepped back when he knew I had seen him. I assumed he did this so I would not feel threatened by him. But his gesture did not produce the desired response because his sudden appearance out of nowhere was enough to send the hair on the back of my neck standing in full alert.

'Do not be afraid, Mr. Van Laan,' Luang spoke with a clipped Thai accent. 'I am only here to talk.' His smooth ceramic knife slipped into his hand from under his sleeve as he spoke, but it was not yet needed. The time to kill was not right. First, words needed to be exchanged.

'May I turn on some lights?' I asked. 'It would be easier to talk if I can see you.'

'Do as you wish,' he replied, seemingly unconcerned.

After turning on a few lights, I asked him, 'Would you like something to drink, a glass of wine, perhaps?'

He casually sat down on a couch near the leather chair where I had been reading. I found his audacity unbelievable. His composure was calm as if he was completely at ease and comfortable, arriving at my house uninvited. As alarmed as I should have been, I couldn't help but be curious. Everything he did was unconventional. Who was this old man anyway? He was Thai, that much was obvious from his appearance. So was he blood relation to Nue, the man I had killed. And what did he want to talk about?

Perhaps because I had been bored for so long, I almost welcomed his appearance.

Not completely...

A voice inside my brain was screaming that this is all wrong in so many ways. How many men had come with him? And more importantly, what was his real motive for coming? Sandy's words of caution began to course through my brain, overpowering all other thought. I could hear her loudly tell me, 'This guy is here to kill you.'

I poured a glass of wine and placed it on a coffee table across from where he was sitting. Then I stood very still for a moment, wondering what to do next. I had options. I could run. I could ask him to leave. Or I could sit and talk to him.

When I was a kid, I didn't like fighting. I avoided physical fights at all costs. Mostly because I was a skinny, runt of a kid, didn't really grow tall and strong until high school. My chosen form of defense was to talk my way out a fight and if that didn't work, I ran. I was fast. I thought fighting was stupid and solved nothing. Besides I didn't like getting hit, hurt by kids who were bigger and stronger than me. I had learned this the hard way. I had been hit, hard many times. I knew what that felt like. My friends and I boxed for fun with gloves. It was fun. Fun as long as you could call a truce when you wanted to stop, when you had enough, when you had been hit enough times. I knew how to fight if I had to. I just didn't like fighting very much.

He took a sip of wine.

'Do not be concerned about your friend in the other room,' Luang announced without my asking. 'My man is looking after him. He is not hurt.'

Now I was really worried. Apparently, Buddy was in no position to help me.

'I would like to see my friend.'

'He does not need to be your concern.'

'How can I not be concerned? Have you brought an army? Do you intend to imprison me like Sophon?'

'Only one man came with me tonight,' Luang replied honestly. 'This man is visiting with your friend in the other room. If you do not believe me, take as long as you wish to look. I will wait here until you are satisfied, I am telling you the truth.'

I thought about what he said. I could check on Buddy, but what good would that do. It could be an ambush. I felt safer where I was, where I could see him.

'Why are you here?' I asked.

'We need to talk about unfinished business between me and you, between my family and your company.'

'What business?'

'We own almost half of the stock in your company. We have a seat on your board of directors. And yet you have not talked to us since you murdered my nephew.'

I didn't know what to say?

Everything he said was true.

SAN FRANCISCO, CALIFORNIA, 5:05 PM.
SANDY

Her watch told her it was after five in the afternoon.

But she knew what time it was. Sandy had looked her watch only a few minutes before and twenty minutes before this. In fact, she had been checking her watch all day. She wondered why. She didn't have a clue. She wasn't late for anything. She had plenty of time to do some shopping before driving to the bay where she was scheduled to meet a girlfriend at a local city restaurant for wine and dinner. Sandy was looking forward an evening of chit-chat, female camaraderie. It promised to be a good time.

So why, she wondered, why had she been constantly looking at her watch along with an uncomfortable feeling she should be somewhere else? Like some big event had been planned and she should be getting ready to go, some party, something important. But to her knowledge, she had nothing special planned. She remembered checking her calendar in the morning. Only one event was posted, dinner with Karen that evening, nothing else.

She cleaned her apartment before going into town for some afternoon shopping accompanied by this strange and uncomfortable feeling, she should be somewhere else. Even though she tried to stop thinking about it, this strange irrational feeling simply would not go away. It had persevered, even became stronger as the day progressed. But with no party to attend, no big social event scheduled; she began to think maybe it was something else, something more important; like she needed to be somewhere to help a friend who was in trouble. It was that kind of feeling; like if she wasn't where she was should be, someone might die.

In the back of her mind, she knew where she could be and who she could be helping, but she had studiously avoided thinking about him, about John Van Laan. That chapter in her book had closed forever.

She began to walk, window shopping; enjoying the sunshine on a great day to be alive in San Francisco, smiling and enjoying the warm weather. Soon she would have dinner with her friend Karen. Then she would go home and get a good night's sleep.

Tomorrow she would feel better.

GRAND HAVEN, MICHIGAN, 8:10 PM.
PHILLIP

Phillip looked at the clock on the wall of his office.

It was getting late, after eight o'clock. Any other night, and he would have been home by this time. But tonight, he stayed in his office and waited in case Luang called him for assistance.

Phillip did not learn that John was in town until Luang called and asked if he could visit. Luang said he had something he wanted to discuss with Phillip.

Of course, Phillip agreed.

At the meeting, the old man told Phillip nothing significant. It was Phillip's job to read between the lines. The old man was crafty. He simply asked the one question, and he gave Phillip nothing in return. Appearing to be in a hurry. Luang asked Phillip if he knew the layout of John's cottage.

Of course, Phillip knew. Phillip knew everything.

Phillip had a friend who had helped build John's cottage. And although Phillip had never been inside the John's home, he knew the layout by heart. Phillip had a photographic memory. His friend had showed him the blueprints. The layout was ingrained in his memory forever. Phillip drew the general layout of John's cottage for Luang, every room, every door.

The old man never told Phillip why he wanted this information, but it didn't take much imagination to understand why. However, before Luang could get out the door, Phillip's curiosity took over and he asked Luang when he was going to visit John. The old man had simply smiled and said nothing before turning to walk out the door. So, Phillip didn't really know the answer to his question, but as he watched the old man walk away, Phillip knew it would be soon, probably tonight.

8:15 PM. JOHN

'Okay, let's talk. Company business or did you come to discuss what happened to your nephew?' I asked, becoming impatient with the disciplined demeanor of the old man.

I had to assume Buddy was out of commission. If not, he would have been in here by now saving my ass. His absence meant only one thing. He was either dead or he was being confined. Either way I was on my own and being on my own was not the plan. I remained standing as the old man sat quietly on a couch, seemingly unconcerned. I was determined not to sit. I was too afraid to sit. I wanted to be ready to run.

Luang ignored my question, silently sipping his wine as if he was contemplating his answer. His silence was unnerving. I wondered what he was thinking. If I was to achieve anything, I had to get the old man to talk.

'Okay, let's start with business,' I finally suggested. 'As far as I know my company has done nothing to break the original deal I made with your nephew before his death. If you have come here to complain about our deal, tell me now.'

Luang thought for a moment before answering. 'Sophon is in charge now. Not me. If you want to talk business, you need to talk to him.'

The mention of Sophon's name did nothing to calm my nerves. My previous meeting with Sophon had been anything but pleasant. But then I assumed Luang knew all about this ugly affair.

'May I assume you wish to continue under the previous agreement?' I asked.

'As I said, you need to talk to Sophon.'

'I'm not sure he wants to talk to me. Perhaps you know about the last time I had the pleasure of speaking with Sophon. My experience with your nephew, being captured and tortured. That didn't exactly create a cordial atmosphere for future discussions.'

'I understand, but then your final meeting with my nephew was also not pleasant. And yet, here we are,' Luang argued.

'What do you want?' I asked impatiently. 'Why are you here.'

'You know.'

'You want to talk about Nue.'

'I do,' he responded as if it didn't matter.' 'Why don't you sit down, Mr. Van Laan?'

I hesitated, not sure I wanted to do anything he asked. Still... this was a conversation I desired, maybe more than he did. Killing his nephew had been an act of outrage taken in a moment of insanity. I needed some sort of redemption, some appeasement if not a full pardon from his family. I didn't really think I had gotten it from Sophon. A reprieve perhaps, a chance to take a deep breath, but that was all I felt I achieved from the young man. I wondered if I could I finally find some peace from talking to this old man? I hoped I could. I wanted it. As much I felt it would never happen, I had to try. I sat down in the leather armchair across from him with my back to the glass sliders overlooking a dark lake night.

'Okay, let's talk,' I agreed.

He waited before asking, 'Why did you kill Nue?'

I retraced the images fixed in my mind when the gun exploded in my hand. It had felt more like my mind had exploded, not that the gun had fired. A flash of light had burst from my eyes. The gun was only a physical manifestation of my mind's desire to inflict great bodily harm on the man standing in front of me. But how could I explain this to the old man in a way he would understand.

'Sophon and I have been over all this,' I said. 'I'm not sure I want to discuss it with you.'

'I do not know what you said to Sophon. He is unwilling to discuss it with me.'

'That's not my problem.'

Luang sighed. 'I am an old man, Mr. Van Laan. Nue was like a son to me. Please answer my question.'

I hesitated. I had this conversation with Sophon. I didn't want to have it again with this old man, but he gave no choice. 'Okay, Nue had just ordered the death of my girlfriend's brother,' I finally answered, giving Luang the short, simple rationale for killing his nephew, hoping this would satisfy him. 'I couldn't let that happen.'

'So you shot Nue to save her brother?'

'Yes.'

'Were you convinced Nue was going to have the man killed?'

'I was.'

'I see, but was it possible Nue never intended to have the man killed? Perhaps Nue was simply threatening to kill her brother to get information from your girlfriend, information about your betrayal?'

'How do you know that?' I asked. 'Did Sophon tell you?'

'No, a man named Phillip told me.'

At the sound of Phillip's name, I immediately became angry.

'Phillip is a liar,' I said emphatically.

'That is why I am asking you,' Luang calmly replied.

'Do you know Nue tried to kill me in Thailand?'

'I know what happened, Mr. Van Laan. And I am very skeptical of what you are implying. Let me ask you. Has it ever been proved that Nue caused the dam to burst?'

'I heard an explosion.'

'Maybe the explosion you heard was the sound of the dam giving way after years of erosion.'

'He tried to kill me many times before this, too many times. I don't need proof.'

'Do you have evidence to support your allegations.'

'Okay, let's just agree to disagree about the events which happened before the night he was killed.'

Luang was silent.

I continued, 'Do you want an answer to your question or not. Because if you do, we need to return to the night your nephew died?'

'As you wish.'

'As I said before, the truth is, Nue had ordered the execution of the brother of my girlfriend. I couldn't let this happen. So, I shot him, one life to save another.'

'I don't believe you. You didn't need to kill Nue. You could have reasoned with him. It is obvious you are a man of words.'

'No, I couldn't reason with him. He was a man of violence. He had demonstrated that too many times in the past. I did not think it was impossible to reason with him. I know.

I tried.'

8:35 PM

Buddy was a former Navy Seal.

He had learned his lessons well. The ropes around his wrists and ankles were strong, but he knew other methods to deal with his captor, methods which don't require fists. He had been taken by the surprise, knocked unconscious before he had time to react. This time would be different. The foreigner looked away just for an instant. That was all the time Buddy needed to make his move. He leaped at the man, planting his forehead squarely into the side of the man's head, stunning him. Falling to the floor he flipped over and kicked at the man's head again.

The man lay silent on the floor.

Buddy thought about finishing the job with a few more well-placed kicks, but instead, he hopped quickly to the bathroom for a pair of scissors. Working the ropes loose and turning the scissors backward, he was able to cut through the ropes holding his wrists.

Finding some adhesive tape in the cabinet, he taped the unconscious man's arms and legs to his bed.

8:40 PM, JOHN

Luang hesitated.

Some indistinct noises we both heard coming from the guestroom interrupted our conversation, loud thumbing sounds like someone falling, a struggle. I instinctively got up to move away from the old man. Luang sat very still, the knife disguised under his hand. It was time.

'You do not need to be concerned about your friend.' he stood.

I wasn't so sure. And I felt a lot better when Buddy appeared with a gun in his hand.

'Would you like me to call the police?' Buddy asked.

'Are you okay?' I asked Buddy.

'I am now.'

'No, don't call the police just yet. Luang and I are having a pleasant conversation.'

Luang nodded in agreement as if Buddy's sudden appearance was expected and sat down.

'Do you have any other men with you?' I asked Luang again, this time in Buddy's presence.

'Only one.'

Buddy nodded.

'Do I have your word?' I asked.

'You have my word.'

'And guns, are you carrying a gun?'

'No,' Luang responded, slipping the ceramic knife into a thin soft cloth wrapped around his forearm, disguised by folds in his shirt.

'Check him,' I said to Buddy.

After giving me his gun, which I held pointed at Luang, Buddy asked the old man to spread his arms and legs. He patted him down, finding no weapons.

'Okay, Buddy, why don't you take a seat near my guest where you can keep an eye on him,' I requested. 'I want to finish my conversation with this old man, now on my terms.'

'Your nephew was a man of violence,' I continued, feeling confident. 'And he was surrounded by men of violence. I could not reason with him.'

'And you, Mr. Van Laan. Aren't you also a man of violence?' When I didn't immediately respond to his question, he continued, 'Didn't you bring men with you the night you killed him, men with guns? And didn't these men kill Nue's bodyguards?' He paused. 'What happened to the bodies of these men, Mr. Van Laan? Their wives and families have been waiting, wanting to properly bury their relatives.'

What he said was true. The CIA had come with Charlie that night. They had no alternative. Nue's bodyguards were heavily armed. I would have been killed if Nue's men had not been taken out quickly by a hail of gunfire from the CIA. Afterwards, Charlie and his guys cleaned the scene, removing all traces of evidence, everything carted away by helicopter, the bodies of Nue's men included. I never asked Charlie what happened to the bodies. I didn't want to know.

Luang waited for my answer.

But I had nothing to say, nothing which would help my case.

'You murdered my nephew because you knew you could kill without fear of ever being punished for your crime,' Luang stated emphatically. 'Isn't that true?'

'No, that is not true. I did it to save a life.'

'I have heard nothing which justifies your crime.'

'Okay, I did it to save my life,' I said, getting impatient with this old man and his arguments.

'Were you in danger at the time?' he asked.

'I had been in danger for a long time. It had to stop.'

'Did killing my nephew erase the danger?'

I looked at him, getting angry. 'No, I guess not. I assume you are here to finish what Sophon wouldn't do.'

He nodded.

'And my latest adventure on the road in Charlottesville, I assume you were responsible for that?'

'You were not taking me seriously,' he answered truthfully.

'I'm taking you seriously now.'

'Yes, I suppose you are,' he responded, looking at Buddy sitting in a chair with his gun pointed at him.

'So, what do we do now?'

'It is time for you to pay for your crime.'

I couldn't believe he had the audacity to assume he could kill me at will.

'Aren't you forgetting something,' I asked. 'Like the fact my friend's gun is pointed directly at you?'

'I am not concerned about your friend.'

'You should be.'

'Just answer my question,' he demanded.

'What question?'

'Why you killed my nephew.'

'I'm willing to admit nothing more than I killed your nephew in self-defense; if not my defense, then to save the brother of my girlfriend,' I answered.

'Nothing you have said has convinced me. In fact, I have a witness at the scene who told me you murdered my nephew.'

'Phillip is not a credible witness,' I replied, assuming he was referring to Phillip. 'He is a liar who will say anything which serves his purpose.'

'I do not know that.'

'Doesn't Phillip want to become the head of my company after I'm dead?' I knew Phillip and I knew what he wanted.

Luang remained silent.

'Well, am I right?' I demanded.

'This has nothing to do what happened that night.'

'It has everything to do with it. You are relying on Phillip's word. He is your witness. But he's lying to you for a reason.'

'We are done here, Mr. Van Laan. It is time you answered my question. Did you murder my nephew?'

'I killed him to save a life, mine. It was self-defense.'

Luang stood up. Buddy also, his gun pointed at the old man.

Luang turned slowly, simply turned, and started walking towards Buddy, slow like he wanted to walk past him and out of the door. Buddy stepped back at first to get out of the way. Then, for some reason, perhaps Buddy thought he should restrain the old man, prevent him from leaving, and take him into custody. Buddy took a step towards Luang.

It happened very quickly. Short quick jabs, too fast for Buddy to react. He was not prepared for an old man. I heard the crack of Luang's fist to Buddy's throat. Buddy gasped and staggered from a second blow to his nose. His gun fell harmlessly to the floor. Another blow to the back of his neck and he fell on the floor, unconscious.

His gun was too far away for me to get to it, nearer to Luang. The old man saw me look at the gun. He took a step towards me.

I saw it then, something shiny in his hand, like a blade.

It was time to go, run, Instinctively I turned to run, pulling the sliders open, out the door without looking back.

Run, run like the wind, one chance to live.

The storm howled in the night. Rain pelted my face infested with ice crystals. I ran across the deck, jumping down the steep banked, sand dune towards the shore, flying into the rainy black night sky, falling, afraid, disappearing into the darkness, tumbling down the sandy embankment. A muffled shot rang out in gray light from town, just enough light to see shadows. Blades of beach grass cut across my face and hands like knives as I fell, turning over and over, down the wet sandy hill in gray darkness, afraid to look behind, afraid to hear more shots in the night, afraid the dark shadow of an old man was following.

A bullet cut through beach-grass near my feet. Another shot was lost in the storm. Reaching the bottom of the bank, I was up instantly, running through wet grass over a small dune, running down the beach to the water's edge, listening to waves crashing nearby over invisible ice dunes in the gray light. The footing was solid near the water, easier to run on the damp firm sand.

Cold wind and wet rain, I was alive. I ran, ran until I was exhausted. Stopping once to catch my breath, listening to the wind howling, hearing nothing, no shots fired, I crouched behind a sand dune, searching the shore for signs of a man, for a black shadow in the night. I saw nothing, only a distant figure of what could be a man standing near the top of my deck, backlit against light coming from inside an open slider.

It could be Luang, but it was hard to see. I was too far away to see clearly, my eyes blurry in cold rain. I turned and continued to run away into the teeth of the storm.

Run from certain death, run, run... breathe and run. Cut and bleeding, I continued to run... run on legs of lead. I ran until the shadows behind me were merely shadows and nothing more, ran until I couldn't run anymore. Exhaustion took over. I had to stop.

Cold and drenched to the skin, the wind covered my misery with an invisible legacy of wild sadness. Exhausted and too frightened to do anything but hide among the cold dunes, I searched for shadows in the night, afraid to believe that the danger had passed, scared that death was still behind me, the little old man stalking me in the night.

In miserable despair, I cowered under the cover of a pitiless storm.

A cold, rain-saturated wind hurried over the lake as the storm rose up in anger and rushed on shore, blotting out the night sky. Waves crashed mercilessly over shadowed ice dunes, pounding the disintegrating ice in anger, crashing, washing over the smooth, penitent, helpless ice. Beach grass, whipped by the wind, cut across my face.

Still, I lingered in fear, helpless, hiding behind a sand dune, watching, ever vigilant for a black shadow determined to take my life.

SAN FRANCISCO, CA, 7:05 PM. SANDY

Dessert was a heavenly, chocolate-covered, ice-cream sundae, the specialty of the house.

Sandy began by taking small bites of the divine delight. Small bites are not fattening, she reasoned. Small bites are not full of calories. Small bites are simply a reward for being a good girl.

Her meal had been a chicken salad with green leaf lettuce, some cheese, and a no-cal dressing. Dinner had been pleasant. Her friend Karen was a talker. Sandy did not have to comment too often to hold up her end of the conversation. Karen was more than happy to hold up both ends. The latest gossip was discussed as tidbits of human irony and minor tragedy. It had been good fun. Nothing really terribly devastating was discussed, no poisoning, destructive talk; only fun stuff to chit-chat away an evening.

Sandy smiled throughout the meal. The view from their table by the window in the restaurant looked over the bay. The weather this evening had been warm for March, with sunshine and blue skies. The sun had set behind red-tainted clouds as they ate. It had been wonderful to see. In fact, everything had been terrific, everything except Sandy. Sandy was not great.

Her nervous tension, her need to be somewhere else, had not disappeared. And now, as she nibbled at her desert with the familiar hum of Karen's chatter in her ear, she knew what the problem was, and she didn't like her conclusion.

John Van Laan was her problem.

As much as she wanted him out of her life, he was not cooperating. He was constantly in her head, smiling at her with that nonsensical smirk on his face. Smiling at her as if to say; see, I told you so. You cannot go away. You can never leave me, not now. You know I am waiting for you to return. You know I need you. You know this more than I do. I get into trouble when you are not here to take care of me. Like today, you know I'm in trouble. You can sense it. You know it. And what are you doing? Having a nice dinner with your friend and eating chocolate-covered ice cream when I desperately need you, want you.

'Sandy,' Karen interrupted.

'Oh, Karen, I'm so sorry. Have I been ignoring you?'

'You have been somewhere else all night, dearie. I have tried my best to keep you entertained, but you are a hundred miles away. What's wrong?'

'Oh, nothing, please forgive me.'

'Man-trouble? Want to talk about it?' Karen asked politely.

'Oh no... not really.'

GRAND HAVEN, 10:25 PM. JOHN

Too tired and cold to care, my body began to shiver violently.

I had to find shelter whether I wanted to or not. I had been outside too long. Adrenaline from my near-death experience had worn off an hour ago. I was cold. I was going to die if I didn't find shelter.

Soft, warm lights from windows in a cottage above the shore beckoned me. I began to climb the beach stairs slowly, exhausted and cold, one step at a time. The stairway was long. The neighboring cottage was far up on a dune overlooking the lake. Each step became a burden. I had to stop, rest several times, leaning against a railing, looking into the night for flashlights or black moving shadows, anything which might be evidence of an old man following me, close behind with a gun. I saw nothing and continued climbing slowly, wearily up one step at a time, leading to soft, warm lights.

When I finally got to the top of the stairs. I wiped my eyes, combed back my wet, sand-filled hair with my hand, and took a deep breath. Knocking on a door, I hoped desperately someone was home to hear me.

Thankfully, a man appeared at the door after repeated knocking.

A wet, dirty man, a bum most likely, or worse, a druggie, looked at him when he opened the door, appalled at the sight of my bleeding face. An undesirable seeking shelter in his multi-million dollar beach house. He shook his head no. No way was he going to allow a desperate degenerate into his warm home.

I pleaded with him. I said I was his neighbor. He didn't believe me. He refused, yelling at me, telling me to go away. Finally, I asked him to call the police. Call anyone. I told him I was going to lie down on his doorstep. If he did not help me, he would have to explain why a dead body was found on his doorstep in the morning.

He slammed the door in anger. I hesitated, wondering if I should go somewhere else for help.

I was cold, so cold, and dead tired. I didn't care anymore; I lay down on his doorstep and closed my eyes, shivering uncontrollably in the pitiless storm.

SAN FRANCISCO, 7:30 PM. SANDY

'Come on, you can tell me. I'm your friend.' Karen pleaded.

Sandy and Karen were sipping after-dinner hot coffee while continuing to chat. Everything seemed fine on the surface, but Karen knew something was amiss. Her friend Sandy was not her usual effervescent self, full of charm and calm composure. Something was obviously bothering her.

'You've got man-trouble. It's all over your face,' Karen said with a smile.

'I'm fine.' Sandy tried to deflect her friend's attention.

'Tell me. Is it that guy from Virginia, the one you keep going to see?' Karen was a woman on a mission now.

'No, no. That's so done,' Sandy replied.

'I don't think so. I think you need to tell me all about him, sweetie. It's time to get that man off your chest.'

Sandy took another small bite of the partially neglected, chocolate-covered delight in her bowl, noticing for the first time the desert was fast disappearing. She had not intended to eat the whole thing, just savor a few sweet morsels, just taste-test it. She couldn't remember taking that many bites.... But one more small bite was okay, wasn't it?

As the sweet chocolate circulated freely in her mouth, she relished the experience to its fullest, thinking maybe it would be good to tell Karen about John Van Laan. Karen wouldn't tell anyone. She could trust Karen. They were best friends.

Maybe she would feel better if she told Karen about John Van Laan.

GRAND HAVEN, 10:35 PM. JOHN

Hypothermia can kill.

Eventually, your body stops shivering from being cold, and your mind slowly slips into unconsciousness as your organs shut down one after another. Then you are dead. No more you. Only a cold, stiff, frozen body remains of what used to be you. Your eyes no longer look, and your mouth no longer issues words of wisdom, sadness, laughter, or stupidity. Nothing works, no breathing in and out, no heart pounding, no nerves rattling, no brain functioning. No thoughts, no words, no visions, no dreams. No nothing.

Somewhere in a cold, confused dream world, Mary smiled at me; wonderful Mary with long black hair, caring Mary. Mary, the girl from my teenage fantasies. She was a beautiful girl in high school. Captain of the cheerleading squad, queen of the prom, everything a guy could ever want. All the guys wanted Mary at one time, me included. My friend David got her. I never had a chance once they started dating. So, when I opened my eyes to see her smiling at me, I wondered for one brief second if I had died, gone to heaven, and returned to a new life in which Mary was my bride, my love, not David's.

But that's when I saw David's smiling face standing next to her and knew that my heavenly apparition was not real. I was still alive on this earth, trapped in the same old, tired body.

Wrapped in warm blankets in some sterile-looking room full of lights and medical machines, an IV dripped into my arm, monitored by a nurse in a white uniform. Mary was sitting on a chair next to my bed, smiling at me. When I tried to respond to her, pain was instantaneous; not too much pain, just some bumps and bruises pain, obvious evidence that my former miserable existence was still functioning on some level.

'So how you doing?' David asked while I was mesmerized by Mary's pretty smile.

'I would do a lot better if you let Mary crawl under these blankets and keep me warm,' I smiled at her while ignoring David.

My lips hurt when I smiled. Couldn't help it, and even though it was painful, I reached up to feel the small cuts that covered my face. It was then I remembered wet cutting beach grass, and immediately, all the sordid details of last night's adventure rushed through my recently frozen brain, and I frowned.

'So, what happened?' David saw the look on my face.

'Can we talk about it later?' I answered, not particularly enthralled with the idea of reliving the experience, even in words.

'Sure, I can wait, but the police want to talk to you now.'

'Look, do me a favor and keep them away, will you?'

'I'll try.'

'Say, have you seen a guy named Buddy?' I asked.

'Yes, he's sitting in a chair outside your door. Looks beat up, worse than you, but he says he is fine. Mostly, he looks mad,' David replied. 'Says he is not going anywhere as long as you are in here.'

'How'd I get here?'

'Some guy found you lying on his doorstep, half dead. He called 911. Buddy called me after he woke up at your cottage, and we found you here.'

'Okay, good. Now, as I was saying, I'm still feeling cold. So maybe you wouldn't mind if Mary crawled in bed with me to keep me warm tonight.'

'Sorry, she's taken,' David said with a sigh. 'Get some sleep, my friend. I'll be back to pick you up in the morning. Don't worry, doc says you will be fine by then.'

CHARLOTTESVILLE, VIRGINIA, THURSDAY, MARCH 11, 10:50 AM. HELEN

Even though Helen received numerous calls every day, this morning had already been one of those days; one of those mad, rush, rush days when bad news circulated the globe so fast, she couldn't put out all the fires fast enough.

However, this was one caller she did not expect to hear from.

'John Van Laan's office, may I help you?' Helen said into her receiver for the hundredth time that morning.

'Helen.'

'Yes.'

'It's Sandy, Helen. Sorry to bother you. And well, I don't quite know how to ask you, but... I just had to call?'

'You and everyone else.'

'What do you mean?' Sandy asked.

'I assume you are calling because you heard about John's latest escapade.'

'No, I haven't heard anything.'

'Oh, so why are you calling?'

'I felt something was wrong. I couldn't get the thought out of my head. I called to satisfy myself that it was my imagination and nothing else.'

'Well, it ain't your imagination, honey. He almost died last night.'

'What happened?'

Helen told Sandy the story. By this time, she had repeated the sorry tale so many times she had refined it to the point where she could tell it in less than three minutes.

Sandy listened silently.

When Helen was finished, Sandy thanked her and hung up.

GRAND HAVEN, MICHIGAN, 11:20 AM.
JOHN

The tall pines along Lake Shore Road swayed in a stiff breeze, driven by the backside of last night's storm.

Permanently bent at the top from being constantly buffeted by prevailing westerly winds off the lake, the rich green pine needles of these verdant conifers supplied badly needed visual vibrancy to an otherwise dull brown landscape of leafless trees. A constant wet drizzle swept across the cool gray scene. Dark clouds hid the sun. Spring was still absent. Cold winter, unwilling to release its ruthless grip on the land.

'So, what will you tell the police?' David asked nonchalantly in his usual legal demeanor, staring straight ahead while driving.

We were in his car on the way to my cottage from the hospital. I was sitting up front with David. Sullenly residing in the back seat of David's four-door luxury Lexus, not talking to anyone, was Buddy who looked like a big loser in a professional boxing match. One of his eyes was black and blue. And he had a nasty bruise on the side of his neck accompanied by a permanent scowl on his face. He was not a happy man. He had been taken twice in one night. That had never happened to this Navy Seal before. He prided himself on being always alert and ready for anything. But last night had not been a good night for Buddy. His reputation, along with his face, had taken a severe beating.

David picked us up at the hospital in the morning. Always self-confident with an even temperament, he was a hard man to get riled. And I had tried. On more than one occasion, I had tried, but I always failed to get a rise out of him.

'Hey, remember when I drove off this road?' I answered him, hoping to deflect our conversation to something more pleasant.

'Yes, I remember,' he replied. 'How could I forget? I thought I was going to die. You almost flipped the car.'

We were in high school at the time. It was summer, and I was in a hurry. I was always in a hurry back then. A car in front was going slow down on this two-lane road, inhibiting our progress. A quick glance and I attempted to pass the offending vehicle. However, automobiles in those days didn't have powerful engines like today. They were big, heavy metal cars with limited horsepower. Step on the gas, and it took a long time for the Detroit iron to get up to speed. I had made an error in judgment. I wasn't accelerating fast enough to make it around the car I was passing in time to avoid a head-on collision with another car that came over a hill, driving directly at me from the opposite direction.

Now, regrettably, I would have been fine after hitting the brake to slow and ease back in behind, except the car I was passing realized the circumstances didn't look too favorable for me and decided to help by slowing down about the same time I hit the brakes to fall in line behind him. The unfortunate result of these two simultaneous reactions was that we were both slowing at the same rate of speed. And this unhappy set of circumstances meant I was stuck in the left lane with an oncoming car headed straight for me. If I didn't do something quickly, a nasty accident was in my foreseeable future. So, I did the only thing I could do at the time, and this was to pull off the left side of the road down a rounded gravel shoulder. As I was working hard to keep my car from rolling over off the shoulder into a ditch, the oncoming vehicle passed innocently without incident, honking madly. The next challenge was to get back on the road again without spinning out or, worse, hitting one of the unforgiving old oak trees that lined the road. Fortunately, I was able to maneuver out of my predicament in a cloud of dust and gravel, merrily traveling down the road again, no harm done. David had remarked at the time, 'That was fun.'

'You didn't answer my question,' David said, ignoring my feeble attempt to derail our conversation.

'What did Buddy tell the cops?' I asked.

'You can ask Buddy. He's sitting in the backseat.' David replied.

'Buddy doesn't look like he wants to talk to anyone.'

David sighed, 'Buddy said to ask you. Said he wasn't at liberty to answer their questions except to give them his rank and serial number.'

I smiled, 'Sounds like Buddy.'

'So, what are you going to say? Sooner or later, you're going to have to talk to them.'

David had shielded me from the cops while in the hospital. Said his client wasn't in any shape to talk.

'I'm going to tell them I took a walk on the beach for fun and got lost in the storm.'

'Come on. Do you really think they are going to buy that?'

'No, but it's what I'm going to say.'

He didn't respond.

He knew me too well to attempt to change my mind.

12:15 PM. JOHN

Cell phone was ringing when we entered my cottage.

Buddy was first in the door carrying a bag of fast food and hamburgers purchased at a take-out restaurant window on the road home. David followed with the drinks in hand. I filed in last, burdened only by remnants of my depleted self-confidence. I was alive and kicking, but just barely after my last near-death escapade.

I made only a half-hearted attempt to locate my cell phone before it stopped ringing. The truth was I had no desire to talk to anyone. I purposely let the phone take voicemail while noticing the missed call came from an area code I didn't instantly recognize, although it looked familiar. I decided to check it out later.

David was staying for lunch. He said we needed to talk.

I agreed, not because I wanted to hear what he had to say, but because I wanted to talk to him about a plan, one of my lamebrain plans, one I had conjured up while during a sleep-deprived night laying in a hospital bed. I badly wanted to find a solution to my Luang problem. And although my solution made perfect sense to my recently frozen brain, I wasn't totally confident it would to anyone else. Given hypothermia, I thought it might be the better part of wisdom to ask for a second opinion. It was possible I was simply being delusional.

Buddy placed the bags of fast food on the dining room table.

Through the dining room sliders, a dismal, greenish-gray, white-capped lake greeted us with wet drizzle obscuring our view. A few brave seagulls could be seen guarding the shoreline, searching for scraps of dead fish, occasionally surfing the wind, rising high over the sand dunes.

We gathered around the dining room table to devour the paper-wrapped hamburgers and greasy fries, washed down with Diet Pepsi. It's not exactly gourmet, but definitely good if you are hungry. No one talked at first, viewing the lake as they ate their burgers in silence. An irritating tune began to emanate again from my cell phone, disturbing our temporary peace. It was a tune I had chosen when I bought my cell phone to alert me to a call. For some time, I had been determined to change the tune because every time I heard my phone ring, I hated the obnoxious song, but I never actually got around to doing it.

The caller ID displayed the same area code as before. Seemed someone badly wanted to speak to me. Two calls in less than a half hour.

Curious, I answered.

'John?' a female voice I instantly recognized as Sandy's replied.

'Yes,' I walked my phone into my bedroom and closed the door, not wanting David or Buddy to overhear our conversation.

'You okay?' she asked.

'I'm fine.'

'What happened? Helen told me you almost died and ended up in the hospital.'

'Nothing important,' I responded, happy I had given limited information to Helen. Knowing that anything told to Helen would soon find its way around the globe.

'Did you meet with that old man again?' Sandy asked as if it was a fact.

I had not told Helen about Luang. Only David and Buddy knew this intimate detail. So...

'Who told you that?' I asked, curious to know what she knew and who had given her the information.

'No one, I guessed.'

'Why do you think Luang was here?'

'Even I don't think you are stupid enough to voluntarily wander around on a cold stormy night and get lost. Something or someone drove you outside.'

'Should I take that as a compliment?'

'So, it was Luang?' she ignored me.

'I didn't say it was.'

'Did he try to kill you?'

The memory of seeing a sharp weapon in his hand before I dashed outside reverberated through my weary brain. He had told me he had every intention of killing me, and he certainly had demonstrated his skill on Buddy. So, the answer to her question was a resounding yes. But I didn't want her to know that.

'You don't have to answer,' she said. 'Your silence tells me everything I need to know.'

'I'm fine. Nothing happened.'

'Okay, have it your way. I'm glad you're fine.'

'I'm fine. Thanks for calling.'

'I'm coming.'

Now, these were two words I was not expecting to hear from her sweet lips. And as usual, I was grossly unprepared for this lady. Luckily, my instinct chimed in and rescued me, and I said what needed to be communicated. I didn't want to have to worry about her.

'Don't come. It's much too dangerous.'

'John, I want to be with you.'

'Look, I want to be with you too, but not now. Maybe sometime in the future when this thing is over.'

She didn't answer, so I continued. 'Please stay where you are, Sandy. Where I know you're safe. Okay?'

I could hear my guys talking in the dining room. Suddenly, I wanted this conversation over.

'I don't care about being safe,' she said.

'Well, I care.'

'That's it. You care, nothing more.'

'Yes, I care about you, and I don't want you to get hurt.'

I was obviously not prepared for this conversation. Getting Luang off my back had been the complete focus of my mental energy, not Sandy. Sandy had decided to go home. It was a decision she had made, not me. I didn't like it. But I knew it was best for her. She needed to stay where she was. End of matter.

'I don't want you to come here.' I said with a wince.

'I don't believe you, John Van Laan.'

'Believe me.'

'I don't.'

'Sandy,' I pleated, but she had already hung up.

12:50 PM. JOHN

Greasy fries, Sandy on my mind; sweet, beautiful Sandy.

A half-eaten burger lay mostly ignored on my plate. I was quiet at lunch, saying nothing, buried in a world of personal chaos, nothing making sense. I sat listening to the guys without really hearing anything they said, not eating, picking at my food, and not really hungry anymore. I think David and Buddy were talking about politics, sports, something, I don't remember what. I interrupted them mid-sentence, like a dead man returning to life.

'I have a plan,' I said.

'Oh, oh,' David responded. 'We're in trouble now.'

'I'm never going to have any peace until I get Luang off my back?' I continued, trying to resurrect my carefully formulated plan from the shambles Sandy had made of my brain. 'Isn't that right?'

'I suppose,' David said. 'So, how are you planning to do that?'

'I have to convince him I killed his nephew in self-defense.'

'You weren't very successful last night.' Buddy chimed in.

'Right, but if you remember, he didn't believe me because of what that idiot Phillip told him.' I argued.

'Phillip is involved?' David questioned.

'Yes, Phillip is involved,' I said with disgust. 'Phillip is always involved.'

I explained to David how Luang was using Phillip as a witness, relying on Phillip's interpretation of the shooting.

'So,' David interjected.

'So, this is never going to end until Luang agrees to back off. And he will not back off until I can convince him I shot Nue to save Ilana's brother from being killed. And to save myself, which is the real truth.'

'Makes sense. But again... how are you going to convince him?' David asked.

'Phillip has to tell him the truth.'

'Why would Phillip do that?'

'I don't know just yet, but I need to find a way.'

'Good luck,' David chuckled.

9:55 PM. JOHN

Two loaded guns rested on a table next to where Buddy sat reading a sports magazine in the living room of the cottage.

It was night. The doors were locked and bolted.

Spotlights spread an unnatural, glaring white light over the gray sand dunes outside, covered with waving beach grass, searching for anything or anyone who didn't look as if they belonged. Still, Buddy was not a happy camper. He wanted us to fly to Charlottesville immediately, if not sooner. He said he would feel a lot more secure in Charlottesville. I agreed, but I told him I had an important task to accomplish before we could leave town. After I explained to Buddy what I wanted to do, he suggested I take a gun with me.

'No, I don't like guns,' I replied. 'The last time I fired one, things didn't exactly turn out very well.'

Buddy said he understood, but the frown on his face told me he wasn't happy with my answer. But then, Buddy was never too happy with my answers.

My solitary bedroom was the only room in my cottage where Buddy allowed me any peace. The rest of the time, he was hovering over me, never letting me out of his sight. Telling me to stay away from windows, not to sit next to an inside wall, keep a cell phone nearby, and call him the minute I heard anything that looked or sounded like it didn't belong. Living with Buddy was a lot like living with my mother, constantly being told what to do and how to do it. The only difference was that I dutifully listened to Buddy and attempted to follow his advice, which was more than I ever did for my mother.

A book lay open on a table next to my bed. I had been trying to read but couldn't concentrate. Sandy's telephone call was running through my head, disturbing my peace. I had tried to call her back several times. I didn't want her to come. I was afraid of what would happen to her if she came.

Now, this wasn't completely true.

Real truth was I wanted her, desperately wanted her to come. But I knew she would be in danger if she came. So not now, Sandy. Please don't come now. Now, I need to concentrate on getting Luang and his miserable Thai family out of my life for good, forever. I feared I would die if I failed.

They wanted me dead, and it was only a matter of time before they accomplished their goal. I knew it. Luang knew it. And that was probably why he told me exactly what he intended to do. He wanted me to know he was going to kill me. He wanted me to know I was a dead man. He wanted me to think about death. And it was working. I was thinking about dying, and it scared me.

Oh, I could stay alive for a while. I could run. I could hide. I had money. But for how long? And what kind of life is running and hiding to stay alive? Nothing but a miserable existence, constantly looking over my shoulder, always afraid. My only other choice was to live in the confining cocoon which Buddy had concocted for me in Charlottesville. But that didn't feel like living, Felt more like being buried alive. I couldn't live in Buddy's artificial cocoon for very long without going stark-raving mad.

I began to wonder if death was the only rational solution to my problem. Was Luang right? Should I simply give in and let him kill me? Because wasn't it true that I had killed a man? Guilt is a heavy burden. Guilt for another man's death is an especially heavy burden. I had learned this lesson the hard way.

Luang had tried to convince me I was guilty, as had Sophon. They both tried to convince me I deserved to die, and I was beginning to think they were right.

Sophon had been curious. Looking back now, I sensed his questions were the questions of a young man who wished to learn about life. He had been told what to think and what to do for most of his life, but like all young men, he questioned the wisdom of his elders. He wanted to live on his own terms. So, he had questioned me.

I'm not sure I convinced him of anything; I only gave him enough information to cast doubt in his mind. Or perhaps he just couldn't do it, pull the trigger to kill me. Maybe he wasn't a killer in his heart. I didn't know.

The old man was a different puzzle. It was clear he never doubted his mission. He was determined to do it, kill me. However, like Sophon, he wanted to talk first. I thought I knew the reason for his wanting to talk. If he could convince me to accept his verdict, then perhaps I would let him kill me, make his task easier. In his mind, it was about justice and honor. And the more I thought about him, the more I began to understand the old man. His was an interesting tactic, his desire to talk to me first. He wanted me to accept my fate, to see the world from his perspective. There was a symmetry to his actions. In a way, I admired the old guy.

But my view of what happened when I killed Nue was different from his. Not much, but still different. In fact, if he knew how close my perspective was to his, he would have known how easy it would be for him to do exactly what he had set out to do, which was to convince me I deserved to die.

If he had known my background, he could have used it to accomplish his goal. I grew up in a world dominated by guilt. I lived with guilt my whole life. I was Dutch, born and raised in a Dutch Reformed Church, a church mired in the mud of guilt. It was the basic living, breathing building block of our religious doctrine. The church depended on guilt for its very existence. Because without guilt there was no need for salvation, no need for the church to exist. Even with salvation, we were never free of guilt. Guilt was something we lived with from the time we were born to the time we died. The church's foundation was built on the bricks of guilt. It used guilt as a tool to demand attention and take the resources of its members.

And truth was, I was not immune to this doctrine.

I was, and still am, a product of my upbringing as are most of us. I am a man who lives under the umbrella of my religious heritage. I am a man who lives with guilt. And when I consider my unfortunate act of killing Nue, when I take the time to really think about it, I know I am guilty. I alone did the deed. And this is a heavy burden, a burden which does not easily fall from my thoughts.

I long to relive the day I shot Nue and do it differently, but that is not going to happen. I can't change what is done. And that's why I knew it wouldn't take much for Luang to accomplish his goal, to convince me I needed to die. Which made it even more important for me to find a way to convince him I was not guilty. I had to convince him as much as I needed to convince myself. I needed to find a way to escape my guilt.

My mind wandered, looking for any path out of my guilty gutter, a mental gutter that had been constantly consuming my thoughts. Round and round, I went, thinking the same hopeless thoughts, all leading to death.

Sandy offered a different path. Someone to think about other than death. She became my only hold on sanity.

Was Sandy really coming? I didn't know for sure. Although I assumed it was true. She always did what she said she would do. She never second-guessed herself. So, I had to assume she was coming. And maybe it was good, her coming. She could help me stop thinking about death, stop thinking about guilt, and start thinking about living again. She could help me escape Luang's mental trap. I could think about her instead. Think about something besides death.

Sandy became my hope.

Sandy, with her wavy blond hair, her easy smile, and her long elegant body; everything about Sandy was easy to think about. She was bright. She was determined. And when she said she would do something, she did it. So, I had to assume she was coming, and I was both glad and afraid for her at the same time. I wanted to see her. I desperately wanted to be with her. If I had only a short time to live, I wanted to spend it with her.

Still, I was afraid, afraid for her, afraid for me.

I didn't want Sandy to die with me.

FRIDAY, MARCH 12, 7:15 AM. JOHN

If I knew anything about Charlie, I knew he was an early riser.

I was also an early riser, and we had freely discussed our peculiar personality disorder on more than one occasion. We were both workaholics. And we agreed the only way to get our work done was to go into the office early before the telephone started ringing. Get in and do some real work before our day was swept away with the buzzing noise of telephones and meetings and emails and all the obligations which so occupied our time. We hardly had a minute to think, much less get any real work done. So, if Charlie was in Virginia, I knew he would be in his office early.

I tried his cell phone first but got only voicemail. As a result, I was forced to go through the protocol nonsense of maneuvering through several layers of worthless bureaucracy to make the phone on his office desk ring. Fortunately, he answered, which was good. I needed to talk to him.

'Charlie.'

'Oh no, please don't tell me John Van Laan is calling me at 7:15 in the morning.'

'I am.'

'Shit.'

'Nice, very nice. Is that any way to greet an old friend?'

'You're not a friend,' he said in jest. 'You're nothing but trouble.'

'Okay, have it your way. How would you like to do me a favor?'

'No...'

'I need some muscle, Charlie,' I said, ignoring him. 'I need the kind of muscle only you can supply.'

'And if I agree, which I won't, just how much trouble will this get me into?'

'A great deal of trouble.'

I described what I needed from him and why. He listened. He listened to it all without saying a word. First, I told him about my recent meeting with Luang. Then I explained what Luang promised to do: kill me. I concluded by telling Charlie I would be a dead man if he didn't help.

He listened before asking. 'So, why exactly do you think this involves me?'

'I just told you. Because I'm a dead man if you don't help.'

'Sounds like your problem, not mine.'

'We're friends. You like me, that's why...'

'I already told you we're not friends.'

'So, you will help me?'

'No.'

'Charlie.'

'Just how many laws do you think I'll have to break to do what you're asking?'

'I don't know, and I don't care.' I replied.

'And how many CIA directives?'

'What difference does that make?'

'Well, there is the matter of my career, you know, my job.'

'We are talking about my life here, Charlie. Not just some old job.'

'We are talking about my life too,' Charlie responded.

'So?'

'So, I'm not going to do it.'

'You have to.'

'Why.'

'Because you have helped me before.'

'What are you talking about?'

'Do you remember how many laws you broke when you covered up my killing, Nue?'

'So?'

'So, if you had just turned me over to the authorities like I asked, I wouldn't be in this mess.'

'John, I saved your fricken ass.'

'I know, but look at the mess you made of it, my ass that is... My ass would be better off rotting in a jail cell right now. At least I wouldn't be running for my life.'

'You know, John, your sense of logic is very interesting... warped, but interesting.'

'What's your point?'

'Okay, say I follow the logic in your argument. Would it go something like this: I saved your ass once, and therefore, I'm obligated to save it again? Is that about right?'

'I guess.'

9:55 AM. JOHN

Phillip was a man ruled by many habits.

Breakfast was always at the same time and the same place, a restaurant on Washington Avenue in the center of town, Grand Haven. A big plate of hash browns, two scrambled eggs, sausage patties, and white bread; all washed down by too many cups of black coffee. After breakfast, he rolled into his office every morning no earlier than around nine-thirty. By this time, the numerous cups of the black liquid energy drug he had at breakfast, were running rampant through his veins, having a major effect on his behavior. The coffee had him wired and ready to go, ready to do his worst, ready to treat the world as only he knew he could, simply as his stage, his place of glory, a role so wonderful only he could play the lead. He was eager to hear the world applaud the truly wonderful person who was Phillip Palmer, the hero of his imagination, the legend in his own mind, the master of all he surveyed. Phillip Palmer, the greatest actor on the stage of life.

He was ready.

And we were ready for Phillip.

Buddy had both his guns loaded when we entered Phillip's office, one in his coat pocket and another one in his hand hidden under his suit coat. Nothing illegal, he explained, because he had a permit to carry a concealed weapon.

Phillip's secretary, Martha, looked up, open mouth, stunned as I bypassed her desk without asking permission, leading Buddy directly into Phillip's office.

'Hi John,' was all she had time to say.

Martha and I knew each other from an earlier life. We shared a mutual dislike. I didn't trust Martha, and she didn't trust me to treat her boss fairly, not after all the stories Phillip told her, all the negative stories about me.

'We are going to take Phillip for a short walk.' I smiled at Martha. 'We will be right back. No need to be concerned.'

I closed the door after entering his office so Martha could not interrupt. Phillip said nothing when he saw Buddy's gun, temporarily at a loss for words, something which didn't often happen to Phillip, almost never.

'Hands on your desk where I can see them,' Buddy said.

'No! What the hell is going on, John?' Phillip asked.

'I just want to talk to you. Don't be alarmed,' I replied. I'm not going to harm you.'

'No fucking way...'

'Shut up,' Buddy took hold of Phillip's arm and, in one fluid motion, had it behind his back with Phillip bent over his desk while Buddy patted him down. Finding no weapons, Buddy gently shoved Phillip away from his desk. I had warned Buddy that Phillip might have a gun on his desk. Phillip liked guns.

Phillip massaged his bruised arm as Buddy pushed him towards the back door exit in his office.

'Got a coat?' I asked Phillip.

He nodded.

'Put it on. We're going for a walk.'

'Why?'

'We need to talk.'

'Why not talk here?'

'Too many ears.'

10:45 AM. JOHN

A city park on Washington Avenue near Phillip's office is an open area about a block long in the center of town.

In the summer, it is a pleasant area with flowers and green grass shaded by tall oak trees. However, that day, the trees were starkly barren and brown. Mounds of shoveled dirty snow lined the concrete walkways. A stone monument to local forgotten heroes of ancient wars stood in the center.

I have often wondered why we make monuments to commemorate dead soldiers. Wars are terrible events filled with misery beyond understanding. The young die horrible deaths in wars. I wondered, if they had a choice, would these soldiers want their deaths remembered by having their names carved into a stone monument to commemorate a war? Or would they rather have their life remembered, the life they lived before the day of their screaming unnatural deaths? The life they could have lived if they had not been unnaturally killed in a war?

In early March before the flowers bloom, the park is empty most of the time, too cold for local pedestrians. It was a good place to have a private conversation.

The sun felt good on our backs as we walked a couple of blocks to the park. Yesterday's storm clouds had been washed from the sky by a harsh northwest wind. The normally dull gray clouds of early spring had been replaced by blue-sky sunshine. But it was still cold, the wind cold, a hard cold against my exposed skin. I pulled my jacket collar up around my neck for warmth. Buddy walked on one side of Phillip. I walked on the other. Phillip didn't look really happy. Every time he slowed, Buddy gave him a jab in the middle of his back, which instantly got his attention and got him moving again.

A bench near the middle of the park was a good place to talk. When I sat down, Phillip took the clue and sat next to me. Buddy stood next to Phillip in case the idiot decided to bolt.

'Okay, what do you want to talk about?' Phillip said. 'This has been fun but a little too dramatic for me.'

'Your friend, Luang, paid me a visit recently,' I replied, ignoring his comment.

'Luang, what kind of name is that?'

'Don't play dumb. He told me he has been talking to you.'

'Okay, so I know the old man. So what?'

'So, I need your help.'

'You have got to be kidding.'

'I'm dead serious. You need to tell Luang the truth about what happened the night I killed Nue. Because you're the only person Luang will believe.'

'I already told him what happened.'

'Yes, but you left out one important detail. You didn't tell him. Nue had just ordered the execution of Ilana's brother. You must have forgotten that.'

'So what?'

'So, he needs to hear it from you. And he needs to believe it was not an idle threat. He needs to believe Nue actually intended to have her brother killed. And this was the reason I shot him. To prevent Nue from having Ilana's brother killed.'

'And why should I do this for you? Are you going to promise me a job like the last time? You do remember that, don't you, John.'

'I'm not going promise you anything this time,' I replied

'Well then, I guess this conversation is over.'

'No, it's not. For once in your life, you're going to tell the truth.'

'Why.'

'Because it is the right thing to do.'

Phillip looked at me as he always did on occasions like this. Like he thought he was smarter. He assumed he could rework the truth to fit his needs. He could spin the truth, make it sound like the truth even when it wasn't when it was a lie.

'John,' he began, now on his stage. 'Luang and I are friends. We have an understanding. He is ...'

I let him talk. At some point in every conversation, Phillip needs to take the lead for no other purpose than to aggrandize his person. He needs to be the star in his life. He needs to be a man of the hour. He needs to be heard.

As he rattled on, I listened, not because I believed him but because I was curious to hear what he would say. Perhaps he might make a mistake and tell me something interesting; some valuable information. But apart from what I already knew, I learned nothing of value. Still, it was important to verify he had the ability to contact Luang. At least, I hoped he could. Finally, I cut him off. If I didn't, I knew he would have continued to talk and talk and talk.

'So, will you call Luang for me?' I pressed him.

The question seemed somewhat puzzling to him because he didn't answer immediately. 'And if I do?' he lied.

I knew he had no intention of doing anything I wanted him to do unless he somehow benefitted from it.

I continued, 'I want you to ask him to call me. I want to set up a meeting with him. And I want you at the meeting. I want you to tell him the truth this time.'

'I already told him the truth. Didn't I say that before?'

'Yes, but we both know you left out a few important details. This time, you will tell him the whole truth. And you will do what I ask because if you don't, there is a distinct possibility you will be charged with the murder of Nue. His death is still an open case, under investigation at CIA headquarters. And it is no small matter. Apparently, the CIA is under pressure from the government. Thailand wants it solved. One of their important citizens is missing, and they want to know what happened to him. I was recently told the CIA is very close to a breakthrough in the case. And unfortunately for you, that breakthrough may include your indictment for murder.'

I paused to let this new information sink in. 'Now, do you understand why it is important for you to be at the meeting?'

My statement seemed to stun him, but only temporarily. He vigorously objected and I let him rattle on before interrupting his tirade. 'I expect to hear from you by next week. You will have Luang call me to set up a meeting. And you will be at our meeting. It will be at my cottage. Do you understand?'

I paused again to make sure I had his full attention. 'If Luang doesn't call me as I have requested, you can expect to see Federal Agents at your door with some rather nasty legal papers in hand, an arrest warrant for murder with your name on it. And don't try to run. You are being watched. You are currently a suspect in a murder case. Any attempt to run will result in your immediate arrest. Do you understand?'

For once, the man was completely silent.

SAN FRANCISCO, CALIFORNIA, SUNDAY, MARCH 14, 6:55 AM. SANDY

Sunday was a difficult day.

Sandy was up early to arrive at the San Francisco airport on time. Just keep moving, she told herself. Ignore the frustration; ignore the people, the nonsense. Flying is simply a means to an end. It doesn't matter how ridiculous: how cramped the seats, how narrow the isles. And the wait, especially the wait. She hated waiting at the gate, waiting for the plane to leave the terminal, waiting for it to take off, waiting for a toilet on the plane, waiting for the trip to come to an end while enduring inhuman conditions followed by one final exasperating wait while standing in a crowded aisle to get off the plane after it landed. What marketing genius convinced us flying the friendly skies was fun?

It was worse than riding a bus.

CHARLOTTESVILLE, VIRGINIA, 8:55 PM, JOHN

It was a long day for me in Charlottesville.

Not because of time lost to busy nonsensical activity, but because my time was spent burdened by a heavy sense of frustration.

Although...

I should not have been feeling down. I had a plan, and it was in place. I thought it had a chance of working. So, I had hope, some hope. But what if it didn't work? I didn't want to dwell on that. But I did. I couldn't stop thinking it wouldn't work because nothing had worked in the past. My confidence level was low. Like I was searching for something that can't be found. Searching but never finding.

Ever feel like this, like you will never find what you are searching for, the one thing you want more than anything else? You know it exists somewhere, but you simply don't know where. And although you don't want to give up, you know deep in your gut... you know you will never find it.

So why try? Why, when the last thing I wanted was one more uncomfortable confrontation with that old man, one more time of trying to get him off my back? Get him and his family to leave me alone. I didn't want to do it. It all seemed so futile, unnecessary, and wrong, like being caught in a bad dream, a vision of gloom, a time of cold, hard rainy days filled with anguish and fear. I was tired, dead cold, tired of it all.

Last night was bad.

I dreamed of being encased in dark, smelly caves beneath the ground. Cold, hard rock walls everywhere I looked; no escape, just a maze of endless rock tunnels leading nowhere. I woke up feeling more exhausted than when I went to bed.

Buddy and I flew home to Charlottesville after meeting with Phillip. We simply left him sitting on the park bench alone. I had no doubt I had his attention, his full attention. And it was true, what I told him. Charlie was having him watch. I did not lie to Phillip.

So, I wasn't concerned about Phillip. He couldn't run. He had to cooperate whether he wanted to or not.

Friday and Saturday at the office were okay. Busy with phone calls and work. They weren't bad days. But Sunday was another story. My world closed in around me on Sunday.

'Undertoad,' the undertoad had me by the ankles. That was what we kids called the strong current in the wind-whipped rough waters of Lake Michigan. We called it the undertoad.

The accepted term for these currents was 'undertow.' But for us kids, 'undertoad' seemed like a better name for the animal who lived in the rough waters of the lake. It grabbed you and pulled you under, dragged your helpless body out to deep water where you could drown. Or at least that is what our parents told us would happen. Beware of the undertow, they warned us. Don't go out too far; the undertow will get you.

We, kids, mostly ignored our parents, having too much fun, laughing and playing in the big waves, and body surfing until we were dead tired. We laughed, and we played, but through it all, we were afraid of the undertoad, the big ugly brown toad who could grab our ankles in his big wet mouth and carry us off to drown in the angry waters of the lake.

That was how I felt on Sunday; like the big ugly brown undertoad who lived in the lake had me by the ankles and was dragging me underwater where I couldn't breathe, where I would die a slow, painful death, fighting and splashing and kicking for my life until I was too tired to care.

It was night, too early to go to bed.

I thought about reading a book, hoping it might make the undertoad go away. I had stuffed a book from my cottage in my suitcase before I left. But it wasn't working. I simply could not keep my eyes open. Ever try to read when you are sleepy? Your eyes close involuntarily in mid-sentence. You wake up in spurts, aware you have no idea what you just read, rub your eyes, and try to read again. That's how it was for me. I couldn't read, but it was too early to go to bed.

I didn't want to wake up in the middle of the night thinking about the undertoad.

GRAND HAVEN, MICHIGAN, 9:05 PM. BEN

Agent Ben Spenser of the CIA couldn't believe his eyes.

The guy was actually on the move. And from what Ben could observe, it didn't look like an ordinary run to the grocery store for a carton of milk. Suitcases had been hastily thrown into the back seat of his car, and his foot was on the gas as soon as he was out of the driveway.

Ben followed Phillip Palmer's car, staying far enough away so Phillip wouldn't suspect a tail but close enough so Ben wouldn't lose him. Hitting a quick dial on his cell phone, Ben called Rob, his backup. They were working the guy, taking alternate shifts. Ben called because he might need help if the guy really was on the run.

This was not supposed to happen. This was supposed to be an easy assignment.

Just watch the guy, Charlie told them. We don't expect him to run, but if he tries, stop him and tell him to go back home and do what he has been told. Charlie said he doubted that would happen, but just in case.

The guy's car turned onto 31 and headed north towards a drawbridge. Already Ben was getting out of range of where Rob would be any help. This didn't look good. But then, maybe he was wrong. Maybe the guy was simply going for a video.

A cold March mist spit on Ben's windshield, forming a thin layer of moisture, quickly freezing in the chill air. He turned on the defroster and hit his wipers. It was hard to see in the glare. Nothing ahead but a pair of hazy red tail lights receding into a dark night. Ben had to get closer. He didn't want to lose the guy.

Rob answered, 'You called.'

'It looks like our guy is running.'

'You're kidding.'

'Not kidding. He threw some suitcases in his trunk and took off in a hurry.'

'Does he know he's being followed?'

'I don't think so.'

'Where are you?'

'Crossing the drawbridge on 31, headed down a ramp on the other side.'

'What's he doing?'

'He is driving fast like he is trying to get away.'

'You have to stop him,' Rob stated categorically.

'I know, but we're headed into a small town on the other side of the draw bridge. I don't want to draw the attention of the local cops.'

'Hold on. Let me get a map,' Rob said.

'Okay.'

Rob returned. 'My map shows the road running through town into a less populated area. Wait until you get outside of town to pull him over.'

CHICAGO, ILLINOIS, 8:15 PM. SANDY

A board inside the terminal building announcing arrivals and departures gave Sandy the bad news she feared.

After landing at O'Hare International Airport outside of Chicago, her plane traveled for what seemed like going on an interminably long, cross-country trip over endless miles of concrete runway across the plains of northeastern Illinois. It felt as if she was spending more time ricing on the runway than flying in the air.

Once the plane finally taxied up to the gate, she anxiously waited to get off, waited for all the passengers in front of her to leisurely collect their luggage, and slowly meander up the narrow aisle. She waited patiently even though she was in a hurry. When it was finally her time, she hastily walked through the enclosed tunnel. Her departure out of San Francisco had been delayed due to heavy fog and this had occurred after time lost due to a minor mechanical problem with the plane. Nothing had gone right. She was afraid she might miss her connecting flight to DC out of Chicago. In which case, she feared she would be forced to spend the night in a small motel room at the O'Hare Airport.

As soon as she was out of the plane, she checked a board, which gave her the news she had already suspected. Flight 731 to Dulles had departed on time. Disgusted with the bad news 'arrival and departure' board, she wondered why all the flights she needed were on time. And all the flights she flew were delayed. Something was amiss in the wonderful world of air travel. The goddess of airplane travel apparently didn't like her.

After being informed by an airline employee at a ticketing counter; no more flights out that evening, sorry, the employee attended to the tedious task of rebooking Sandy's flight for the morning and giving her a voucher for a motel room. She was stuck in Chicago for the night. She briefly considered taking a taxi to midtown Chicago. Perhaps she might enjoy her forced sojourn in the windy city. But it was already past eight. By the time she retrieved her luggage, booked a room and took a taxi into town, it would be late, too late to enjoy a good meal in a hotel restaurant by the lake. In the morning, she would have to get up early to take a long taxi ride to the airport. It wasn't worth it. She decided to stay at a motel near the airport. Maybe catch an earlier flight out if one was available in the morning.

Wearily, she leaned over to pick up her black and brown overnight bag. That's when she noticed a man standing only a few feet from her. Oriental, maybe Thai, brown eyes and straight black hair.

He didn't bother to look away, returning her look with a stare, surveying her physique at leisure, apparently enjoying what he was viewing. She found his stare disconcerting, but perhaps this was his custom. Perhaps it was considered proper for a man in his world to observe pretty women without concern of appearing to be obtrusive. Perhaps staring at pretty women was to be expected. Maybe even a compliment where he came from.

As if to affirm her suspicions, he nodded to her.

She decided that returning his gesture might appear to be an invitation. Enough of this nonsense. Sandy simply ignored the man's arrogance and walked away without glancing back. And it wasn't until she was in her motel room for the night that it occurred to her. She wondered if there was a different reason the man was observing her. Perhaps he was an employee of Sophon's family, and he was following her. Perhaps intending to kidnap her again, like in Belize?

A shiver of panic passed over her. The memory of those days and nights in a bedroom in Belize rushed over her like a wave. The thoughts of not knowing what would happen, not knowing if she would survive... or worse, being raped, beaten, and forever scared... wounds which never healed.

The deadbolt on her door clicked shut. The chain was securely placed on its hook. Sandy sighed and went to the small motel bathroom to wash her face.

It had been a long day, and she feared it might be an even longer night.

SPRING LAKE, MICHIGAN, 9:25 PM. BEN

A cold mist fell like rain when Ben stepped out of his car.

Pulling up the collar of his trench coat to prevent the moisture from dripping down the back of his neck, he briefly wondered if he could disguise his true identity. He was not a policeman. He planned to try to act like a policeman, but he wasn't sure he could pull it off. Just have to wing it, he thought. At least the flashing red light in his official CIA car had worked. Phillip Palmer had voluntarily pulled off the road outside of the town of Spring Lake on a dark two-lane rural road leading to Interstate 96. He had been speeding at the time. So maybe he was not surprised when he looked in his rear-view mirror and saw an intermittent red light reflecting off the metal roof of a car behind him.

'Please step out of the car,' Ben said with authority as soon as Phillip turned down his window.

The bright headlights from Ben's car lit the scene with an eerie light that seemed to glow in the misty night air. It all seemed so surreal, especially to Ben. He had no CIA training for dealing with speeding drivers. But fortunately, he was no stranger to being pulled over by the cops. Ben was a speeder by nature. He had been pulled over many times in the past. He was well aware of the fact that ordering a guy out of his car without probable cause was not standard police procedure. But he wanted Phillip out of his car. He didn't want to give Phillip an opportunity to run. A car chase could get messy.

'Why have you pulled me over?' Phillip demanded.

'Speeding, now get out of the car.'

Phillip reluctantly opened his door, perhaps aware somewhere in his warped mind that something was amiss.

'Turn around, put your hands on the roof of the car, and spread them,' Ben said.

Phillip did as he was told, but he couldn't resist turning his head to look at the policeman who was ordering him.

'Hey, you're not wearing a uniform,' Phillip said.

'Shut up and do what you are told.'

When Phillip turned again, Ben smacked him on the back of his head with an elbow and spread his legs at the same time forcing Phillip to lean on his car against his will.

'Eyes forward,' Ben said, patting Phillip down.

A gun in a holster under his shoulder was easy to find. Ben reached inside Phillip's coat to pull the gun out, along with Phillip's wallet.

'Got a permit for this?' he asked.

'Yes, I carry jewels worth thousands of dollars. I have a permit to carry a concealed weapon.'

'Well, your permit is permanently revoked,' Ben said. 'No more guns.'

'Hey, who are you anyway?' Phillip started to turn again.

Ben shoved the back of Phillip's head forward, banging it on the metal roof of his car. Opening Phillip's wallet, he read Phillip Palmer's name on his driver's license, confirming what Ben had already suspected. He wanted to be certain before he issued his warning. Turning him around, Ben handed Phillip his wallet and briefly showed him his CIA badge. After Phillip saw the badge, a light of recognition flashed in his eyes.

'Do you know why I stopped you?' Ben asked.

Phillip nodded.

'Good, now go home and do as you have been told. One more instance like this and we will arrest you and hold you indefinitely. It's your choice. Stay home, or we will be forced to place you in a CIA jail. Do you understand?'

Phillip nodded affirmatively.

'Say it,' Ben demanded.

'Say what?' Phillip asked.

'Say you will do what you have been told.'

FLYING FROM D.C. TO CHARLOTTESVILLE, VIRGINIA, MONDAY, MARCH 15, 2:35 PM. SANDY

Sandy couldn't stop wondering if the man sitting behind her on the plane was the same man.

Thoughts of him, the man who had stared at her last night in the Chicago airport; these thoughts had run randomly through his mind during the night. While dozing off and on, afraid to sleep, afraid of the man in the airport, afraid of her memories of the kidnapping, afraid of the panic and the rush of fear... afraid of fear which could pass over her in endless waves of panic. It was not until shortly before dawn that Sandy finally got some sleep.

In the morning, she felt somewhat better.

It helped to see a hint of gray light appear on the eastern horizon outside the window of her motel room, illuminating a dull sky, clouds racing overhead in the wind. Knowing the night was over gave her hope. Lights from buildings at the airport reached out to her. Car headlights filled previously empty roads. The restless activity restored a sense of balance in her world and gave her some peace of mind for a few minutes, a time when she was able to shut out the memories of those days in Belize. For whole minutes, she actually forgot about that man, the man who looked Thai, the man who looked like one of her kidnappers, the man who had looked at her in the airport, the man who embodied her fears.

She showered in the morning and dressed in clean clothes: jeans, a sweater, and her long leather coat to shelter her against a raw wind and cold March rain. Her stomach felt queasy. She wasn't hungry. No need to find a restaurant for breakfast before her flight. She decided to go directly to the airport terminal. It would be safe inside. Her plane wasn't scheduled to fly for several hours, but the airport seemed like the safest place to be, better than a lonely motel room.

Fortunately, no one was loitering in the empty hall of the motel when she stepped out of her room. She had feared the hall, feared she would see the man, but the hallway was empty; no one was in sight. Once inside the airport, she felt safe. Not like in the night. In the night, panic had swept over her when she closed her eyes. Eventually, she turned on the TV, something to occupy her mind, anything to take her mind off the fears that seemed to be quivering through the inner fiber of her being. The mindless moving images on the TV screen helped her calm down until, eventually, her eyes closed, and she slept for a brief time, unconscious until she woke up after hearing a sound in the night, probably something from the TV. She took a deep breath as panic washed over her. And then she waited, waited for the panic to slow, to subside, to ease so she could rest again.

It had been a long night.

She was glad when it was the morning, glad to be moving again. She was happy to return to a world of living, breathing people. Unconcerned people are people going about their business, traveling, and living their lives. They were people who knew nothing about her fear; people who seemed happy, smiling, frowning, laughing people... not panicked people, not like her; normal people. She could do this, she told herself. She could be strong. Still, she looked for the man, looked over her shoulder as she walked, looked and listened, afraid of seeing him.

As usual, her flight was delayed, but she had become accustomed to waiting. She breathed a sigh of relief when her plane finally moved from the gate, slowly at first, pulled back, hesitated, stationary, engines revving, moving finally, beginning its arduous land journey, taxiing over the endless concrete prairie lands of O Hare Airport, standing in line at the end of the runway before finally taking to the skies; the noise of the powerful engines, the rush of acceleration; lifting into the air, turning, rising, leveling off. Soon, she would be in Charlottesville. Soon, she would be with John again. It would be okay then. She would be strong then. She would not be afraid.

But on the last leg of her journey, on the late afternoon flight on a small commuter plane to Charlottesville from DC, just when she was starting to feel better, she saw him again, the man who embodied her fears.

He didn't stare at her this time. He looked down when she stood to allow another passenger to go to the bathroom. He lowered his face making it difficult to determine if he really was the same man she saw in Chicago. But he looked the same. His hair was the same. He was wearing the same suit. Or was it the same suit? She wasn't absolutely sure. Maybe it wasn't him. Maybe...

She sat very still in her seat as a new wave of panic hit her. She knew it would come. She waited for the inevitable shock to attack her. Breathe deep, take long, deep breaths, she told herself. Don't think about this man. Put him out of your mind. Just take a deep breath and think about what needs to be done, nothing more.

She could do this. She could. She told herself she didn't have to think about that man. She would think about what she had to do. Call John when she arrived at the Charlottesville airport. Ask him to come. Or send someone. Send Buddy... yes, Buddy would know what to do. John would understand. That's it, call John and ask him to send Buddy.

She leaned into the uncomfortably cramped airplane seat and tried not to think about the man who was sitting behind her; she tried instead to think about being with John again, about how good it was going to be to spend time with John.

CHARLOTTESVILLE, VIRGINIA, 4:55 PM.
JOHN

My company car waited outside at the curb.

Our driver stayed with the car.

I went inside the airport terminal to look for her. Buddy went with me.

She didn't sound too good when she called. That's why I didn't get mad at her when she told me she was at the airport. I should have been mad because she came even though I told her not to come. But that didn't seem to matter when I heard her voice. Something in the tone of her voice seemed amiss when she asked me to send a car for her like it was really important to send the car.

She had never asked for a car before.

In the past, she had just showed up at my doorstep with no announcement, no warning, just walked in the door, found her way from the airport, taxi, I assumed. Not this time. This time she called from the airport and asked me to send a car. Plus, she asked me if Buddy could please come with the car to get her.

Buddy, why Buddy? Buddy was not my driver. Buddy was security. She knew that. I knew that. Something was wrong. I didn't ask her to explain; I just agreed to send Buddy with a car.

I grabbed Buddy on the way out and decided to go with him. We rode together to the airport in the company car with my driver. I didn't say much to Buddy on the road; I only told him Sandy was at the airport and had asked for him. I was afraid something might be wrong. We needed to go.

He didn't question me. He was like that. He understood things.

When we didn't see her at the curb, we went into the terminal to look for her.

He insisted on coming with me. Buddy wouldn't let me wander around the building alone. I didn't like that, but I understood. Although I argued we would have a better opportunity of finding her if we split up. Buddy disagreed and said we had to stay together. He was not going to let me out of his sight.

I wanted to yell at him, but his mind was like concrete. Never could convince him of anything.

We walked and we looked at winding hallways, people, people everywhere, women, some pretty, some not so pretty. Some with black hair, not Sandy. Sandy had blond hair. Some women with blond hair like Sandy, hoping the woman was Sandy, but no, the woman with blond hair turned and she was not Sandy, no flashing eyes, no smile for me. Just this look on her face like, why are you staring at me, buddy? Buzz off. Sorry, I'm looking for someone, hoping she is here, wanting to see her. Excuse me, sorry, I wasn't trying to bother you. Just want to find Sandy. But no Sandy, no sight of her anywhere. Only long halls filled with people, lights and boards and advertisements, food booths and drinking fountains.

No, Sandy.

NEW YORK, N Y, 5:25 PM. LUANG

It is easy to disappear in a place filled with eyes.

Eyes looking everywhere, eyes seeing everyone, eyes looking but not seeing, not seeing anyone. Too many people, masses of people, all different people, all nationalities of people, poor people, rich people, people who try to appear rich, people who appear to be poor but are rich, smart people, dumb people, beautiful people, ugly people.

Do you know how hard it is to stand out in a crowd? Do you know how hard it is to be noticed in a crowd? It is difficult. It is much easier to disappear in a crowd.

Luang walked the sidewalks filled with seeing and unseeing people. Even on a cool, blustery day in March, New York's sidewalks were full of people. It was the same as in his city, Bangkok. Same as in any big city, always sidewalks filled with people. He could disappear as he walked with no one seeing him. And he liked to walk. This was the one activity that he liked as much as gardening. He liked to walk, and he liked to watch people without being seen. So, he walked, and he thought about a telephone conversation he had earlier in the day.

That strange man had called him again and left numerous messages saying it was urgent they talk. Luang had finally called him to stop the strange man from bothering him. Phillip Palmer was the name of this odd man and it was strange how sometimes things worked. Luang surely had not expected to hear what Phillip told him. Phillip had said John Van Laan wanted to meet with Luang.

So why would Mr. Van Laan want another meeting? At the last meeting, the American had learned Luang intended to kill him. Luang had told him this to his face. So why would John suggest another meeting? He had to know he might be killed. Didn't this man understand the danger he was in?

It was an opportunity. Luang could not afford to avoid any opportunity which allowed him to complete his mission. This was his destiny, after all. He would call John as requested and schedule a meeting with him, assuming it was not a trap, hoping it was not a trap.

Luang did not want to be caught in a trap.

Luang did not want to be caught in a trap.

CHARLOTTESVILLE, 5:35 PM. JOHN

My cell phone buzzed.

Caller ID indicated my office was calling, probably Helen. I was in no mood to talk to Helen at the time. I was at the airport looking for Sandy. I wanted to see Sandy. We couldn't find Sandy.

I was starting to worry.

Habit took over, and I hit the call button.

'Sandy is here,' Helen said.

'Where?' I was surprised.

'She's at the office,' Helen replied.

'But I drove to the airport to get her. How can she be there?'

'It's a long story. She can tell you when you return. In the meantime, would you mind getting her luggage? It seems she didn't have time to retrieve it.'

'Sure, no problem. Buddy and I will be her baggage, boys. Tell her we will be along shortly.

And please tell her we expect a tip when we return.'

6:05 PM. JOHN

My cellphone rang.

My cell phone number is not common knowledge to anyone except friends and family. If anyone else wants to talk to me, they are obliged to call my office and my secretary, Helen, takes their name and telephone number. Unknown callers are told, I will return their call when I am able. Known persons are given the option of leaving a detailed message on voice mail for a return call. The point is that talking to me is not easy, and only a few people have my personal cell phone number, only the people I know and trust. So when my cell phone rings, I normally pay attention. However, when it rang that evening, I was otherwise occupied. Burdened down might be a better way of describing my sorry situation at the time.

Buddy and I were hauling Sandy's luggage up the stairs, up the back entrance to my apartment from the garage and this was no easy task given the suitcases were extremely heavy. Apparently,

Sandy intended to stay more than a few days this time. I began to wonder what she had in them. The strain on my back was uncomfortable.

However, that didn't mean I wasn't anxious to see her.

The little lost-girl drama played out at the airport had intensified my desire to see her. It made me realize how much I missed her. So, when my cell phone rang, I wasn't highly motivated to answer it. Someone else was on my mind, and I badly wanted to get that person's heavy luggage up the stairs so I could see her smiling face and give her a hug, her warm, beautiful body close to me. Ask her what happened at the airport, why she had disappeared. What had caused the fearful minutes of searching for her?

I was halfway up the stairs when my phone rang. Buddy was halfway down for a second load. When he heard my cell phone, he politely took her suitcase from my hands so I could answer. Caller ID told me nothing. I thought it might be a wrong number, but the force of habit made me answer it anyway.

'Mr. Van Laan,' said a voice with a Thai accent.

'Luang.' I recognized his voice.

'Phillip Palmer gave me your number and said you requested a call.'

'Yes, thank you.'

'What can I do for you?' he asked simply.

'I would like to meet with you again, this time at my invitation.'

'Why would you do such a thing?' he asked. 'You know my intentions.'

'Yes. You made that very clear. And that's why I need to talk to you.'

'What more can we discuss?'

'I'll have someone with me you need to hear.'

'Who?'

'Phillip Palmer,' I replied.

'I have talked to this man many times.'

'Yes, but this time, I want to be there when he tells you the truth.'

Luang was silent for a moment. 'Is this a trap?' he asked.

'No, I want to talk, nothing more.'

'But we have talked, Mr. Van Laan.'

'This time, I want to talk to you in depth.'

'I think you are setting a trap for me. Do you think I am naive?' he asked.

'This is not a trap.'

'How do I know you are not lying?'

'Because if you do as I request, I give my word I will not attempt to detain you when you want to leave.'

What I said was true. I had no intention of stopping him. Besides, I assumed he had a diplomatic passport. He couldn't be held even if I wanted him arrested. But I didn't tell him that. And I didn't tell him I was about Charlie. I didn't tell him I was planning to ask Charlie to have a chat with him. If things didn't go well, I would let Charlie deal with the old man. But Luang didn't need to know this, not now. He didn't need to know what Charlie would tell him. That could wait until later and only if necessary.

What I didn't tell Luang was that if he didn't agree to stop bothering me, Charlie would inform him that he and his family would be permanently barred from ever entering and doing business in the United States of America from that day forward. This was the biggest gun I had in my arsenal. If I couldn't convince the old man to stop trying to kill me, then I would let Charlie have his way. This was the deal I made with Charlie. That's why he agreed to help me.

'No guns?' Luang questioned.

'No guns, I promise. Just come to my cottage to talk... no trap,' I replied truthfully.

Talk was the only weapon I planned to use.

11:40 PM. JOHN

What is it about the way a woman looks at you after a long absence?

You, no one else, only you... her eyes see you.

And then there is the smooth resistance in her lips when she offers a kiss? You hold her close. She is near. She is resting in your arms and nothing is more important than the feel of her hair brushing against your face, the smile on her lips when you lean back to look into her eyes. The gentle curve at her waist, the small indentation at her spine, or the way she moves quietly in your arms with her breasts against your chest. Holding a woman's body close, a woman you love, holding her in your arms after thinking she was lost. Some moments can become lost in time, especially moments you have longed for. Moments lost to your wildest imagination; your mind completely absorbed in her naked body resting on sheets made of wind, her eyes the color of the blue sky, her breasts like clouds over a vast landscape. The ever-increasing wonder of her body, the smooth, soft touch of the skin on her thighs, the rise of her hips, her hair falling like warm rain on a hot summer day across your face... her voice passing through your mind like a breeze through the trees at night.

She is sleeping now, and you can rest with your eyes closed, reliving a vision that is playing through your mind. The vision of her lovely body as you made love to her.

Earlier, she had told me all about her trip while we ate some food she found in the refrigerator, leftovers from frozen dinners Helen bought for me. The food was bad. The wine was good, and her story was full of fear. It was in her eyes. She was afraid.

The man sitting behind her on the plane, she saw him again at the airport in Charlottesville when she got off the plane. That's why she decided not to wait for us to come. She left the airport quickly and grabbed a cab. Ran away from the man she thought was following her, wanting to kidnap her.

Was she sure about the man? I questioned.

She said she wasn't sure, but she was afraid. So, she ran. She went directly to my office, never stopping until she was at the door, sitting in a chair next to Helen's desk. Only then did she finally feel safe.

I simply let her tell her story without comment. Thought maybe she would feel better after she told it. I had no idea whether the man was real or not. It didn't matter. What mattered was she had been afraid. I could see it in her eyes. I could feel the fear in her words as she talked.

She seemed to calm down after she finished telling me. Wine helped. She was much better after we finished dinner.

It was late by that time. We went to my room. We needed to be together. We needed time together, time to shed our fears. We made love and she slept in my room, in my bed. Not the guest bedroom.

She slept with me in my bed with her brown and black shoulder bag resting against the wall inside my bedroom.

TUESDAY, MARCH 16, 7:30 PM. JOHN

Whatever he was doing, it must have been important because Charlie never returned my call until well after seven that evening.

It was a rather uneventful day for me, except for the fact I spent most of my time thinking about Luang when I wasn't worried about Sandy or wondering why Charlie hadn't returned my call.

I left several messages for Charlie. Told him it was urgent, but it seemed my good buddy, Charlie, was busy with something or someone more important than me. Because he didn't return my call.

Now, that was worrisome because I badly needed to talk to Charlie.

Sandy on the other hand, was making good progress recovering from her strenuous cross-country trip. No more panic attacks. Hopefully, they were a thing of the past. She said they came out of nowhere. She didn't really understand why, but for whatever reason, she had become really scared. Obviously, something was bothering her, something buried deep in her psyche from what happened in Belize. It was something she was going to have to deal with.

I spent as much time with her as I could during the day, a long breakfast in the morning and a break for lunch. And we had a delicious dinner which she prepared in the evening. Helen helped by having groceries ordered by Sandy, delivered to the apartment. So, the day had gone rather well. Her smile had returned, her mischievous grin along with her dry sense of humor. The Sandy I loved was back and I was happy for her.

And then Charlie finally called.

I took his call in my apartment; didn't let it go to voicemail like most calls. I really wanted to talk to him. And I was so involved in my discussion with Charlie that I didn't realize Sandy had come into the room and was listening to our conversation.

'You aren't serious,' Charlie replied after I told him about my proposed meeting with Luang. 'Do not tell me you are thinking about meeting with this guy, just you and Buddy without any guns.'

'Right, except Phillip is also going to be there.'

'That wasn't our plan.'

'I changed the plan.'

'John, why don't you just shoot yourself in the head and get it over with?'

'Charlie, I have to get this guy off my ass.'

'Your dead ass, you mean.'

'I need this meeting, Charlie, don't you understand?'

'He's going to kill you. I understand that.'

'He won't. He knows he can't get away with it.'

'I don't think he cares,' Charlie said. 'You don't know these people. They don't think like we do.'

'It's a chance I have to take.'

'It's a dumb ass move, and you know it.'

'It is the only move I have.'

'Okay, but don't do it alone. Let me help.'

'Look, Charlie, I had to convince him the meeting wasn't a trap. He wouldn't come if you were in the room.'

'John, why don't you let me just take care of this guy for you?'

'How you going to do that, Charlie? Sure, you can keep him out of the country and cut off his family and his business from doing business in the US. But that won't stop him from retaliating by sending someone to kill me?'

'I suppose,' Charlie admitted.

'So, you agree, this is the only way.'

'John...'

'Charlie, just help me, will you? Have your guys make sure Phillip is at the meeting. That's all I'm asking. If my plan doesn't work, Luang is all yours.'

'Okay, it's your funeral. I'll make certain Phillip is at the meeting even if I have to drag him there myself. What happens after that is your responsibility.'

'You're the best.'

'And you're an idiot.'

'Agreed, but I'm your idiot friend.'

'Not anymore.

'Thanks, I love you too.'

I put the phone down. When I looked up, I saw Sandy sitting in a chair looking intently at me.

'Who were you talking to?' she asked calmly.

'Charlie,' I replied, knowing it would be a mistake to lie. She had heard too much.

'And who are you meeting with?'

'Would it help if I said it was none of your business?'

'No.'

'Okay, then I won't tell you.'

'You're going to meet with the old man again, aren't you?'

I took a second before answering her question. 'Sandy, this is something I have to do.'

'When are you meeting him?' she asked with a steely-eyed look on her face, a look which told me this conversation would not be favorable, not for me anyway.

'No more questions, please.'

'When,' she asked, ignoring my request.

'I'm leaving Thursday morning for Grand Haven. I'll be back Friday night.'

'I'm going with you.'

'No.'

'John, I'm going even if I have to go by myself. You can either take me along and make sure I'm safe, or you can leave me behind to do it my way.'

Damn, women never listen. And this woman never ever listened.

'Okay, you can come,' I said. 'But on one condition. You can't be at the meeting. You must stay with one of Charlie's guys. Agreed?'

'Agreed.'

WEDNESDAY, MARCH 17, 11:40 AM. PHILLIP

Phillip wasn't looking for a call from Luang that morning, but it came anyway.

'Yes, I will be at the meeting,' Phillip replied to Luang's question. 'Did he tell you why he wants me there?'

'I know why,' Luang replied.

'Do you want to know what I'm supposed to say?'

'It doesn't matter.'

'Then why are you coming if you already know everything?' Phillip asked.

'That is not your business. I simply called because I wanted to know if you would be at the meeting.'

'Okay, now you know. What do you want me to do?'

'Nothing.'

'That's it, nothing?'

'Nothing. One more question,' Luang asked. 'How are you traveling to the meeting? Are you driving alone?'

'No, I am being delivered by some of John's CIA friends. I guess he doesn't trust me to just show up.'

'Is the CIA staying with you at the meeting?'

'No, they made that very clear. They will drop me off before the meeting and leave.'

'They will not be there?'

'No.'

'Good.'

'But you still want me to come?'

'Yes.'

'I can do that,' Phillip replied, delighted to know that he would have the opportunity to witness it all.

CHARLOTTESVILLE, VIRGINIA. 4:35 PM.
JOHN

Normally, he didn't make a habit of calling me. I usually called him.

So, when Helen announced David was on the phone, I was surprised, but it only took a second to guess why he was calling. Charlie had been talking to him, and he knew what I was planning. And David didn't like what I was planning any more than Charlie did. So, David was calling to talk me out of it. I sighed and resigned myself to the fact that I would have to defend myself to a lawyer who made a career out of convincing a jury to do what he wanted them to do.

'I know what you're going to say. So, save your breath,' I said before he could say one word.

'Nice to talk to you, too,' David replied, disregarding my opening foray.

'Somehow, I don't think you intend this to be a particularly nice conversation,' I continued on the offensive.

'What makes you think that?'

'You have been talking to Charlie, right?' I asked to confirm my suspicions.

'Yes, Charlie called me,' David confessed.

'So, this isn't a social call.'

'What, calling a friend to discuss his impending death? Isn't that a social call?'

'I'm not going to die,' I replied flatly.

'I think the odds are against you this time, pal.'

'I have beaten the odds before.'

'John, you can win the game of life many times. But you only get to lose once.'

'Good point.'

'John, don't do this.'

'I'm just going to talk to him. I'm not planning to arm-wrestling him.'

'John, I have won a lot of court cases by following one simple rule: get to the main point fast. Lay it out to the jury and make sure they clearly understand it,' David began his oration.

'You're a good lawyer.'

'Thanks, but that's not the point. My point is that this man wants you dead. And he's willing to do whatever it takes to accomplish his goal. Inviting him to your house only makes it easy for him.'

'That's right.'

'You agree.'

'I do. I wouldn't expect him to come for any other reason.'

'John, then walk away.'

'I can't. I can't run anymore. David, I'm tired of running and hiding. Don't you understand?'

'Are you saying you're ready to give in and let him kill you?'

'No, never. That's not why I'm doing this. I'm doing it to convince him to stop trying to kill me. That's the only way I will ever get some peace.'

'But you admit he's coming to kill you.'

'Right.'

'That makes no sense.'

'Look, if I don't give him the opportunity to kill me, he won't come. And if he doesn't come, then I can't convince him to stop trying to kill me.'

'John, that's idiotic nonsense. He doesn't want to discuss anything with you. He only wants to kill you.'

'I'll just have to convince him otherwise.'

'So that's it then.'

'What's it?'

'It, you're it. You're a dead man.'

'I didn't say I was going to make it easy for him.'

'When are you coming to town?' David asked.

'I will be in Grand Haven around noon tomorrow.'

'We'll talk more tomorrow.'

GRAND HAVEN, MICHIGAN, THURSDAY, MARCH 18, 11:40 AM. JOHN

Sandy was unusually quiet on the chartered flight from Charlottesville to Muskegon, Michigan.

After renting a car at the airport, we, meaning Sandy, Buddy, and I, headed for my cottage near Grand Haven. Our only stop was at a local grocery store on the road for supplies.

A cold rain fell lightly. The windshield wipers were on a slow, intermittent cycle. The road was wet, and the clouds looked low and heavy, like they were falling out of the sky.

March has always been my least favorite month of the year, especially when I was a boy and lived in this town. Now I remembered why. The weather is normally terrible in March, with cool, rainy days and frost-bitten nights. Winter storms off the big lake lash out with all the fury old-man winter can muster. He knows his time to beat us into cold, numb, mindless pulp is coming to an end. That's why he makes the most of a month, which is dismal by any standard.

'You're quiet today,' I said to Sandy while sitting in the rear seat of the rental car with Buddy up front driving.

'I don't know what to say, John,' she replied.

'We could talk about the weather.'

'I don't care about the weather.'

'Okay, how about talking about your sister? How is your sister?'

'John, I don't want to talk about my sister.'

'Well, maybe I do.'

'Okay, she's fine, the kids are fine, her husband is fine.

'Are you going to see her when you are in town?'

'No.'

'Have you told her you're coming?'

'No.'

'How do you think she will feel when she finds out you ignored her?'

'I don't think she will be very happy.'

'I see.'

'Can we talk about something else?' Sandy asked.

'Like what."

'John, this might be the last full day of your life. I don't want to spend it talking about my sister.'

'Okay, what are you in the mood to talk about?'

'John, stop.'

1:25 PM. JOHN

The thermostat was set at fifty-five degrees.

That's the temperature maintained inside the cottage when it is unoccupied in the winter. Fifty-five degrees indoors can feel downright freezing when you step inside, hoping to get warm.

My first act after a long absence from my cottage is always to open the drapes over the sliders. A wind-whipped, dull-green Lake Michigan greeted my view. White caps dotted the water's surface to the horizon. A late winter storm was pounding the cottage, shaking it occasionally as if it was shivering in the cold.

After turning up the thermometer, I went to look for Sandy, hoping some heat might thaw my relationship with her. We had not spoken since her outburst in the car.

'Sandy, look, I'm sorry,' I began. 'I don't want you to be mad at me.'

She answered with an all-knowing stare, which indicated, I assumed, that I was an idiot.

I began to say something repentant to her. I don't remember what, but I never got a word out before being interrupted by the sound of my backdoor opening.

Charlie was the first person inside. Apparently, he had been monitoring our trip with the help of inside intelligence. The militia had been alerted to our landing on the beach. The shore artillery was loaded and ready to start shooting.

Sandy must have known all about this counter-assault, which was why she had waited until reinforcements arrived before firing her guns.

David was next inside, calm and prepared as usual. I should have known he would be in on the action. He had his trial face on.

Buddy looked unconcerned through it all. Apparently, he was their inside guy.

2:55 PM. JOHN

'John... why won't you listen to these guys?' Sandy finally joined the argument with a wail so shrill even I was surprised by the intensity in her voice. 'Why do you always think you know better than everyone else in the world? They are trying to save you from dying and still you argue with them.'

Now, this was a harsh indictment.

Everyone in the room became suddenly silent, content to let her have at me. The discussion had reached a critical mass. Sandy's explosion was the final assault. Logic had failed. David's oratorical skills had failed. Charlie's lesson in Oriental culture had failed. Buddy's Navy Seals 'leave-no-man-behind' rah-rah nonsense had failed. Everyone had failed, everyone except Sandy. Sandy didn't need logic. Sandy didn't need speaking skills. Sandy didn't need to try to con me. She needed nothing but what came from her heart. She was their last hope. Everyone knew it. I had no defense from her barrage. I was a baby seal in her waters, and she was a big, bad killer whale.

'Well, do you?' she indignantly asked.

'No, Sandy, I don't think I know better.'

'Then why won't you listen to them?'

'I have been listening.'

'No, if you had been listening, this discussion would be over.'

'But I have been listening. I just happen to disagree.'

'And if your thinking gets you dead.'

'I'm not going to die tomorrow.'

'That doesn't seem to be the consensus of opinion.'

'Okay, maybe I'm wrong. But if I'm wrong, then I alone will pay the price, no one else.'

Now, this was the wrong answer. I may have been making some sense before this stupid statement. But now, I was dead in the water.

'Do you really think that's true, John?' Sandy lit into me with all the guns firing. 'Do you really think no one else in this room will pay a price if you die tomorrow? How about me, John? Will I be affected by your death?'

She had me. She had me big time. They all knew it. I knew it. We were done here. Nothing more needed to be said.

'I'm sorry, Sandy. I didn't mean it like that.' I tried to backtrack.

'Of course, you meant it, John. You always mean it. It's always about you, no one else. It's that right, John?' She stormed out of the room.

Everyone sat silently, watching her disappear, listening to a bedroom door slamming shut. Charlie finally spoke after a few minutes of uncomfortable silence. He had previously moved away from the discussion after a particularly heated and frustrating interchange between the two of us.

'So, John... Are you still going through with this?' he asked.

8:40 PM. JOHN

A black night lived outside the rain-distorted windows of my cottage.

Music on a stereo played in the background, something classical, I don't remember what, Yo-Yo Ma, I think. I wasn't listening. Too many thoughts were racing through my tired brain. I was only vaguely paying attention.

Sandy was in the kitchen cleaning, rinsing and putting dishes in the dishwasher, something to do to take her mind off her fears. David had gone home, Charlie to a motel. Buddy was in his room, and Charlie's men were stationed outside somewhere in a car, keeping guard for the night. In the morning, the CIA guys were scheduled to leave after delivering Phillip, meaning the stage would be set for my meeting, and the cottage would be unguarded except for Buddy.

Contingency plans had been made despite objections from all sides. Everyone knew their role or lack thereof. Mostly, we had argued about what they would not do, would not interfere, would not arrest, would not protect, would stay out of the way, and let me do my thing. They didn't like it. Charlie, especially, was upset. None of this made any sense to him and his way of thinking. He liked being in charge. He liked dictating events. Force was his tool. Power was his culture. Control was his method.

After Sandy's outburst, I finally agreed to some of my companion's suggestions. Charlie and his guys would not be very far away after dropping off Phillip, only a short distance up the road from the driveway. Listening devices were installed in the cottage. Charlie would be able to hear me if I needed help. He could be inside the back door of the cottage in a matter of a few minutes. However, this halfhearted compromise failed to satisfy anyone. No one said it. Everyone knew he would probably be too late to help.

Later in the afternoon, we ordered take-out pizza for dinner, had a few beers, and tried to forget about the whole thing. For some reason, I did not understand, probably just to relieve the tension, we began to act like a bunch of teenage boys lacking parental supervision. Boys will be boys. The conversation got rowdy. Sandy got up from the table without a word and left the room and her early departure signaled an end to our inappropriate conversation. The party was over. The guys hastily finished eating and said goodbye for the night.

I eventually went to the kitchen to find Sandy even though I had nothing I could say to her, nothing she wanted to hear. I didn't know what I hoped to accomplish. Just knew I needed her. I kissed her lightly on the cheek as she was working at the sink cleaning dirty dishes.

Dutch girls clean in times of tension, retreat to the kitchen and clean the dishes. I remember my mother doing this more than once when things got unsettled at home. My father would follow her into the kitchen and help. It was their time together to patch up their relationship. I picked up a rinsed dish to put it into the dishwasher, hoping to ease the tension.

'Don't do that, John. I have a method for this dishwasher. I'll just have to rearrange everything if you try to help.'

'What can I do?'

'Stay out of the way.'

Ignoring her instructions, I went into the dining area to retrieve the remaining dirty dinner dishes soiled with dark red pizza sauce, greasy knives, forks, and glasses still partially filled with stale beer. I brought all of it to her like a penitent kitchen boy, hoping this would help.

Help what, I didn't know, just seemed to be what I should do.

She didn't rebuke me this time, let me bring the dirty stuff to her, taking each piece, one at a time, rinsing it before placing it in the dishwasher; all done without comment, without acknowledging me in any way. When nothing remained to be retrieved, I stood beside her and watched her work because I didn't know what else to do.

'What are you doing?' she finally asked without looking up.

'I'm watching a beautiful woman work in my kitchen. It's like seeing a vision.'

'I'm no vision,' she said.

But she looked like a vision to me, even in jeans and a sweatshirt with an old apron draped around her waist. Yellow rubber dishwashing gloves covered her beautiful long fingers like the white gloves of a princess. Every once in a while, she jerked her head and ran her hand over her forehead to push an irritating strand of blond hair from falling over her big blue eyes.

I smiled at her.

She turned to look at me. 'What are you leering at?'

'You, you beautiful thing.'

'I don't look beautiful,' she said.

'You do to me.'

'Well, then, it's true that beauty is in the eye of the beholder.'

'It is true.'

I reached around her and turned off the faucet. Lifting her off her feet and placing my arm under her legs, I picked her up.

'Put me down, John Van Laan.'

FRIDAY, MARCH 19, 1:55 AM. JOHN

I had to get up.

Lying in bed, unable to sleep, is like slow torture.

It was the middle of the night. Didn't matter. My muscles ached. I was tired of tossing and turning. The cottage was cold and dark with only enough light from the outside spotlights shinning through the windows to see outlines of the walls and furniture. Putting on a bathrobe, jeans, socks and an old baseball hat to get warm didn't help. It was cold inside the cottage, the thermostat set at sixty-two degrees. I turned up the heat a few degrees.

The storm which had lashed the cottage all afternoon was slowly subsiding through the night hours. Wind no longer pelted the windows with sheets of rain. A strange stillness crept into the cottage. Only the sound of lake waves pounding the beach outside, disturbed the otherwise tranquil quiet.

My confidence had vanished like a storm, and I was left with nothing but lingering doubts. It was as if a new mindset had taken over my fractured brain. A less confident one filled with concerns and questions, like fearing I was making a big mistake. What my friends said to me was finally beginning to register. Reason had started to take hold, grabbed my brain by the balls, and squeezed until all the nonsense I had been spouting that afternoon was gone.

The words Charlie said... or was it, David... I couldn't remember who said, 'You lose the game of life only once.' Those words kept replaying in my head like a broken record.

And the question Sandy asked. Did I have the sole right to gamble with my life? Wasn't she right about that? Didn't what happened to me affect other people? Obviously, it affected her. I was being selfish. I had been considering only myself, my stubborn, foolish, selfish self.

Earlier that evening, I had carried Sandy from the kitchen directly to the bedroom, where we made love. Or should I say where she allowed me to make love to her after first resisting, fighting me, pounding me on the chest? I didn't press her. Waited until she calmed down. We kissed. She put her arms around me. After taking the covers off the bed and getting undressed, we lay naked together for a long time, touching and kissing like we had all the time in the world.

When we were done, she turned away. No smile of satisfaction rested on her face, only a tear in her eye. I didn't look, didn't want to look. I didn't want to know if she was crying. I just wanted to hide the moment away, to remember it for the future.

And this was when it started... my doubts, I mean. After we made love, this was when doubting started to take habitation in my troubled brain.

Because maybe I didn't have a future.

2:20 AM. JOHN

I don't remember how long I sat in the dark that night, listening to waves crashing on the beach. Just sitting and thinking and wondering if I should cut and run.

No one would blame me. I could leave and let Charlie clean up the mess I left behind. He wouldn't care. He would love to deal with Luang. He would know how to handle the old man. Force, power, take control; Charlie was my guy.

'What are you doing?' she startled me out of my wide-awake nightmare.

I turned on a light to see her face. She was dressed in my old bathrobe over her pajamas, a terrycloth robe, light brown. The neck and belt of the robe had been unraveling slowly from use. It was still useable. She had adopted the robe after finding it in a closet. I think she washed it by hand first. Anyway, she looked cute in the old thing.

'Come sit by me,' I said, raising my arm so she could snuggle under my protective embrace. 'It's cold.' I grabbed a blanket and covered her bare legs as she settled next to me on a couch.

'I asked you a question,' she said.

'What?'

'I asked what you are doing out here in the cold?'

'Thinking maybe I should pack my bags and get out while I'm still alive,' I honestly replied.

'Is that what you really want?'

'No, what I really want is to forget about the old man, pretend he doesn't exist.'

'But that's not possible, is it?'

'No.'

'Then maybe you should do what you have planned,' she said after a moment.

'What are you talking about? You have been against this from the beginning.'

'I know, but I have been thinking. Maybe you need to follow your instincts.'

'What?' I couldn't believe what I was hearing.

'Maybe you're right. Maybe this is the only way,' she continued, undeterred. 'Maybe it's worth the risk.'

'Why have you changed your mind?'

She was silent for a minute before continuing. 'No one ever really knows how life will turn out,' she finally said. 'People take chances all the time. Sometimes, they take big chances. Because if they don't, their life could be much worse.'

'Sandy, I don't think I will ever completely understand you. Just when I think I know you, you say something... or do something that blows me away.'

10:05 AM, JOHN

'Your man must wait in your car,' I demanded, standing about six feet from the old man.

Prior to Luang's arrival at my cottage, I had been given a thorough indoctrination in the protocol of avoiding death. Buddy had warned me; do not get too close, do not take your eyes off him, and do not greet Luang with a handshake when he walks in the door. This and other polite gestures will get you instantly killed.

His man, I didn't know his name, but I did know he was the same guy who had come with Luang the last time. And although he didn't look particularly lethal, kind of small and short under a gray tunic, I remembered what he did to Buddy, and I, therefore, assumed he was trouble.

'You have a man with you,' Luang nodded at Buddy. 'You would not wish me to feel at a disadvantage, would you?'

'We agreed that only Phillip, you, me, and my bodyguard would be at our meeting,' I replied.

'I said I would come if they were the only people you had at the meeting. I did not say I would come alone,' Luang countered.

Our meeting was not off to a good start, not following the script I had written for it in my head. We were arguing when I hoped we would be finding common ground to agree, where we could find a way to live in peace.

Luang sensed what I was thinking. 'I can leave,' he pushed the one advantage he had. He assumed I wanted this meeting, perhaps more than he did and he was right.

'Okay, your man can stay.' I made a quick decision. 'But you must ask him to sit in a corner of the room where he is not anywhere near us.'

'And your man,' Luang demanded. 'Will he also sit in a corner?'

I looked at him. I wanted to tell him to shove it, to get the hell out of my house and leave me alone. But that would have accomplished nothing. So, I made another decision I was afraid I would regret later. 'Yes, he will also sit in a corner.'

I was fully aware that this was not the plan. This put me in danger. This was not what Buddy said should happen. Buddy had demanded he sit between me and Luang, act as shield in case the old man tried anything.

I nodded to Buddy and he gave me a look which begged the question, obviously not happy. But he did as he was told. He and Luang's man found chairs in a back corner of the great room where they could see us, but not interfere.

Phillip silently observed this mini-drama with a smirk on his face. Sitting comfortably on a couch where he had a view of the lake through the sliders. Dressed in his usual splendor, black sport coat and bright red tie, he had been delivered fifteen minutes earlier to my cottage, courtesy of Charlie's guys.

Open drapes revealed a cool, crisp, blue-sky day outside. A stiff breeze from the northwest was blowing long lines of white-capped waves over the vast rolling waters of the big lake stretching across the horizon. Yesterday's storm had wind-cleaned the smooth sands of the beach. Waves monotonously washed on the shore below the dunes, crashing in disturbing regularity as puffy clouds rode a windy sky. Seeing the sun in the morning had given me hope. Blue sky days in Western Michigan are rare in the month of March. The sun was a good sign, or so I hoped.

Sandy had gone with the CIA guys after they delivered Phillip. This was the plan, but not before she made one last appeal to stay.

She didn't want to go. But I had insisted, said it was too dangerous.

She had argued and said we were in this together. She wanted to be with me.

I said this was true, but it served no purpose to have her needlessly in harm's way. She had to go. Although she had no real basis for disagreeing with me, that didn't mean she was a happy camper. No kiss, no hug for good luck was offered before she left. She simply put on her coat and walked out the door without saying a word.

A pot of hot coffee and a plate of cookies had been placed next to coffee cups and saucers on a table between the couch and several leather armchairs by the fireplace, all prepared according to plan. The furniture had been purposely spaced so that Luang would need to take a stride or two before he could attack. This was supposed to give me time to react, time to be ready for his blow, time for Buddy to shield me... all a bit lame, according to Charlie.

Without waiting for Luang, I headed for the great room where Phillip was already seated, one step forward for each step Luang took following me. At one point, he stopped as if testing to see if I was deliberately keeping a safe distance from him. I continued walking.

Looking around, he said, 'I did not have the opportunity to compliment you on your home when I was last here. This is truly a wonderful place.'

'Thank you. Coffee and cookies are on the table. Please help yourself.'

The plan was to let him decide where he wanted to sit first. Then, I would choose the chair that was the farthest from him. Stay as far away as possible. That was Buddy's advice. But Buddy was sitting in a corner of the room. Buddy was no help. He was too far away. And Luang's man would certainly interfere should Buddy attempt to intervene. This was also not the plan, but there was nothing I could do about that now.

Luang eventually chose one of the leather armchairs, which looked directly at the lake. He smiled when I took a seat opposite him across the coffee table with my back to the fireplace and the sliders.

Waiting patiently, I assumed he was hoping I would serve him, but that was not going to happen. Don't serve him, Buddy warned. You will be vulnerable while leaning over with a hot cup of coffee in your hand. And never stop watching the old man; never look away for a minute. Don't drink coffee, and don't reach over to take a cookie.

Stay where you are and never take your eyes off the old man.

10:10 AM. DAVID

David pulled his car off the road, parking behind a plain black Ford with a US government plate.

Charlie was sitting in the Ford, waiting for David on the corner of Lakeshore Drive and M 45 at a small parking area designated for exercise nuts who liked to use a paved bike path parallel to the road. David, as usual, was late. Lawyers are always late. Time is money. Bill by the hour. That's a lawyer's creed.

Charlie was irritated. Nothing in any of this made sense to him. And David's late arrival only made matters worse. Charlie had only reluctantly agreed to let David go with them after making David promise to stay out of the way if anything happened.

As soon as David was in the back seat, Charlie yelled at his driver to get going. The meeting had already started. Charlie did not want to be this far away.

Although... Why bother, he thought. He would not be close enough to help.

What difference did it make?

10:15 AM. JOHN

In all events, protocol rules and order are required.

Even in an event which is meant to end in death; even then a proper agenda must be observed, first things first.

I wondered if Luang had such an agenda in his mind. Would he want to talk first? Would he want to hear what I had to say? Or would he simply seize the first opportunity to kill me?

I wished I knew how Luang planned to kill me. Once again, Buddy had patted him down after he entered, and once more, Buddy found nothing. But I remembered a knife in his hand the last time he was here. I had told Buddy about the knife, but Buddy did not find one. So maybe I was wrong, my imagination creating a false reality.

Luang poured a cup of coffee. I wondered if this was the first time he ever poured his own coffee or did a servant always pour his coffee for him? He acted unconcerned however, sipping coffee before selecting a cookie from the tray; apparently in no hurry to kill me.

Phillip was sitting quietly upright on the couch next to Luang. He had already had several cups of coffee since his arrival, which was not unusual for him. The man lived on coffee.

It was time to begin.

'Phillip,' I said calmly. 'Perhaps you would like to tell Luang what really happened the night his nephew was killed.'

Phillip smiled. 'I have already told him.'

'Would you mind repeating it so I know we have all heard the same story?'

'Phillip has told me my nephew ordered the death of the brother of your girlfriend,' Luang interjected without looking up. 'It is not necessary to make him repeat the story.'

'When did he tell you?' I asked Luang.

'He told me in a recent conversation when we were discussing this meeting.'

'Did he tell you before?' I asked.

'No, he did not.'

'Why not?'

'I suppose because it did not serve his purpose at the time,' Luang replied.

'So, he lied.'

'I suspect Mr. Palmer lies quite often,' Luang commented.

Phillip remained uncharacteristically silent during this exchange. Usually, he defended his deviant lying behavior with vigor. I guessed this time; he knew he had no defense.

'Did he also tell you about a man named Manuel, a friend of your nephew, about how he was hitting my girlfriend when I arrived?' I asked Luang.

'No, he did not.'

'Your girlfriend attacked Manuel first,' Phillip suddenly came to life.

'To stop him from ordering the death of her brother,' I countered.

'Is this true, Phillip?' Luang asked Phillip.

'Manuel was defending himself from this crazy woman who was hitting him,' Phillip said.

'Crazy because she thought her brother was about to die,' I countered. 'And to set the record straight, Manuel was doing more than simply defending himself. He struck her hard more than once. He was obviously enjoying himself, beating a defenseless woman.'

'That's not what I saw,' Phillip said.

'You're lying,' I countered, raising my voice.

Phillip stared at me. I stared back.

It was then that I remembered Buddy's advice to never look away from Luang. Never allow your eyes to wander. Never let your defenses down. I glanced back at Luang who was standing up. When he saw me look at him, he seemed to relax and take a cookie from the tray before sitting down again.

The moment had passed.

10:25 AM. SANDY

A bright sun warmed the interior of their car parked on the shoulder of the road.

In a nearby pond a couple of white swans paddled lazily in the water as Sandy stared out the window of the car, looking into space, seeing but not really taking notice of the swans.

David sat next to her in the back seat with Charlie up front and Ben, his CIA colleague, behind the steering wheel. They were listening to a small speaker Charlie rigged on the dashboard. Several listening devices had been installed at John's cottage yesterday, along with small video cameras, which were digitally recording the event from several hidden locations in the room.

The entrance to John's driveway was a short distance down the road from where they were parked, perhaps a quarter mile away. The distance made it physically impossible for Charlie and his men to get inside the cottage in time to stop a sudden attack. Charlie had made this fact crystal clear to John. He was impatiently convinced his only role in this mess was to clean up after the crime had been committed. But in case he was wrong, Charlie had brought a man with him from Langley, a counter-terror specialist. This guy occupied the front seat of a second car parked in front, along with Rob. These men were younger faster and better trained in combat than Charlie. Charlie was good, but he was a lawyer first and a gunslinger second. These men were former Marines who had been trained for combat before they were hired by the CIA. They were prepared to save John's life if they could get inside in time.

From the backseat of Charlie's car, Sandy was half listening, half afraid to listen. If something went wrong, she would be forced to helplessly listen to the sounds of her lover's death. It was not something she wanted to hear. The sounds would be buried in her memory banks forever. But she had asked to be in the car because as long as she could hear John's voice over the speaker, she knew he was alive.

With eyes not really seeing, she watched the swan floating in the pond. And with ears only half listening, she heard the words of a conversation between two men who came from very different worlds.

10:30 AM. JOHN

'Mr. Van Laan, are we done talking to Phillip? Or do you have something else you want him to tell me?' Luang asked, mocking my feeble effort to convince him I wasn't guilty of killing his nephew.

'No, I wanted you to know what really happened that night,' I replied.

'I now know.'

'Does it make a difference?' I asked. 'Do you feel different now that you know what your nephew and his friend were doing that night? Do you understand why I had no choice? I had to stop them from committing a completely unjustified crime.'

Luang sighed, 'No, I am not convinced. I don't think my nephew ever actually intended to have this brother killed.'

'How can you say that? Phillip told you he ordered the killing.'

'I believe Nue was attempting to extract information from your girlfriend by threatening to kill her brother. He was putting pressure on her to talk, but I don't think he intended to have her brother killed.'

'What do you say, Phillip?' I asked without taking my eyes off Luang. 'Did it sound to you like Nue was simply trying to put added pressure on Ilana? Or did he really intend to have her brother murdered?'

Phillip pondered the question for a moment as if he was actually thinking about it. Then he answered evasively as he usually did, 'I don't know. It's hard to know what's in a man's mind.'

'Phillip, you were there. Don't give me some sappy, nonsensical answer. You know Nue was serious about killing her brother. He was frustrated. Ilana had withheld valuable information from Manuel. He wanted to punish her by killing her brother.'

'I don't know,' Phillip stated. 'It's possible he thought she had additional information which could be helpful.'

'How can you say that? You know she told him everything she knew.'

'How would I know that, John?' Phillip asked. 'Did you tell me? All I got from you was lies, like your promise to make me COO of your company? That was just a lie, wasn't it?'

'We will never know, will we?' I replied.

'You know it was a lie. Why don't you tell Luang what you promised me?'

'As soon as you decided to help Nue, the deal was off,' I responded, not wanting to delve any deeper into this subject.

10:35 AM. SANDY AND CHARLIE

Sandy could understand only about half of the words which came from the speaker mounted on the dashboard of Charlie's car.

Most of the conversation was simply jumbled noise to her. But that was okay. She didn't really need to understand the content of the conversation. Everything she wanted to know could be learned from listening to the tenor of the men's voices. Like the tone of John's voice which told her the conversation was not proceeding as he hoped. His voice was getting higher and louder. It was obvious he was getting frustrated.

Charlie listened in a different way. He was taking in every word. He knew the whole story. He had been with John the night John shot Nue. Charlie understood John was losing. Phillip's testimony was no help. And Charlie knew Phillip was right about one thing. John never intended to make Phillip a COO. John only promised Phillip the job because he wanted Phillip to help him with his plan to trap Nue into admitting he had tried to kill John on several occasions. That information captured on tape could have been used against Nue, indicting him for attempted murder. But before the trap could be sprung, Ilana had been forced to tell Nue about Charlie. When Nue learned a CIA agent was traveling with John, the cat was out of the bag. John's attempt to trap Nue was dead.

And that's when everything went wrong.

10:40 AM. JOHN

'Please stop.' Luang entreated. 'I have no interest in forgotten promises. I only want to know what happened.'

He paused before continuing. 'You were convinced Nue was trying to kill you,' he said looking at me. 'You thought he wanted you dead so he could take control of your company. Isn't that true, Mr. Van Laan?'

'I suspected as much.'

'And when you heard my nephew order the death of your girlfriend's brother, it was as if he was ordering your death. Is that right?'

'Yes, in a way, I guess that's true,' I answered, amazed at the old man's insight.

'So, you killed him?' Luang said.

No one spoke for a moment.

'Did you know what Nue was doing to me?' I asked.

'I knew my nephew was using methods which were very forceful.'

'Then why blame me. It was self-defense. Kill or be killed.'

'I don't know that is true. I believe he was simply trying to scare you, scare you into giving up your stock. I don't think he ever actually intended to kill you.'

'How can you say that? What will it take for me to convince you? Do I need to tell you about all the times I almost died? I will if that's what it takes, I will. I don't care if it takes all day,' I said looking directly in his eyes.

'No need for that. The fact is, Mr. Van Laan, you are alive. This is proof enough he never intended to kill you. If he wanted you dead, you would be dead.'

Phillip sat back on the couch after this comment. Up until this time, he had been sitting on the edge of his seat intensely listening to the discussion. But now, he sensed; it was game over. Luang had won.

'Doesn't matter,' I countered, not ready to concede defeat. 'Doesn't matter if Nue never really intended to kill me. ... because that's not why I killed him. I killed him to stop the murder of Ilana's brother. I killed him to stop Manuel from beating Ilana half to death. I killed him to stop him because I believed he was trying to kill me. How many reasons do you need? I was justified.' I argued, while hoping to appear calm, wanting to logically convince Luang that nothing short of killing his nephew would stop him. I wanted to do it with objective reasoning. I wanted to act like Luang, be calm, unemotional. But I couldn't. As much as I tried to act calm, I could not.

'I don't think so, Mr. Van Laan.' Luang stated in a calm voice. 'I think you killed him to get him out of your life. You murdered him to get rid of a business rival.'

10:50 AM. DAVID

As he listened, David looked out the window of the car at the pond where a white swan was gracefully swimming along the shore, searching for food.

He knew the gig was up. John was making a mess of things. The arguments which they agreed John should use to convince Luang to walk away were weak from the beginning. David always suspected John might lose his case, but he never thought it would be over so quickly. Luang had taken every point John hoped to make and destroyed them one by one. John had no defense. It was murder in the second degree, unpremeditated, but murder even so. That would be a jury's verdict if this case was tried in a court of law. David glanced at Sandy wondering if she fully understood how badly John was losing.

Sandy only looked lost, like she was far away somewhere in another world.

For a moment David questioned why he had come. This whole affair was a mistake from the start. It was, as Charlie had said, a weak plan which had almost no chance of success.

10:55 AM. JOHN

'Maybe you're right.' I countered, getting more upset by the minute with the old man, his calm logic getting on my nerves.

'Maybe your nephew never intended to kill me.' I said, 'Maybe he only wanted to scare me. But even if this is true, I still have one question for you. How many people needed to die in his scary game? How many? Do I need to count them for you? I will if I have too.'

I paused. When he didn't immediately object, I continued. 'Okay, let's start counting. Please stop me when you have heard enough. First, my girlfriend, then my best friend, and then two of my business associates died. That's four. And let's not forget about all the people who died in the flood, who rode the river of death in your country. How many villagers died that day, maybe several hundred?'

'People die every day.' Luang said. 'Catastrophes happen. Dams collapse. Death is as much a part of life as is life itself. You know this, Mr. Van Laan. Why do you ask me these questions?'

'Sure, people die. But some deaths are needless. Those villagers didn't need to die. My girlfriend didn't need to die. She was young. Her life was just beginning. Tell me why she needed to die.'

'Did my nephew have a gun in his hand the night she was killed?' Luang asked.

'His bodyguards were armed.'

'To protect Nue,' Luang simply countered.

'No, they had guns so they could kill me if I didn't agree to sell him my company.'

'Did they shoot you, Mr. Van Laan?'

'No, the CIA came to my rescue first.'

'So, his bodyguards never tried to kill you.'

'They never had the opportunity.'

'So, can we agree that Nue's bodyguards are not important to our discussion?'

The old man was smart; he had an answer for everything. I was getting nowhere. 'It's not enough, Luang,' I finally said out of sheer frustration.

'What is not enough?' Luang asked me.

'Your unemotional, logical defense of your nephew, it's not enough.'

'What are you saying, Mr. Van Laan?'

'I'm saying, it doesn't matter how logically you dismiss everything I have tried to tell you. Because people don't live by logic alone. Life is not reasonable. Life is full of fear and love and hate and other illogical emotions. We live and die by our emotions. Our deeds, our acts, they don't make us correct or logical, they make us happy, they make us sad. They make us who we are.'

He just stared at me like I was a mad man.

'How do you live?' I fairly shouted at him. 'Do you live by some logical scheme? Or do you live for happiness? Do you try to avoid being sad?'

He said nothing.

I continued, 'When a situation becomes so bad that we see no way out, when the pain is too great... then sometimes we do terrible things, things we regret.'

Luang sat passively listening, appearing to be unconcerned, uninterested.

'Take a step back, old man,' I demanded with as much passion as I could gather. 'Think about what your nephew had been doing to me, killing people I loved, threatening to kill me many times, too many times,' I said. 'Then ask yourself, what you would have done if you were me.'

He did not answer.

'Answer my question. What would you have done?' I demanded.

11:05 AM. SANDY

Sandy was now trying to understand every word of the conversation.

Because something had changed. The tone of John's voice had become urgent. Something new was happening. She didn't immediately understand what it was, but she knew time was critical. Time was running out. If John had any hope of convincing Luang to leave him alone, he had to do it now.

She buried her head in her hands.

11:10 AM. JOHN

'Your arguments are unconvincing,' Luang finally responded after a moment of silence. 'You have simply confirmed what I already know... You murdered my nephew.'

'How can you say I murdered him?' I screamed at him. 'Have you lived in my shoes? How many times in the last few years have you been shot at? How many times has your car been rammed off the road? How many of your friends and lovers have died because of one man?' I paused to take a breath. 'Answer my questions. How many, Luang, how many?'

'My path has been different from yours. That is all,' he calmly responded completely ignoring my pleas. 'I am not a murderer like you.'

'I am not a murderer.'

'You killed my nephew.'

'I did.'

'Then you are a murderer.'

'No.'

'How can you say you are not a murderer?'

'Because there is a difference between a man who kills to save another person's life... or himself... and a man who kills for pleasure or gain. I don't deny what I did to your nephew, but I am not responsible for his death. I am not a murderer.'

'You killed my nephew.' His eyelids narrowed and his lips got real tight. It was the first time he showed any emotion.

'Yes, I did... And not a day goes by when I wish it never happened.'

'Are you apologizing for murdering him?' Luang demanded.

'No, I won't apologize. Because he alone bears the responsibility for his death, not me.'

'That is nonsense,' Luang said, raising his voice.

'Is it? Is it really? Who created the atmosphere of fear and terror which led to his death? I didn't. He did. He did it for gain, for control of my company, something which didn't belong to him.'

'Nonsense.'

'Nonsense, really? I don't think so. And what about you, did you approve of what your nephew was doing to me? Did you know? Were you happy with your nephew's actions?'

'What I thought was not important.'

'Answer my question. Did you know what he was doing?'

'I did. I knew what he was doing, but the decisions were his,' Luang responded once again retreating to a realm of calm composure.

'Did you approve?'

'It was not my place to approve or disapprove.'

'But what did you think? Did you think his methods were good and just?'

'It was not...'

'I know it wasn't your place,' I interrupted him. 'That's not what I'm asking you. I'm asking if you approved. And if you didn't approve, then what did you do to stop him?'

'I could do nothing to stop him.'

'Nothing, really, nothing?' I fairly screamed. 'He was your nephew. He was your brother's son. Surely you talked to him. Didn't he come to you for advice? You are the old wise man of your family, aren't you? Couldn't you have done something to stop him?'

'This is getting us nowhere, Mr. Van Laan.'

'On the contrary, this is everything. Because if you did nothing to stop him, then you are just as guilty for his death as is he.'

'Not true.'

'Did you approve of his actions, Luang? I'm asking you. Did you approve?'

'I did not,' he finally admitted.

'Then why didn't you stop him?'

'Because as I have told you. It was not my place.'

'What, one man in control, nothing you could do, chain of command? Is that right?'

'That is correct.'

'Well, bullshit, Luang. You had a responsibility and you did nothing. You did nothing to stop him and now your nephew is dead and you want to blame me. Well, I played a part in his death, but so did you.'

'You alone pulled the trigger.'

'Yes, but you were with me the whole time. You lived every painful day with me because you knew what was happening. And you did nothing to stop it,' I screamed at him. 'You are just as guilty as I am.'

'Enough. You alone killed my nephew,' he yelled, leaping towards me with a sharp blade in his hand.

11:20 AM, CHARLIE

The sounds of a struggle burst out of the speaker on Charlie's dashboard like something alive had suddenly invaded his car.

Sandy's eyes opened wide as if she could see across the wireless void between the speakers and the mayhem of fear which existed inside John's cottage.

Charlie yelled into his phone at the guys sitting in the car in front of his.

His colleague immediately jammed the car's transmission into gear. Gravel from the rear tires shot back, beating a panicked staccato rhythm on the windshield of Charlie's car. Both cars accelerated, quickly covering the short distance to the cottage driveway entrance. It took less than a minute, but seconds are a lifetime when death is stalking.

Tires screeched, the two cars turned and sped down the quarter mile driveway, brushing against outstretched limbs of trees planted too close for speeding cars to avoid.

11:25 AM. JOHN

My mind had been so deep into arguing with the old man that it took me a fraction of a second too long to react to his attack.

Even though I had planned for this moment, even I knew what to do, rehearsed it over and over in my mind many times. Fall off the chair, roll away from him, roll towards a black wrought-iron fireplace poker which I had placed within reach on the floor, use it to keep him back until help could come. This was what Buddy taught me.

Problem was, I was too slow.

Luang was on me like a cat, leaping over the coffee table in one fluid motion, a knife in his hand to cut deep into my neck. I pushed back, falling out of my chair away from his assault, causing the blade to miss its primary target, cutting my shoulder.

Undeterred, he moved swiftly around my chair as I rolled helplessly on the floor, reaching for the iron poker, getting it in my hands, holding the iron bar up in time to block his blade from cutting me a second time. Wildly rolling onto my feet, swinging the iron poker, I luckily hit his arm, knocking the blade out of his hand, skipping across the floor out of reach. That didn't stop him from charging me. His blade was an easy weapon, but he knew how to kill with his bare hands. Taking the bar in one fluid motion, he twisted my wrists, forcing me to release the bar to stop the pain. But his actions exposed his head and before he could crush my throat with the bar, I swung, my elbow driving hard into the temple of his skull.

He fell backwards, temporarily stunned.

No fear, I was not afraid. I was fighting for my life, going full out, no holding back. This gave me an edge. Lack of fear allowed me to close fast, hitting him hard in the stomach with my fist before he could recover. He fell, staggered, caught his breath, preparing for my next attack.

I hesitated, not sure why. He stepped to the side; iron bar ready to strike. I charged, head down like a bull before he could swing, driving him to the floor, we fell together against a table. He cried out in pain. I rolled over kicking him in the knee as we lay on the floor.

Quickly up on his feet, he leaped at me, his hands driving into my side and face, pain instant. I tried to avoid his blows, but he would not stop until I lashed at his legs, driving my foot into his ankle, feeling it buckle under him, he fell hard. I was on him before he could react, flailing away with no purpose than to stop him, blows to his head, neck, mid-section; fists, elbows, hard and fast until the old man screamed, my hands bloody and bruised.

I stopped... looked down at him.

A hurt old man looked back at me, blood on his face, his hands up as a shield from my blows. He didn't look dangerous anymore. But then neither was I. I could hardly breathe. I was exhausted. Still, I found one last ounce of energy somewhere deep inside, enough to pull him from the floor and throw his limp body on a couch.

Phillip had retreated to the other side of the room while Buddy and Luang's man were holding each other in a stand-off.

No one moved.

I stood, bent at the waist, trying to get my breath. When I could talk again, I yelled at him. 'Is this what you want, old man? Do you want this to go on and on and on until more and more people are killed? Is this really what you want?'

He stared at me, gathering new strength into his old body while he lay on the couch.

'I asked you a question?'

'I heard you,' he replied through blood stained lips.

'Then answer me. Do you want this to continue, more blood, more killing? You and your nephew started this. And I did what I did. I admit it. I killed your nephew. It wasn't right. It solved nothing. But neither will killing me solve anything. So, here's our dilemma. Do we stop now? Do we decide to end this now and live in peace? Or do you want the killing to continue? More deaths following us to our grave?'

'What are you saying?' he asked.

'I'm saying this needs to end. Walk away and it's over. We both win. Or kill me and it continues.'

'Are you offering me the opportunity to kill you?' he asked, disbelieving.

'Is that what you want?' I replied in anger.

Charlie's two combat veterans ran inside with guns drawn. Nothing was happening, the room oddly quiet. They hesitated. Everyone was stationary. Charlie charged in behind, almost knocking down one of his guys.

'Get back,' I yelled with a high pitched, scream.

They involuntarily froze.

'No one interfere.' I shouted with as much authority as I could muster, still trying to breathe.

No one moved.

'Is that what you want?' I repeated my question to Luang. 'Do you still want to kill me?'

He didn't answer so I picked up his knife from the floor and handed it to him. He took the blade, looked at it before getting up off the couch. I moved so my body shielded him from the drawn guns behind us.

Memories of the time Nue had offered me a gun to kill him ran randomly through my brain. Nue did it for reasons which proved to be a lie, but I was not lying. I wanted this to end, end now. I didn't care what it took.

'Okay, if you still want to kill me, do it,' I yelled at Luang in frustration. 'Kill me and the carnage continues. Your violent act will surely lead to more violence. Next time it could be someone in your family who dies. It's your choice, Luang. Kill me now... or promise me this is the end... Promise me you will return to your family and swear to stop the violence. Do this for me and I promise you I will find a way to make my company work to help you and your family. Do you understand? I promise I will make it work.'

He looked at me, standing stationary with the knife in his hand,

'What do you want old man... more blood, more violence... or peace?' I demanded, convinced he would listen to reason and not kill me.

'I understand,' he said simply. 'But you need to understand that I must kill you. I don't have a choice. Honor demands that I kill you.'

'No, I only understand we all have choices in life. You can choose what your culture dictates. Or you can decide that violence works for no one. No one wins. Everyone loses. Death and destruction follow... Make a choice, Luang. But first understand that you alone are responsible. No one else, the responsibility for what happens in the future is yours alone.'

'As I have said, I have no choice in this matter. My family expects me to do what I have come to do.'

'No, the decision is yours alone. Don't blame your family or your country for what you do.'

Guns clicked behind me. 'Don't do it,' I yelled. 'Do not kill this man. He is my guest and I will not allow him to die in my house.'

'Stand down,' Charlie ordered.

'Okay, Luang.' I looked at him. 'What's it going to be? Do you want the violence and death to continue... or do we work this out peacefully?'

11:35 AM. SANDY

The driveway to John's cottage was sheltered by overreaching branches of tall oaks and towering pines.

In the summer the branches of these old trees formed a green canopy over the pavement enclosing it in a shaded woodland. It was a different world from the open lake side of the cottage; darker and more mysterious in the twilight of morning and evening. During the day it was a natural forest filled in the spring with berry bushes and wild flowers where the sun found openings through the trees to nourish the plants with light. But on this March morning and it was a cold lifeless place waiting for spring.

Sandy stood for what seemed like an hour next to Charlie's car parked in the driveway under the spreading branches of a tall, barren oak. She was afraid to go inside the cottage, fearing what she might witness when she ventured inside. Finally, hearing no gunfire and observing no movement, she could wait no longer. She had to know. Climbing the steps to the back door, she went inside.

The cottage was eerily quiet when she walked inside. Everyone standing inert, like lifeless manikins, very still. John's face was hidden with his back to her. He was alive, but what was he doing? And what was the old man doing, his face bloody, his eyes steady with something shiny and sharp in his hand?

Charlie had a gun in hand, but it was helplessly pointed down at the floor.

None of this made any sense to Sandy. She wanted to yell at them, tell them to stop this madness. Get the old man away from John, but everyone in the room seemed paralyzed, afraid to move.

The sight of Luang's knife hand swiftly shotting towards John's heart, broke the spell.

Sandy screamed.

SUNDAY, MARCH 21, 5:35 PM. SANDY

Driven by harsh winter winds, invisible grains of sand flowed undeterred across a beach temporarily unmarred by human habitation.

Endless lines of dull green waves rode across the lake to assault its cold windswept visage, the beach existing as it must have for thousands of years before man disturbed its natural order. The sound of the constantly crashing waves was mesmerizing, one after another, fast and furious, harsh and unrelenting, pounding the cold damp sand in a continuously clashing clamor which never paused. It was very disconcerting; this never-ending noisy racket, offering Sandy no peace as she stood by the windows of the cottage with a bitter frigid rain beating against the glass, distorting her view.

The California coast where she lived was different. The distance between ocean waves is longer. Pacific Ocean waves are each given their time to rise up, one after another, before dissipating their energy on the shore. Not like the waves on this big lake in the middle of the country which all rush together against the beach in mass hysteria; interfering, overriding, overpowering other waves where no order exists, nothing more than total confusion, an unrelenting, crashing commotion. She didn't like this lake anymore. It was undisciplined. No peace lived on this lake, only confusion and hurt. She turned away from the disquieting scene below her; closing the drapes over the windows.

A cold damp wind, blowing at twenty-five to thirty-five knots, was invading every cool, unguarded corner of the cottage with a draft, forcing the furnace to work overtime to heat the interior of the cottage. Adjusting the thermostat up a few degrees, Sandy went into the kitchen for a cup of hot coffee. But when the clock on the wall told her it was almost evening, she decided a glass of wine might better serve her needs; warm her internally, drive away the demons. Finding an open bottle of Merlot in the pantry, she poured a glass and took it to the living room.

A spiral notebook lay on a corner of the desk where John worked when he was at the cottage. She noted it was well worn, pages curled and used. Tears formed in her eyes when she realized it was his personal journal.

Opening it, she read John's last handwritten entry.

5:45 PM. JOHN

Perhaps his heart simply wasn't in it.

Or maybe my arguments had created a small element of doubt in his mind, enough so he was not as fully committed as he should have been when it came time to kill me. I like to think that was the reason, but I am not sure. Or perhaps it was because he was an old man who had taken a beating and that was why he was too slow.

I guess there is no value in speculating why. But for whatever reason, Luang moved just slow enough that I was able to catch his wrist, deflect his arm before he could drive his knife into my heart. Call it the will to survive, call it whatever you want. When the time came, I could not let him kill me. I thought I could. I had told him I would not try to stop him, but at the last second, I raised my hand, slowed his thrust... not completely, just enough so his knife missed my heart, cutting me in my side instead.

Smashing my fist into his face, I drove him back.

Charlie leaped, knocking us both to the floor, grabbing Luang's wrist as I rolled away in pain, blood seeping steadily from the wound in my side.

Sandy was with me through it all, pressing a cloth to my side to stem the flow of blood as I lay on the floor until an ambulance arrived. She smiled at me as the paramedics worked on me during the ride to the hospital, siren wailing. She held my hand while I waited to go into the operating room. And when I woke from the surgery to repair the damage, she was sitting next to my bed, smiling, waiting for me to open my eyes. I spent two nights in the hospital. She slept in my room both nights. And then she came home with me to my cottage for my recuperation.

The wound was not terribly serious, mostly a flesh wound and cut muscle, no vital organs damaged. It took the surgeon less than an hour to sew me up. But the wound to my soul was deeper, a wound which will likely never heal. I have tried to understand why he did it. And I am still deeply disappointed I could not convince him to stop.

But perhaps I understand.

The death of his nephew must have hurt him badly. Or it could be the demise of his family's wealthy birthright which hurt him even more. My company had in a few short years drained the lifeblood from his family business. More than anything else, that was probably the problem. It must have been difficult for the old man to witness the fall of his family's fortunes after hundreds of years.

Not in his lifetime; he could not allow this to happen in his lifetime.

Or maybe the truth is that violence always triumphs over peace. The mind of man will always find war more attractive than peace.

Sandy came into the bedroom where I was reading a book and curled up next to me under a blanket.

'Are you cold?' I asked her.

'I can't seem to get warm in this place,' she said, snuggling up against my side.

'Be careful, I'm still tender down there.'

She smiled and moved away, but not so far that I couldn't run my hand through her blond hair.

'Thanks for staying with me.'

She responded. 'I was so afraid.'

'I know. I was afraid too.'

CHARLOTTESVILLE, VIRGINIA, FRIDAY, MARCH 26, 5:45 PM. JOHN

It was the end of another work-week.

I was healing, able to move around without too much pain.

Normally Friday afternoons are like every other day. A little slower maybe, but still busy. Work goes on around the clock. The telephone doesn't ring as often on Friday, but it never totally stops ringing until I stop answering it. So, Fridays are like most days. I sometimes work well into the evening, even on Friday; but not this Friday. This evening and all other evening will be different from now on. Sandy has informed me that life, as I know it, must change. No more late nights in the office. Like tonight for instance, we are going out for dinner, the two of us; Sandy and me.

Luang flew home to his native Thailand under a diplomatic passport. Nothing anyone could do to stop him leaving. I didn't really mind. I didn't see him as a threat anymore. I saw only a broken old man.

We had one more talk before he went home. Charlie brought him to the hospital in handcuffs at my request. I told Luang I would work with Sophon to find a way for his family to benefit from the sapphire business. Not in the same manner it worked for them in the past when they dominated the world of sapphire. But they could still have a role to play if they chose. It was up to them to decide now, decide if they wanted to work with me.

He didn't say much, just nodded a few times during our conversation.

Charlie, as expected, thought I was wasting time talking to the old guy. And it could be Charlie was right. He has been right most every other time in the past. So, I had to assume he was right this time. But still, I had to try.

Phillip was released to once more retreat to his life of lies; a life where he is the star and all he surveys is under his power and influence. I hope to never see Phillip ever again.

And oh yes, I don't want to forget the good news Helen told me. Ilana called her. They are good friends, Helen and Ilana. Ilana wanted Helen to hear her good news. She is engaged to Todd, her bodyguard. Wedding date not yet set, but it will be soon. I'm glad she is happy. I hope her brother approves.

Sandy came into my office and stood over my desk with a smile. It was time to put down my pen, time to go to dinner, new rules, Sandy rules; no more late nights working.

Soft red lipstick brightened her full fresh lips. Long silver earrings set with small green sapphires shined behind strands of curly blond hair. She didn't have to say a word. Her smile communicated everything I needed to know.

It was time to go home.

THE END

See below for excerpts from Book 7, AFRAID TO HOPE

GRAND HAVEN, MICHIGAN, FRIDAY, AUGUST 3, 2000, 8:15 PM, JOHN

I turned and she was gone.

And because the memory of all those times when I should have been more careful, when I had not been alert; when grief and pain followed... those memories were still too fresh in my mind. I became increasingly anxious, couldn't help it. I searched for her, searched the crowded sidewalks in town, the many faces who strolled with me that warm summer evening. Strangers, people I did not know; they were not my friends, just someone who by chance existed in this time and place with me; just coincidence, nothing more. People who could not help me.

Sandy, I needed to find her, find her quickly. My imagination was ramping up, panic lying just below the surface. Already my irrepressible brain was visualizing dire circumstances, seeing her dragged off in a car speeding away, angry men covering her mouth with tape to keep her from screaming.

A girl turned, a tall girl with blond hair who looked like she could be Sandy. She wasn't Sandy. Just another pretty blond haired girl, not the pretty blond haired girl I loved. I quickly turned away, didn't want the woman to think I was staring at her.

Walking the sidewalk, searching, becoming slightly desperate. No panic yet, but I knew what would happen next. I could sense my heart rate increasing, breathing shortened. The first small wave of adrenalin would soon wash over my mind, passing quickly, a forecast of what was to come. Fear would take hold of me soon. Fear would come, fear and the fear of fear. I needed to find her, find her fast to stop the fear from taking over. I needed to see her smiling face.

I picked up my pace.

We had gone into town to window shop. The main street in the resort town of Grand Haven was busy that day. Noisy tourists roamed the sidewalks. Hotrods and convertibles cruised the main street lined with rows of attached old two- and three-story buildings.

Shops mostly, commercial businesses, some storefronts remodeled, some simply covered with a new coat of paint. Restaurants and beach wear shops, hair salons; all the normal businesses. It was a busy time, filled with happy vacationers escaping the heat of big cites, flocking to this lakeshore resort town. Shops were making money, selling goods. Restaurants were clogged. Lines of impatient customers stood on hot sidewalks waiting outside for an inside, air-conditioned table.

I tried to reassure myself.

She couldn't have strayed too far, just got lost in the crowd. Tall blonds were common here. This was West Michigan after all. Tall Dutch girls with blond hair are standard fare for this region. I told myself I didn't need to be concerned. I would find her soon. She was just down the street, inside a shop, looking at the merchandise.

Calm down.

8:20 PM, PHILLIP

Even though it was past eight in the evening, Phillip was still sitting in the reclining chair at his desk, mostly because he had nowhere else to go, no friends to visit, no wife or family. He was a loner by nature.

His office was a mess; papers in piles on his desk, his credenza, the floor. Cigarette ash overflowed a corner of his desk, covering an ashtray which should have been emptied days ago. He had taken up smoking again. After years of living without the filthy weed, he started smoking again after Martha quit. With her out of his office, with no mother figure to tell him what to do: he was a free man.

Phillip's long-time accomplice, confident and secretary, Martha, had finally given up trying to maintain a sense of order in his otherwise cluttered existence. She had resigned weeks ago, walked out; decided she had no future working for this man. Despite his promises, his sweet-talking promises; she quit because she just didn't believe him anymore, didn't want to hear any more of his tales of future success, no more lies. She was convinced that he would never amount to anything more than what he already was and that was a colossal loser.

Still, he was a mystery.

She often wondered how a man who was so intelligent, so capable of sweet talking anyone; how could a man so full of promise, fail so miserably. She didn't understand it. She couldn't stop thinking about him even as she packed her personal belongings in a cardboard box.

Phillip spoke not one word to her as she prepared to go, no thanks, no wishing her good luck, no nothing. He simply went about his business as always. On the phone mostly, or writing memos, looking through his papers. He ignored her.

Didn't even look up when she walked into his office to say goodbye... just sat looking down, scribbling on a sheet of paper. It had been six years. She had worked for him for six long years. She had given him her dedication. She had endured him, cared for him, protected him and this was how he treated her... not so much as a thank you.

Could it hurt to say thank you, she wondered.

She turned one last time to look down the hall into his office before closing the door.

She was gone and Phillip occupied his office complex alone without interference from anyone. In a way it was great. It gave him a new sense of freedom. Anything was possible now.

An errant ash fell lazily from the tip of his tapped cigarette, landing on the top of the heap covering his ashtray before almost succeeding in falling on the floor as he sat quietly with his phone in his hand; anxiously waiting in anticipation of the next great challenge in his life, dreams to be had, legends to be lived. He was the star of his show and he alone knew to what exalted heavens his fame would rise.

But first, he had to deal with one man, the one man who stood in his way, the lone obstacle to his rise to power; the man who had been holding him down when this should have been the time for his star to shine. John Van Laan was the name of that man, a man he hated more than any other man.

Phillip Palmer put down his phone and leaned back in his chair.

A plan began to take form in his muddled mind as smoke rings rose in the air, a plan which was a stroke of his genius brain, a plan which would finally bring him everything which should have belonged to him for years.